"An inspiring and explosive novel that shows how two people confront the misperceptions in their lives."

—**LARRY KIRSHBAUM, literary agent and publishing advisor**

"As a combat decorated and wounded veteran, I was truly captivated by Carol's storytelling. Phoenix Walker captures the mindset, roller coaster and daily heroics of my experience after being injured. All around excellence."

—**DOC JACOBS, Bronze Star with Valor and Purple Heart-decorated Navy Corpsman, CEO Doc Jacobs Foundation, author of** *There and Back Again*

"In this most worthy novel, the protagonists' lives are shattered and they re-emerge champions, showing a true test of character. Phoenix is all of us, unconquerable until we're conquered. A tale of sacrifice and rebirth; heroism is in the details."

—**SSGT AARON MICHAEL GRANT, author of** *TAKING BAGHDAD: Victory in Iraq With the US Marines*

"Carol Van Den Hende has written a wonderful, heartbreaking yet heartwarming novel, perfect for our times. I couldn't put this book down and was captivated by the main character, CEO Phoenix Walker. I highly recommend reading *Goodbye, Orchid*, and sharing it with everyone you know."

—**MICHELE KESSLER, chief executive officer at REBBL Inc.**

"A human drama that traverses every emotion, *Goodbye, Orchid* reminded me how life can change in a second. It's a beautifully written tale about the power of true love to overcome deep-seated misbeliefs. Phoenix and Orchid's story will forever live in my heart. Highly recommend!"

—**GORDANA GEHLHAUSEN,** *Project Runway* **couture designer**

Goodbye, Orchid

by Carol Van Den Hende

Published by

köehlerbooks™

3705 Shore Drive
Virginia Beach, VA 23455
800-435-4811
www.koehlerbooks.com

CAROL VAN DEN HENDE

Goodbye, Orchid

a novel

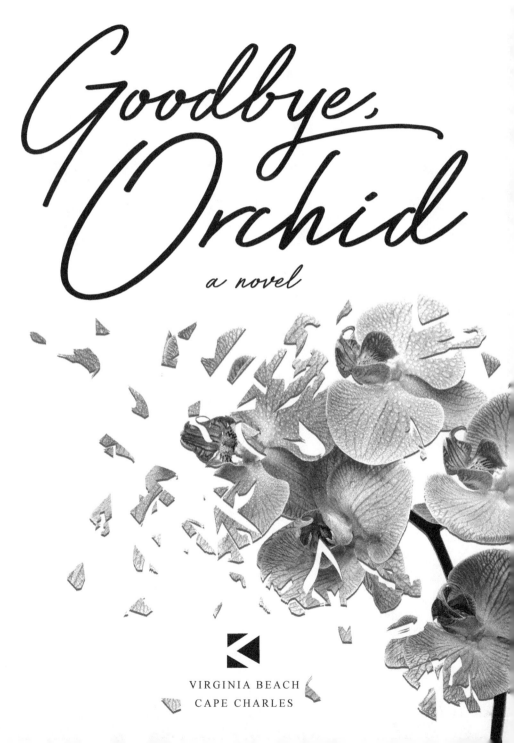

VIRGINIA BEACH
CAPE CHARLES

DEDICATION

For my humorous hubby who proves that love

really does conquer all. To Joshua and his

kitty-shaped spot in my heart

"I'm beginning to like you

So you probably won't get what I'm going to do

I'm walkin' away from you

It probably don't make much sense to you

But I'm trying to save you."

—Jack White, *A Martyr For My Love For You*

Mortality tests for willingness,

traces a finger along one cheek.

A snake's bite—or black widow's caress.

You ready, Golden Boy?

–July 29

CHAPTER 1

TEMPORARY GROUND

Phoenix

Phoenix never believed today was goodbye. Even though hellos come with goodbyes. Like black holes and Stephen Hawking. Like doughnuts and doughnut holes.

But today's goodbye wasn't the end of something.

Orchid's kiss, petal-soft, had changed everything. That was last night. Today, she stood before him, in a leather-edged tunic layered over tights. "It's not too late to come with me," she said, her laugh tinkling like the metal bangles on her arm. She and Phoenix stood at the mouth of the TSA pre-check line before airport security, parting a stream of passengers. Lodged like two boulders in a brook. Her flight was boarding in minutes.

"I'm not going to spoil your moment in the spotlight," he replied.

She reached up for a hug. Her slender frame made Phoenix feel even taller than six feet. Yet, there was tenderness too. *Mentor, I'm her mentor,* he recalled, slipping from her embrace.

"Spoil my moment? You know I wouldn't be going to China if it weren't for you. You always encouraged me." Her voice rose above the hum of conversations around them. Her lashes were ringed kohl black. Pale skin and ebony hair framed her dark eyes.

"Who, me? You did all the hard work. Stop giving me the credit *you* deserve. You're going to be awesome," Phoenix said.

"Thank you. Thanks for seeing me off."

"How else was I going to get rid of you?" he asked, his voice oddly gruff.

"Shut up. I have abandonment issues, you know that." She blinked, then her left cheek dimpled. He knew better than to think that she was joking. He wasn't going to tell her, but if it came to it he'd protect her from a 787 Dreamliner crashing through the windows of their terminal.

Orchid tiptoed up to kiss his cheek. The edges of their mouths brushed. *Crap.* He stepped back and her hopeful expression came into focus.

"You better get going or there won't be any China," he said and released her elbow. It struck him that their stance mimicked Michelangelo's *Creation of Adam*, their hands nearly touching, as if heaven was in those millimeters between.

"I don't want to leave you," she said.

"You have to. You have exactly ten minutes to get through security."

She held his glance for a beat too long and opened her mouth. "This thing between us—"

He shook his head to stop her words before it was too late. "Don't go all dramatic on me," he said. What he really meant was, *Don't screw up our magic, the thing that keeps it real.*

So real that she'd comforted him when he confessed it was too late to live up to Dad's expectations. *Gone one year today.* That had led Orchid to trust him with memories of the accident that had killed her parents. The one thing they shouldn't talk about was them. Phoenix's ex, tough mouthy Tish, had said it best. *You break women until there's nothing left,* Tish had said as tears fell down her face. And she never cried.

"You better go," he said, distancing himself from Orchid's reach.

She looked at him as he soft-pedaled back, keeping the attraction between them at arm's length.

Her mouth opened and closed. "Do you want to talk about last night?"

The previous evening validated every feeling Phoenix had suppressed since starting work with Orchid on a *pro bono* project months earlier.

Standing in the airport he recalled what his brother, Caleb, had said the first time he'd seen them together. "You two are hot for each other."

"You're going to miss your flight. We'll talk when you're back," Phoenix said.

She sighed and ran a hand with rings on every finger through her silken hair. "You're a piece of work, Walker."

She used his surname when she was pissed.

"And you are a magnificent marketer about to wow the world of beauty. Now go," he said, and watched as she passed through security to board her overseas flight.

Tish's accusation rattled his brain. *Orchid is not a woman I want to break.*

Later that morning, after working out and showering, Phoenix pulled on a white button-down dress shirt and tailored slacks. He was leaving his apartment to see Mom. She was in town for some flower show. Or a color seminar. And most of all, to be with her sons on the anniversary of their dad's death.

Phoenix held the elevator door for Mrs. V and her dog. They chatted until the lift descended to the lobby.

"How's Elton feeling today?" he inquired about her panting little terrier.

She told him about the pup's joint issues. They walked out into the sunshine together. She bent to lift Elton's paw in a miniature wave.

Phoenix waved back, then turned right toward the subway station.

As he strode, he couldn't stop thinking about Orchid. *What makes her so different? Did something shift when she confessed her secrets? She had worked so damned hard to raise money for military vets; even when she couldn't bear to see their injuries, it was like she felt their pain as if it were her own.*

At the 86th Street station, he descended the steps two at a time. Energy buzzed to his fingertips. Down below, the cavernous space echoed empty except for a homeless man seated on the ground. This guy looked worse off than most. Phoenix fished for a rumpled bill. The vagabond scowled over his bulbous nose at the lone single. Phoenix was distracted by a square of paper that tumbled out with the money. He walked towards the track and unfolded the note. It read, *I'm going to miss you more than you know.* Orchid had pressed a lip-shaped kiss print into the blank spot below the words.

He'd miss her too, until her return in six weeks.

At the edge of the platform, he punched up a song from Orchid's playlist and plugged in his AirPods.

"Where have you been all my life?" wailed Rihanna. *Indeed.*

He stood without noticing his physical surroundings, lost in thought about Orchid. *Sleek hair; slender; smart; strong.* Orchid sparked tenderness and more. Like no one else he'd ever known. On a whim he texted Caleb, both thumbs a blur.

You were right about Orchid.

Eighty thousand pounds of steel mass squealed towards the station. Phoenix stepped forward. Rihanna belted out a ballad over the sound of metal on metal, *"Are you hiding from me, yeah? Somewhere in the crowd—"*

In his peripheral vision, he noticed a figure swaying towards the gaping hole in the ground. "Hey!" Phoenix shouted, turning as the beggar stumbled right for the open track.

Without thinking, Phoenix dropped his phone and bounded forward. He grabbed the guy's coat to pull him away from the blurred train speeding towards them. The man jerked back. His bearded mouth screamed with fury. For a moment, they swung with wild centrifugal force. Suddenly, the guy yanked himself free. Phoenix tripped backwards. His feet scrambled to find purchase. Until there was just air over the edge of the platform.

With a split-second to grasp at nothing, Phoenix crashed through the empty space to thud onto the track. He could feel the train's screech judder. The sickening crush of steel slicing bone. *Fuck!* He could barely breathe. The air filled with screams. He attempted to lift his head. Except he couldn't move. *Broken until there's nothing left*, he wanted to say.

CHAPTER 2

I JUST DON'T KNOW WHAT TO DO WITH MYSELF

Veronica

At Sarabeth's Restaurant, Veronica Walker cut a fine figure, handsome and refined. Her graying hair was coiffed stylishly, and she wore a tapered cardigan.

She sat alone, wondering what could possibly be delaying her normally responsible son. Phoenix was already forty minutes late. She regarded her watch again, as if that could make him appear faster.

The young waitress checked her iPhone, with a different reason for noting the same duration. "I'm sorry, ma'am, Sunday mornings are our busiest time. If you don't order, I'll get in trouble with my manager."

Veronica glanced at the menu. "Four Flowers mimosa, hold the flowers."

"Anything to eat?"

"Okay, leave the flowers."

When the waitress stayed waiting for an order, Veronica cleared her throat. "Please give me a few minutes."

The waitress nodded politely. "Certainly," she said, and left the older woman.

This was not like Phoenix. If it were Caleb, she could be confident he was most likely asleep in a strange woman's bed, hungover and disheveled. *But Phoenix?* He'd texted he was running a little late. This was more than a little. Maybe the anniversary of her husband's death was making her edgy.

Veronica's phone vibrated on the table. *Must be Phoenix. Thank the Lord.*

She answered with no preamble. "Phoenix Walker, is that you? Do you know how long I've been waiting?"

She didn't recognize the woman who spoke. "Hello? Is this a family member of Mr. Phoenix Walker?"

Her tone struck Veronica with fear. Time slowed. "Yes. I'm his mother."

There are moments when self-preservation inspires the brain to slow the speed of input, because it can only absorb so much at a time. Veronica heard "accident," "train," "surgery" and then her mind shut down. It couldn't be him. He was on his way straight here.

"Where?" she asked. She pushed against the weight of the news to stand up, her focus narrowed to the one place she needed to be right now.

Veronica grabbed her Louis Vuitton satchel. She caught sight of her waitress, champagne flute in hand, mouth wide with surprise. For the first time in her life, Veronica fled without paying and didn't give a damn.

"How is he?" Veronica was overcome by desperation. She stood up from the hospital's plastic chair. Her high-heeled feet, swollen from pelting pavement, complained at bearing her weight. She ignored them, angry at her own weakness. Phoenix was who mattered.

"We don't know yet. I just came to check on you. You have someone coming?" The nurse's hand hovered near her, as if ready to comfort a lost child.

"Yes, I'm about to call my other son, Caleb. Here's a picture of him." She bent to pull up the home-screen photo on her phone.

"So handsome," the nurse said, eying not Caleb's features but Phoenix's. It was often the case, that even as people complimented her boys, they lingered on Phoenix's tousled hair and blue eyes. Both were good-looking, but Caleb frightened strangers off with his scowl and tattoos. In contrast, Phoenix's warmth held universal appeal. The screenshot had been taken years ago. It showed young adult boys, virile with the lie that nothing could harm them.

Fear rose in her throat. "It can't be him. Please don't let it be him," she pleaded, both with the nurse and an omniscient being. The rigid seat caught her collapsing mass.

CHAPTER 3

MANY SHADES OF BLACK

Caleb

Traversing the narrow corridor leading to his New Brunswick tattoo shop granted Caleb Walker a few minutes before starting work to grieve his father's death. His dad had been the ballast against his mother's bias, and it was now a year since he'd died.

The room was empty in the morning before weekend opening hours. The interlaced black and white linoleum tiles echoed with each scrape of his booted heels. Caleb looked around at the walls dotted with framed prints of the shop's best work, ornate tattoos of celebrities, pets, kids, and arcane symbols. From the number of tattoo revisions the shop undertook, he knew that sometimes the things people initially loved would later become the bane of their existence.

He fingered the small animal skulls atop a metal-rimmed glass case. The yellowed bone reminded Caleb of the dead animal that had led to his first love. He lapsed into fifteen-year-old high school memories, and one particular blue-sky day. Caleb had only dug the squirrel's grave a foot deep when an attractive teen girl drew closer.

"What happened?" Her voice had lilted.

"Dunno." He shrugged, lifting his dad's shovel. "Just found it. Figured I better bury it before animals get him."

She knelt, ruffling the squirrel's fur.

"Hey, don't do that." He dropped one denim knee onto the soil inches from her hand. "It might've been sick. You don't want to get whatever killed it."

She sat back, cornflower blue eyes round with respect. "You're smart. You must be Nixy's brother."

"Yeah, that's right. You're here to see Mr. Straight-A, huh?"

She snickered. "What's your name?"

"Caleb. And Nixy's my brother," he had said, pleased at the ease in swapping importance, mocking his twin's newly bestowed nickname.

So what if she was captain of the swim team? Beneath the stylish bangs and clear braces, she harbored a dark streak that wanted to touch dead animals. Phoenix, student president, star athlete, could have any girl. *Why not leave this one—pretty on the outside, fucked up on the inside—for me?*

The phone interrupted his reverie. Caleb checked his mobile. Ah, it was off. *Probably Mom trying to guilt me into coming into the city, when all I want is to be alone on the anniversary of Dad's death. I'll tell her I'll come in tomorrow.*

He grabbed the old-fashioned black handset before the answering machine kicked in.

"Yeah?" He listened to the voice on the other end with growing alarm. "What the—"

His free arm steadied himself against the telephone stand, his only stability against the failure of his legs.

Why was his ex-girlfriend the first person Caleb thought to phone? *Because she's my business partner,* his distraught brain reasoned before he punched up Sascha's number.

"Caleb, you're not calling to scold me for missing Mass, are you?" Sascha's morning voice was coarse.

"Sascha. Thank God I got you," he said, sounding as bereft as he felt.

Her tone changed from playful to attentive. "What's wrong?"

"Um, something terrible's happened." He could barely get the words out, feeling as if he was lost and far away.

"Where are you?" she demanded. "What's wrong? Do you need help?"

He could hear her scurrying around. He pictured her in her cramped apartment. "Talk to me," she ordered. "Where are you?"

"I can't talk," he said, realizing that the road had blurred before him. "I need to pull over."

"You're driving? . . . That's not safe. Get your ass off the road."

He breathed in short bursts. Phoenix might die before he could get to him.

"Are you having chest pains?" she asked, probably recalling how Caleb's dad had died from a heart attack.

"No, it's not me," he said. "It's Phoenix. He's been hurt. I need to get into the city. Can you open the shop for me?"

"Who cares about the shop? Where are you?" she asked again.

"I'm still in New Brunswick. I pulled over on Easton Ave."

"I'll be there in five minutes. Don't you dare move," she commanded.

When she arrived, Caleb was leaning against his pickup, head in his hands.

Sascha's Fiat screeched to a halt behind his truck and she jumped out. The familiar petite figure with auburn hair and head-to-toe red latex approached.

"What happened?"

"There was an accident." He couldn't get any more words out.

"Get in," she said. "I'll drive you to the city and you fill me in on the way there."

He folded himself into the space that was ridiculously small for his large frame. He felt too upset to make his usual tease about her choice of a miniature vehicle.

"Where to?" she asked.

"Columbia-Presbyterian Hospital. Take the GW Bridge."

Her foot slammed the accelerator. The car took off like a rocket. "Phoenix is in the hospital?"

"Yeah."

He couldn't offer more. His brother was unconscious, in surgery. Maybe dying?

"Honey, I'm sorry. You want to tell me what's going on?"

She had saved Caleb time and again. *She deserves to know.* Maybe it'd be a relief to get the awful news off his chest.

"Mom called to say Phoenix never showed up. He was in some freak accident. On a subway track. He got hit by a train."

"Aw hell." Her words exploded.

He felt like a jerk for dragging her into his inner torture. He faced her and put a calming hand on one leg. "You need me to drive?"

She kept her eyes on the road. "I'm . . . I'm okay. Sorry. I just . . . *what* happened?"

"I don't know much either. Just that he's in surgery. Mom said he lost a lot of blood. She said I better come right away."

Sascha's eyes froze open with shock. And then they filled.

"No. Phoenix? How can this be?"

"I know," he said, his voice flattened by emotion.

She sped through the automated toll lane, seeming not to care that she blew away the speed limit.

"Could they be wrong? I mean, if it was a train accident, how do they even know it's him?"

"Shit, don't say that," he groaned. He rocked back. "I don't want to picture him so fucked up that we can't even tell it's him." The idea of Phoenix on the ground, crushed by massive metal wheels made him nauseous. It was as if half of him had been crushed.

She put the George Washington Bridge behind them and headed downtown into Manhattan. They rode in silence through city traffic. At stoplights, he glanced around, half expecting to see Phoenix striding along the sidewalk.

Finally she pulled up to the emergency room entrance. "You go first. I'll meet you in there."

"Thanks." He bolted out of the car.

She lowered the passenger's window and shouted. "Hey, it's going to be okay."

Without a response, he jogged through the emergency room doors. He could only hope they'd arrived in time.

Caleb found his mother seated in the waiting area. She got to her feet and met him with an unsteady gait. He wrapped an arm around her and frowned.

"He's not—?" he asked, alarmed at Mom's puffy eyes.

She shook her head but clung to him, almost as inconsolable as when Dad had died. Then she pulled back and regained her composure. He recognized the effort it'd taken her, and once her stoic expression was locked in place, it looked like nothing could shake it.

Sascha hurried towards them.

The older woman looked up as she approached. "Hello, Sascha. Thanks for driving Caleb."

"Mrs. Walker, I'm so sorry. How's Phoenix?"

His mother shook her head, eyes filling. "Not good."

Sascha looked from his mom to Caleb, fear in her eyes. "Don't tell me—"

"They, um, amputated . . . the train amputated his leg and hand," Mom said.

Caleb had seen clients swoon over the sight of blood, but not him. He considered himself tough as steel. But now, he felt his stomach churning.

"He's going to survive, right?" Sascha said.

"As long as he makes it, nothing else matters," his mom murmured.

"He's a fighter. He's gotta be okay," Caleb said, as much to himself as anyone else.

When his father died unexpectedly, Caleb had descended into anger. He became wildly volatile, swinging through moods as if shifting gears in his truck. Phoenix grieved, yet exhibited an inner strength that drew him closer to their mother. Putting aside his ad agency work, he'd stayed with Mom for nearly a month. Mom had said she couldn't conjure anyone more dependable to help her organize her affairs and get her bearings. Caleb envied their relationship but suppressed jealousy.

Now, instead of dispensing support, Phoenix was the one who needed it.

They all sat, lost in their own private thoughts, slumped into the slick plastic seats. Caleb couldn't tell if minutes or hours passed waiting. He released a shuddered breath.

"Are you okay?" Sascha asked, peering at Caleb.

He shook his head. "It's hitting me really hard."

"Aww, luv."

He buried his face into her shoulder. All the petty jealousy with his brother, the drama with Sascha. He would shove it all aside, if only Phoenix would get better.

A nurse came over to the trio. "Mr. Walker's out of surgery. We'll let you know when you can see him. It might be a while."

Caleb turned to Sascha. It comforted him having her there, but wasn't he being selfish? "Thanks for driving. Do you want to go and open up the shop?"

"Forget the damn shop, I'm waiting here with you," she said.

His mother straightened. "I know it's going to be tough to see him like this. But we're going to be strong for him. It's not going to help if we fall apart. Understand?"

She looked so determined, it was impossible not to believe her conviction.

CHAPTER 4

IN THE COLD, COLD NIGHT

Phoenix

Phoenix floated downstairs two or three at a time. His movements were effortless, effervescent. His body seemed suspended, capable of fluidity that defied gravity. He sank slowly, a burning at the edges disturbing his cool darkness.

Quiet. Silence. Once, his mom took them to vacation at a Relais-du-Silence chateau. He resisted that amount of solitude and stillness. Now, it beckoned to him. He answered its call. *Yes. Now. Okay.*

"Phoenix?" came the whisper. A tug on his consciousness. *No, not yet. Stay silent.* He vaguely recalled some epic struggle. A struggle with gargantuan proportions, like a sweeping Hollywood production. Now, an eerie hush followed the struggle. Blackness beckoned.

CHAPTER 5

INTIMATE SECRETARY

Liv

Monday funday. Liv loved her boss, but wondered how she had landed in the middle of a modern-day "Mad Men." First thing, she sent Phoenix a text reminder of his meeting to present the agency's creative capabilities to a potential client. Not that he needed the reminder. It was more the satisfaction of doing something for a man whose hyper-independence meant he asked for little.

Liv was shocked to realize she'd been at the agency for twelve months. A year ago, job prospects for recent graduates were as scarce as affordable apartments in Midtown. Liv's plan of working in advertising didn't land her a desirable copywriting position. Instead, she could only find administrative roles.

Her sense of candor during interviews didn't win many offers. Except at counterAgency, where her stubbornness amused rather than intimidated Phoenix. She fell in love with the spirit of the unique place—and maybe a little with the guy who orchestrated that spirit.

She had stepped into his airy office, noting the broad expanse of glass opening up over Midtown. The air was scented with fresh orchids.

"Phoenix Walker. Nice to meet you," he'd said, standing to shake her hand. His grip was self-assured without crushing her fingers.

She'd settled into the indicated seat across from the clean sweep of his desk.

He made her feel at ease, then got right down to it.

"Tell me about your career aspirations."

"Honestly?" she asked, studying his blue eyes. His suit probably cost more than she would make a week. Outside his glass wall, she could see that the nearby conference room was abuzz with a creative team brainstorming and drawing on a whiteboard.

"I love to write," she said. "I'd like to be a copywriter."

He scanned her résumé, already marked up with circles and underlines.

"Editor of the school paper, published editorials, finalist in poetry competitions, a degree in English with honors. Your writing skills are coming through. So why apply to be an executive assistant?"

She sat straighter, her palms suddenly damp. She needed to explain the pivot.

"Please don't hold my achievements against me. I'm super-organized, I have great follow-through," she declared. "I'm tough when I need to be . . . and professional. I'm coachable, too. I want to be part of a team."

He angled back into his desk chair with a bemused grin. "Hold your bachelor's against you?"

She knew the game was up. This guy was an advertising wunderkind, just as all the trade rags said. He could see right through her plan to land a spot to pay the bills until she could find a *real* job.

"Mr. Walker, I know I seem overqualified to be an admin, but can't overqualifying for a job be a good thing?"

"If you'll stay awhile," he'd replied.

"Capability and motivation are different things," he'd stated, making the pronouncement sound like a fresh insight. Her fingers twitched with the desire to take notes. She reminded herself she was no longer in school. He proceeded with his inquisition.

"How would you feel if . . . if I asked you to send a reel to a client?"

"No problem," she assured him. *Easy one.*

"Asked you to schedule appointments?"

"Of course."

"Personal ones?"

"Okay."

"Make travel arrangements?"

"I know the duties of an assistant. I can take care of correspondence, calendars, protect your time, make excuses to stave off unwanted calls, serve as your proxy for internal staff and even handle difficult clients."

Is him grinning a good sign?

"I repeat, how are you going to feel about doing all that? When you were the star of your high school paper? When you just earned your degree in the musings of James Joyce? When you want to be a copywriter?"

Crap, tough psychological questions.

Other interviewers would dance around her skills and reject her without giving her a chance to respond. He clearly had seen her potential, but needed to verify his instincts.

She straightened the jacket of her pants suit, borrowed from her mom for the interview. "Copywriting can wait. I'm going to feel like I'm learning about the industry from the ground up. And I'm going to push you for opportunities to be part of the creative process. That's still my strength."

He nodded, as much in control of this interview as he probably was over everything in his life.

"If you fulfill the job's priorities, there are always opportunities. New business presentations that need all hands on deck. Networking events."

Her heart quickened. *I need to go shopping.*

"I still want to know," he questioned. "Do you feel like you're selling out?"

"Do you?" she shot back before she could think.

That bemused grin.

"We sell out every day, but hopefully with our analytics and not our souls. Now, what questions do you have for me?"

Her standard queries about the company had suddenly seemed trite.

"What made you do it?" She waved her hand to indicate the people and rooms beyond the clear glass. "What drove you to create this?"

For a moment, she didn't care about the details of the job. She was transported. She wanted to know more about this agency superstar.

He seemed amused. He studied her, measuring the earnestness of her question. *Who's interviewing whom?*

"I had a type of company in mind that I wanted to work for. Couldn't find anything like it. A place that made me feel like the work was fun and worth doing. A place that stood up to clients and stood for something."

All doubts had vanished. She wanted the job more than anything. Forget about grad school or creative writing.

He stood and offered her an even firmer handshake like they were making a deal.

"Nice meeting you, Liv. See you soon."

"See you" is better than goodbye, right?

"See you soon," she repeated like it was a refrain from her favorite song

Now, a year since the offer had been made and accepted with enthusiasm, she'd learned his style and knew how much sass she could sling back. Her initial awe had morphed into respect, even when he could be moody or overreact to one of her mistakes.

She'd even grown accustomed to his streak of perfectionism. So what if he held her to high standards? They were nothing compared to the standards he held for himself. Even after a year, she loved working for Phoenix. Everything else could wait.

His phone line sounded.

"counterAgency. Mr. Walker's line."

"Liv?" the voice on the other end was washed out. Liv sat up and pressed the receiver closer.

"Yes. Who's calling?"

"It's Veronica Walker, Phoenix's mother." Liv glanced at the time. Nine-thirty on a Monday wasn't impossibly late for Phoenix to arrive, but her scalp prickled with premonition.

"Is everything all right?"

"No. Phoenix's been in a bad accident. I'm at the hospital with him." Liv could hear a muffled sob.

"Oh my God. Is he okay?" Her heart pounded in her ears making it hard to hear Veronica's words.

"I don't know. We don't know. He's still unconscious."

"What happened? What can I do?" Liv looked around the office frantically, as if Phoenix would appear.

"I don't know when he's coming back to work, if he's coming back to work. I have to go." She hung up.

Liv stared at the phone and stood. She glared at the empty desk where Phoenix normally sat. She couldn't go to the person she usually relied on for advice. Her heart lurched at the thought. What did Veronica mean, *if* he's coming back?

Dex. She needed Dex. Stumbling on legs wooden with fear, Liv found Dex in his office, bent back in his chair, tossing a Nerf ball in the air.

"Liv!" he greeted her, sitting up. "How was your weekend—" The question aborted as he turned and saw her face. "What's wrong?"

She shut his door behind her. "Phoenix," she uttered, eager to share the burden of this awful truth. "Phoenix has been hurt in an accident. He's in the hospital. His mom called."

Dex's bearded jaw dropped. He was staring at her. He took a step towards her, as if he could glean more information by being closer.

"In the hospital? Is he okay? Where is he?"

"I don't know. The only other thing she said was she didn't know when or if he'd be back." Her voice lost its power.

A few minutes of pacing and Dex pieced together the start of a plan. He'd call Phoenix's brother. He warned Liv. "This is not a matter of gossip, you understand?"

"Of course not. And don't worry, I'll take care of his meetings."

By afternoon, Dex ushered Liv into a conference room, his normally jovial eyes red.

"It's bad," he said straightaway. "He was hit by a train. He lost a lot of blood. I don't know if—" He stopped, then tried again. "He might not make it."

She fidgeted with her glasses to hide her trembling hands.

"What can we do?" she asked.

"For now, I think he'd want us to keep it business as usual."

That sounded like Phoenix. She nodded.

"I'm going to get the agency together and tell them what happened. I'm going to ask everyone to keep this from becoming a media circus. We're an ad agency, we know how to generate PR and how to avoid it. He's never on social media anyway, so no one needs to know. He wouldn't want our clients losing faith in us."

"Okay."

Despite having avoided church for many years, Liv squeezed her eyes shut and brought her hands together in prayer.

CHAPTER 6

TAKE ME WITH YOU WHEN YOU GO

Orchid

MONDAY JULY 30, BEIJING CHINA

O rchid pulled her suitcase through the echoing terminal at Beijing's Capital Airport. Her brain tried to make sense of the unintelligible pictograms and literal translations. *You're not in Kansas anymore.* She didn't have Chinese yuan yet, so she dropped US bills into the hands of the few beggars who'd snuck into the *uber*-clean terminal.

What would they do if Phoenix were here? He'd probably snag a few tourist brochures and convince her to take far-flung excursions, then research vegetarian restaurants to make sure she ate well. His long fingers would swipe a set of kitty playing cards for her from the duty-free shop. *Wait, no.*

She replayed their goodbye yesterday morning in New York. Phoenix's darkly handsome face and kind eyes shrinking back. His voice exposing his heart, which was in stark contrast to the night before. Sure, they'd drunk a lot, but his words had felt like the truth.

They'd been sitting so close. On the little settee in her living room. He'd studied her, then brushed a lock of hair off her cheek. The spot where his skin had grazed hers left a trace of electricity in its path. "You are amazing. Everything about you," he'd murmured.

She'd read the tenderness in his eyes and leaned in, breathing in his warmth. He'd smelled of Scotch and spice. After all these months of holding back, she'd lifted her face and brought her lips to his. They were soft. He'd returned her kiss. Gently at first, then more urgently. In contrast to their months of professional distance, their closeness sent a shock through her, even more explosive than the hum she felt whenever they were in the same room. Her hands explored his ripped arms and muscular back. Lost in passion, time had no measure. While her brain was still foggy, he'd pulled back and studied her, his lids hooded and eyes wet. She had no idea how she looked. Her lips felt swollen, her cheeks raw from his stubble. He'd stood, unsteady on his feet, either from the booze, or emotion. He bent, his cheek to hers, and said something that she couldn't hear over the buzz in her ears. Then, he'd left. Walked out her door. The next day, he barely wanted to acknowledge or talk about the attraction between them, about the night that should've been a turning point in their relationship.

She hated goodbyes. They seemed so final.

I have it bad, she thought to herself as she waited in line for a cab.

"*Lidu fan guanr.*" She told the driver the name of her hotel, and settled into the back of his taxi. Seat belts would be great, except they were tucked into the fabric cover, unreachable and unusable.

"*Lidu fan dian*," he corrected her, baring teeth brown in the deep crooked crevices.

During the drive, she practiced her Mandarin, and learned that the driver's parents were raising his son in a faraway hometown. It was a common practice for rural citizens to move to China's cities and send their earnings back home.

She glanced at the time. Four a.m. in New York. Too early to call. Instead, she opened her phone and paged through photos. She paused at an image of Phoenix from their day at the beach, his familiar gaze and cobalt eyes framed by thick lashes. It seemed as if an artist had brushed an impressionistic sweep of stubble around his full lips to soften the perfection of a straight nose and masculine brow. *Stop*. To distract herself, she snapped a pic of her agreeable driver, and wrote a post to check on her friends. "Arrived! Miss you all already!" Nothing from Phoenix. After his refusal to talk about their relationship, she wasn't about to be the first to make contact.

Her hotel room smelled like cigarettes, the still-smoldering butts hurriedly ground into bedspreads, tables and any available surface. Tucked in between the pages of her book, she discovered a little reminder of Phoenix. A note from the congratulatory flowers he'd sent, his handwriting a loose and confident scrawl. At the last minute, she'd grabbed the memento as a bookmark, a talisman against anything happening during their time apart. Now, anything related to Phoenix seemed to mock her.

In the morning, a downstairs breakfast buffet featured rectangles of turnip cake, thousand-year-old eggs (hopefully marketing puffery), sweet red bean soup with gelatinous doughballs, and Chinese cabbage in savory sauce. She wanted to share the experience with those back home.

Orchid tapped her screen to post photos for her friends. Chats rolled in from girlfriends wishing her well. Mandy had sent a baby photo, colleagues posted funny memes, and her boss wished her a safe trip.

Nothing from Phoenix. Jerk.

CHAPTER 7

NEVER FAR AWAY

Veronica

When the twins were little, Veronica lost herself in their innocent eyes, one pair bright like the sky, the other pair polished like obsidian. She didn't love one child more than the other. But Caleb sure brought home the heartache. Her husband, John, said Caleb butted wills with her because he was too much like her.

Then John died so unexpectedly. He'd been a part of her. They were supposed to retire in the next few years and travel. Even now, she would forget and turn to tell him something. Especially now, with this accident.

The news of Phoenix's injuries had floored her. She couldn't bear to picture her beautiful son under a train. How could she not have realized that Phoenix was as much a part of her as John had been? Just like when the boys were little, she felt his pain as if it were her own.

She looked past the IV line dripping fluids into him, past the tubes entering and exiting his body. She squeezed his hand.

"Phoenix, please wake up. I need you to come back to me," she murmured. Nothing. Silence. Just the beeping of equipment keeping him alive.

His skin held a gray pallor, which frightened her. His jaw was slack, his body motionless. He lay so still that several times she checked to ensure he was breathing.

He was not dying. The doctors had said so. She worried they might be wrong.

One diminished worry only meant that another took its place. She could barely fathom his loss. She pictured his chubby-yet-firm toddler arms flung around her neck for a kiss, or his child's long legs urging a dirt bike down the steep path behind their summer house. As a teen, he would dive over and over until he sliced through the water with perfect precision.

Unbidden as they were, ugly ideas gripped her. Her mind tried to push away thoughts of his abilities, and now, limitations. How would he take the news she'd have to tell him? The hospital staff assured her that he'd be able to do more than she imagined. She clung to the ray of hope the nurses had given her. "Prostheses are getting better and better nowadays. He'll be able to return to an active life."

She didn't look closely at his bandages. She'd promised she wouldn't cry. She didn't want him to hear her and bear the weight of her grief. Instead, she talked to him. Looking around, confirming Caleb was out of the room, Veronica brushed her lips over his cheek.

"When I first held you, I knew you were a wise soul. I said you would teach me more than I could teach you." She paused. "This is not what you're meant to teach me. Not this."

Then, in a cruel twist, her mind sighed relief. *At least it's not Caleb.* She imagined that losing so much might undo Caleb.

But even in her worst nightmares, she never thought this accident would undo Phoenix.

CHAPTER 8

THE AIR NEAR MY FINGERS

Phoenix

An insistent beeping stirred inside Phoenix's brain. Its fuzzy edges grew crisper, more solid until he could no longer ignore the sound. He assessed himself, struggling to move. His mind waded through semi-consciousness to test out the weariness in his body. Eyelids resisted until he forced them open, only to close against a flash of bright white.

A pressure on his arm let him know he wasn't alone. A familiar voice reached him from far away. His head seemed heavier than possible. So tired.

"Phoenix?" asked the voice again, closer now, and finally giving him the strength to pry open his eyes.

Caleb's face appeared, dark eyes scowling, framed by a blinding whiteness around his head as if the tattooed scoundrel had turned angel.

"Are you okay?"

Phoenix groaned, and shut his eyes, still unaccustomed to the light.

"Are you in pain?" Caleb asked, protectively releasing Phoenix's arm.

Christ, that's what was wrong. Everything hurt. His arms, his legs.

His gut clenched, as he tried to roll into a position that would alleviate the fire incinerating his limbs. Moving was difficult, as if he was weighed down by sandbags.

A chair scraped the ground. "You want me to get the doctor? Or Mom?" Caleb asked.

"Wait." Phoenix's voice croaked from what seemed like years of disuse.

"Water? You want a drink?" His brother leaned so close that Phoenix could feel his breath.

Phoenix's mouth felt as dry as Death Valley in August. He nodded.

He heard liquid trickling into the hollow of a cup. He opened his eyes to reach for his brother's hand, the cup blurry. *Shit.* Wires restricted his movements.

His brother's face came into focus, distraught, with his mouth set in a grim line.

"What happened?"

Caleb's brows furrowed. "You were in an accident. You're in the hospital."

"In the hospital? What do you mean?"

This makes no sense. I need to finish a campaign pitch . . . brunch with Mom . . . Orchid.

He twisted against the pillows, eyes shut again, exhausted by their exchange.

His brother kept talking. Phoenix couldn't concentrate as memories started to unlock.

Orchid at the airport . . . back to my place before meeting Mom. The subway station. The homeless guy with the beard. Oh my God. Losing my balance, flying through the air. . . . His eyes squeezed tighter, shutting out the scenes that clamped around his chest until he couldn't breathe.

Can't be.

He struggled to move. Pain pierced through his leg, as if it was on fire.

Caleb put a supporting hand on his brother's shoulder. Phoenix opened his eyes to find his brother still toting the cup. He reached for the water. Clumsy with grogginess, he knocked it over. The water spilled onto the bedspread. Phoenix instinctively threw out his left hand to steady the cup.

He whiffed air.

Confused, he regarded his arm. Bandages ended inches above where his wrist should've been. Bile spiked in his throat.

"What the—" he yelped, heart pounding from images of bloodied limbs, inanimate, lying apart from his body.

Caleb swallowed. "I'm sorry. They couldn't save your hand or your leg."

Phoenix barely registered the ache in Caleb's voice.

"My hand *and* my leg?" He didn't recognize his own guttural cry, as his future spun 180 degrees around him.

His mom swept into the room, setting a paper coffee cup beside his bed.

"Oh, Phoenix, it's going to be okay," she said, reaching over to press the controls to elevate the head of the bed, helping to calm his flailing as he tried to sit up.

Little by little, the room came in focus, LED bulbs glaring overhead, machines buzzing beside him. He searched wildly around the reflective surfaces of the room. He knew he needed help, but from whom and for what?

"Mom?" he asked, confused. "What are you doing here? How'd you get here so fast?"

"Oh, honey, I've been here three days."

Three days? Looking down, he saw sheets dipping below his left knee. He tried to kick them back to no avail.

"No. God. No. This can't be."

His mom stroked his right arm. He could feel her fingertips. "Shh, I know, sweetie. It feels bad but it's going to be all right."

"Do you see what's missing? There's nothing left of me."

"All the important parts are there," Caleb intervened.

"The important parts?" Phoenix practically screamed. As he lifted his shoulders in a shrug of denial, the sight of his bandaged left arm provided a shocking reminder of his tragedy. Spent, disbelieving, he leaned back into the pile of pillows. "No, please no."

His mother pushed the bed down to a supine position. "Just rest, Phoenix. Everything's going to be okay."

Okay?

His life's dreams, gone, sublimated to nothing. *How am I going to do anything?* A nurse arrived with a sedative and he fell into a troubled sleep.

An alarm shrills. The green glow of the room's EXIT sign indicates head this way, if you can. Are one good hand and one leg enough to escape? Maybe. Crawl, drag, clutch any leg of furniture, any object along the path. Inch a broken body through empty hallways. Follow the fluorescent signs through a darkened labyrinth. Get to the fire door. Moving like an inchworm whose sightless head seeks the warmth of the sun. Work the handle with an uninjured right arm. Flames lick one foot, intact but mateless. Pushing with newfound alacrity, one shoulder abuts the door. One hand scrabbles to do the work of two.

The heavy metal door slams shut. The heat of the flames is gone. In its place are stairs, the simplest of escape routes. For those with feet. Crawling, tumbling, falling, down the stairs until exhausted; unable to perform a simple feat from last week. Last week. The final week of living. Now there is only living hell.

"Carry me." *Arms outstretched, beseeching.*

"Carry you?" *Mother mocks.* "First scramble me an egg," *she taunts.*

"Carry you?" *Caleb mocks.* "First cut me a line of coke."

"Carry you?" *Father asks.* "Get your lazy ass off the floor!"

Orchid turns her face away, as if disgusted by the flailing legs of a beetle unable to right itself. She lifts me, navigating the hard-won steps I spent forty minutes tumbling down. She opens the fire door. The flames are gone. Everything is sterile. The hallway is empty. She pushes through the door to my room and, like an offering, places me on the bed. She wipes clean her clothes as if contaminated.

In the bright white of the light, I see what shocks her. The bandages covering my stumps are gone, discarded in the struggle. My wounds lie bare and ugly. Bloody lines wind around blunt, severed limbs like moss creeping up a tree. I scream. Orchid appears, grimacing.

"What do you need, love?" She turns her back on my disfigurement. At least she called me "love." But then, what's wrong?

"Why are you crying, Orchid?"

"I'm about to be sick."

"Are you ill?"

"Only when I'm here. What do you need?"

"My limbs . . . my leg and hand. Please."

"Okay, love." She departs the room.

"No!" he shouts. "Don't leave, please don't leave."

Real hands comfort him. His mom's voice soothes. "Shh." She wraps one arm around his chest. "It's okay," she says over and over like a mantra. "You're okay now."

In the cruel darkness of that first night, ideas form, amorphous but deep-seated, never to allow what's missing to make him dependent on another. Nor to shackle anyone else to his half-state.

CHAPTER 9

WEEP THEMSELVES TO SLEEP

Phoenix

The morning was rough. Every nerve, physical and emotional, felt raw. His mom didn't want to leave, refusing even the bathroom until Caleb arrived.

"Hey, how you doing?"

Caleb seemed careful to avoid the tubes and tender spots that had pained his brother the day before. Phoenix pressed the button releasing morphine into his veins. Relief snaked its way through his bloodstream, easing the sharpness in his body and letting him care a little less.

Phoenix stared at his brother from his propped position against a pile of pillows. He could offer nothing. Everything he thought was too awful to say, and his mind was a jumble of drugs and pain. He closed his eyes to the sight of Caleb's worried expression. A weird jealousy arose over what previously seemed to be givens—the ability to walk, to care for oneself. Phoenix was always the more capable brother. *This can't be.*

The sound of air compressing from the vinyl chair at his bedside accompanied the pinging of the machines keeping track of his broken body. *Caleb must've eased his mass into the guest seat.*

His mom's heels tapped towards his bed.

"Is he okay?" Caleb asked their mom, knowing the answer.

"He had a bad dream," she explained. "He's going to be okay."

What do they know about being okay? And dream? That was no dream.

No, that nightmare was Phoenix's subconscious screaming in no uncertain terms that he was never going to be the same again. That he'd lost as much as he thought and more. That there was no point to his denial.

"What do you need, dear? Are you hungry?"

He wanted them to leave. He could only shake his head. Even that small motion triggered discomfort.

After a long period of quiet, Phoenix became aware of Caleb's low, murmured voice. He had no way of determining how much time had passed and whether he'd slept.

"No, I'm not going," said their mom, in answer to some question Phoenix hadn't heard.

"You look like crap, Mom."

"Excuse me?" she said this almost as an afterthought, as if she surely hadn't heard Caleb properly.

"You need grub, too," Caleb admonished.

"I don't want to leave."

Paying their mother no mind, Caleb stood. "Something hot. Follow me," he insisted.

"But—"

"Come on, soldier, this is an order." Chalk it up to the unspoken power of twins, but Caleb intuited that Phoenix needed time to himself.

Caleb put his arm around their mom. "C'mon, we won't be long."

Phoenix opened his eyes long enough to encourage his mom. "Go eat something," he managed, his voice cracking.

She studied him a long time, without saying anything.

Phoenix nodded towards the door. "Go."

She fussed over placing the nurse's call button within Phoenix's reach before reluctantly leaving his side.

"You need a haircut," she told her tattooed son, looking up at his overgrown mane.

"Just for that, you're buying breakfast." Caleb said, throwing Phoenix a smirk.

Phoenix watched them move on able legs towards the exit.

The door, half a room away, may as well have been across the continent. The distance to the floor mocked. *Yeah, right. Just try to get down.* He could brace himself with one leg and then what?

Now that he was alone and conscious, Phoenix needed to take a hard look at himself. He flung the sheets off with one hand. It was an alarming sight. His leg ended too early. His arm was a swollen mess of bandages. One fall had truncated his life in half. Framed by nostalgia, his old life seemed full and happy. His new life, he couldn't picture.

This can't be real. Fuck. I can't do this. I need help.

Orchid.

No. Never Orchid.

The one woman who could help, he couldn't imagine in this abyss of horror.

CHAPTER 10

A MARTYR FOR
MY LOVE FOR YOU

Phoenix

Phoenix glanced down at his uncovered limbs and pulled the hospital blanket over his legs. It didn't make the sight any better. Mom helped him straighten the bedspread and smoothed it with one hand.

"Are you cold?"

"No, I just don't want to see—"

"You look fine," she lied. "You're still you," she insisted. He was in too much pain to argue.

She looked like hell. Caleb looked even worse than when Dad died. Which meant Phoenix's half-state between life and death was worse than death.

His mother and brother spent the day taking turns bringing him any small measure of comfort. They helped Phoenix adjust his position, poured him cool drinks, and encouraged him to eat. His mom punctuated the periods when he was awake by reading aloud his correspondences. She skipped business emails to share personal notes from friends and colleagues. Sincere if stuttered expressions of sympathy, especially the impossibility of "get well soon," left Phoenix feeling worse. It reminded him of a world that kept going, even if he might never rejoin it.

Mom skipped from emails and texts over to photos on his phone.

"Who's this?" she asked, showing him a selfie that Orchid had taken of the two of them.

They looked happy. Ignorance is bliss. *If only she knew, what would she think?* A lump rose in his throat when he didn't want to feel anything.

"Who is this?"

"Orchid," he said.

"Is she a friend?" Mom's eyes scanned the pic again.

"Someone I know from work."

"She looks like more than a co-worker," she said, squinting at Orchid's dimpled cheek pressed against his.

"At one point, it looked like that might be the case."

"Does she know about your accident?"

"She doesn't."

"Do you want to call her?"

"No."

Mom leaned back at the sharpness in his tone. "Text?"

"No. She's in China," he said, as if that were an adequate excuse.

"You sure?"

"I'm positive. And I'm tired." He turned, closing his eyes. Would there be more reminders of Orchid? *Hope not. There's no point.*

A knock at the door interrupted his thoughts. Reluctantly, he opened his eyes.

A sturdy woman in dark blue scrubs entered, pushing a wheelchair. He couldn't help but stare at the hulking contraption.

She introduced herself with a firm handshake and explained

she'd come to help him to the bathroom and would first remove his catheter.

"Is that something I could do . . . myself?" he mumbled.

She beamed. "Nope. My specialty."

Caleb led their mom to the window, giving Phoenix a small measure of privacy.

The nurse pushed the bed's plastic handrail down out of the way. She smelled like antiseptic soap and talked as she worked.

"This wheelchair is a one-handed model," she explained. "It's set up as an amputee chair, weighted so that it won't tip back." *Amputee chair? Does she have any sense how much it sucks to need a wheelchair, much less a one-handed amputee one?*

"There, all done," she said, covering his lower half with the hospital gown. "Now, let's get you up."

Finally.

She pushed a button to adjust the bed upright. "You feeling dizzy at all?" she asked.

"Uh, no."

At the sound of the bed's motor being activated, Caleb and his mom returned. *An audience, great.*

The nurse wheeled the chair right next to the bed. "No dizziness? That's good. Your balance might feel different but you're going to swing your legs over the side," she instructed, wrapping an arm around him for support.

He placed one hand on the bed and levered towards the side of the mattress. His weight felt strangely distributed, his left side oddly light, his right side weighted and awkward. He bit his lip. She studied the beads of sweat he could feel forming on his forehead.

"Okay, take a break. What's your pain level?"

"Really bad," he said, as fire rocketed everywhere, the pain refusing to be ignored.

"Very intense?" The woman in blue asked. "You want to wait 'til later?"

"No, it's okay. It's like a six out of ten now." He waited for the waning sensation to catch up with his fib. *I need to get out of bed.* "Or five."

The nurse nodded. She wrapped her arms around his back and braced herself on the bed. Between the stinging pain, Phoenix realized what she planned to do.

"You're going to help me by yourself?"

She paused and looked at him, surprised. "Why not?"

"Aren't I too heavy for you?"

"I doubt it. I weigh more than you."

"No you don't. I weigh—" He stopped, a new realization hitting him.

"Besides, it's just for long enough to sit in that chair," she continued, ignoring or oblivious to the horror washing over him. He was no longer a six-foot, 165-pound athlete. He weighed no more than this stocky woman. He had less agility than a two-by-four.

Caleb stepped over. "You want to show me what to do, in case I ever need to help out?"

Phoenix groaned over the thought of his twin aiding him out of bed. The humiliations kept coming.

The nurse demonstrated the spots where she steadied him for his brother to observe. "Ready?" she asked, and then encouraged Phoenix until he was briefly up on a single leg, and just as quickly, down in the seat. He grabbed the armrest, instinctively seeking to balance himself.

"This is a stump board," she explained, helping him position the swollen mass of his severed leg onto a padded surface jutting out from the seat of the chair. "It'll keep your leg at the proper angle to prevent swelling."

Oh, god. Amputee. Stump board.

He didn't have long to contemplate the unfamiliar phrases that seemed to have nothing to do with him. Being seated instead of prone, he felt like he'd been set adrift in a vast space. Unmoored from the bed, he grew dizzy.

The nurse set them into motion, wheeling the IV pole while guiding his chair.

Mom hurried ahead to open the bathroom door.

The nurse pushed him over the threshold, not just into another room, but into another life. "Okay, we're going to practice transferring onto the commode."

A toilet sat framed by industrial grade handrails. *How the hell am I going to get onto that?* Before he could tackle the seemingly impossible, he caught sight of himself in the mirror, which was angled towards the ground for someone seated. The first sight of his new form struck him with a wave of repulsion, almost a physical force. Framed in the chrome edges of the looking glass sat a disheveled figure in a wheelchair—half man, half bandages, oddly truncated and unsettling in the asymmetry of its body.

The nurse must've thought he was looking at the sink. She pointed out the brush suction cupped to the inside of the porcelain.

"That's so you can wash one-handed. Just pump some soap and scrub your hand against the brush. The occupational therapist will show you."

He stared at her, the magnitude of his adaptations dawning on him one icy trickle at a time. *Does this mean I'm going to become a suction-cup brush-carrying freak?* If he had to think about how to wash a hand, what other thousand things would he have to do differently?

The nurse, moving to the next task, wheeled his chair adjacent to the toilet.

"First, we'll practice. Just put one hand here," she said, indicating the right-hand grab bar, "and an elbow here." She pointed to the wheelchair's armrest. Her stern expression left him no choice. He did as instructed. She steadied an arm around him, helping him push up from the upholstered seat to sit on the porcelain one.

His brother, watching from the doorway, scowled, hands on hips.

Phoenix was clothed and this was just practice, but still, he felt the loss of privacy.

"Sitting to pee for the rest of my life is going to suck," Phoenix said, trying to keep the sharp edge in his voice more ironic than self-pitying.

"Who cares," Caleb declared. "I'm goddamned grateful to see you mobile again."

"This isn't fuckin' mobile."

"Language," Mom scolded.

Caleb's glower deepened. "That's mobile enough. You could've died. I freakin' said goodbye."

The nurse reversed their steps and situated Phoenix back in his chair.

"Sorry. I don't know what's wrong with me," Phoenix said, chastised. Nothing felt right. Not only the burning through his limbs and unclear thinking, but also his moods which swung as wildly as a carnival ride.

The nurse pushed from behind and dragged the IV pole. "Let's get you back to bed. I want to give you medication so I can change your bandages, check the swelling, and let you rest. Then the psychotherapist will be in later."

Psychotherapist? Great. What lies will I have to tell to keep this therapist off my back? That I'm adjusting? Glad to be alive?

Good thing ad guys excelled at spinning stories.

CHAPTER 11

I THINK I FOUND THE CULPRIT

Phoenix

Sascha hid any shock over Phoenix's bandaged injuries with a cherry red pout. "Hullo, luv," she said, cupping his cheek and leaning over his hospital bed for a kiss.

She stood back studying him with a cock of her head, not breaking eye contact.

Smart move; don't look at the missing parts.

Then she loosened the drawstring of her knapsack. "Caleb and I stopped by your place. He's parking the truck."

Out tumbled familiar white T-shirts and navy-blue gym shorts. Folded, the emblazoned logos weren't visible. Even so, he knew which ones represented his undergrad and graduate schools. Not long ago, those institutions seemed to hold importance in his life. Now, nothing did.

"How are you?" she asked, piling up workout gear on top of his bedspread.

"What do *you* think?" he snarled.

"I think you've had a run of tough luck, and it's a good thing you're strong." She stacked the neat pile on his side table, then shook out a shirt and shorts. "How about these?" she asked, holding up the items to model them for him.

He ignored the clothing. "I'll tell you the God's honest truth. I'm not strong enough for this."

She put one hand over his, the flowing sweep of a tattooed pattern made visible as her sleeve hiked up.

"I think you're strong enough, luv. So does Caleb. So does your mom. And you're not alone. Look how many people care about you." She waved a hand to indicate the flowers and cards that lined the dresser top and windowsill. "Now let's get you out of that hospital gown."

"Sascha, are you crazy?" He felt like exploding. "Who cares what I'm wearing?"

With a shake of her mass of auburn hair, she stepped closer. "You're the handsomest guy I know. I bet you'll feel better in regular clothes. How about we give it a try?"

He twisted in bed, trying to escape the burning feeling traveling up his missing leg. At least his IV was gone, no longer trapping his movements.

"Aw, crap."

"What's wrong?" Sascha asked, alarmed at his contorted expression.

He grasped the side rail and sucked in a breath. "It's phantom pain. The cut nerves are looking for the missing limbs and sending back messed up signals. My foot feels like it's on fire. Ironic when I have no leg, right?"

"I'm sorry. Can I get you something?"

"This isn't something an aspirin is going to fix."

Her cheeks flushed. "I am so inconsiderate. I should go. I'll tell Caleb to let you rest." She scooped up the folded laundry and walked across the room. With one hand, she yanked open an empty dresser drawer.

Oddly, he suddenly felt the absence of her concern. "It's okay, don't go."

She paused putting the items away.

"Let's try it," he said, gesturing at the abandoned outfit on the bed.

"You don't have to do it to make *me* feel better. I'm supposed to make *you* feel better," she replied.

"Actually, you might be onto something," he admitted, sitting up. "Do you know this gown opens in the back?"

She came over to peer behind him. "Wow, this hospital gown look is so not your thing. The boxers underneath show promise, though."

"Untie this sack while you're back there, would you?"

She yanked at the knots from top to bottom. "You want some privacy while you get dressed?"

He shook his head. "It's no more than you'd see at the beach." He shrugged out of the surgical green fabric and tossed it onto the ground.

Her gaze traveled from his chest to his abdomen. "Oh my, you'll have to tell me which beach."

"Bad girl." He pulled the shirt over his left, then right arm and over his head.

She handed him the shorts. "Don't tell Caleb. He gets jealous enough."

The bottoms challenged him. He shimmied the shorts up over his uninjured leg, and over the swollen mass of a knee. Then, he balanced his left elbow on the bedrail to inch up one side at a time until he'd wormed the waistband over his hips.

Sascha stepped back to assess the effect. "There's the Phoenix I know."

He exhaled. "The better half, anyway."

"You ad guys, nothing's sacred."

"We're not above going low for a laugh."

"Speaking of ad guys, you know that guy from your office was here right when you were first hurt?"

"You mean Dex?"

"Yeah, I think so. Big guy? Looks like a human teddy bear?"

"Ha, yeah, sounds like Dex."

"And your aunt spent two days here with your mom."

"I must've been a rude awakening for Aunt Betsy's perfect life," he said.

Sascha laughed, a tinkling sound. "Don't worry. She was too busy being shocked over Caleb and me. I guess we've gotten more tatted up since she last saw us. She checked out my outfit like she was trying to decide whether to run, or hide."

Phoenix pictured his aunt's pinched expression. "You're kidding."

"I kid you not. And then she starts sniffing around Caleb like a police dog, all 'are you doing drugs?'"

"He must've loved that," Phoenix mused.

"Not as much as he loved the lecture about how your mom's done enough for him through his teen years, and he better not worry her with his punk lifestyle, or some such b.s."

"Punk lifestyle? She just can't relate to anyone who doesn't summer at the beach and winter at Vail."

He looked down the bed at the white sheets. He wasn't going to be skiing Vail anytime soon.

Sascha squeezed his hand. "I'll tell you what. Let's give your aunt something to talk about. When you're feeling up to it, you come in and we'll design you a tattoo."

"You think some ink's going to distract people from noticing what's missing?"

"Nope. I think you should embrace that with pride, luv. You're a hero. It's survival scars. That's you, nothing to be ashamed of."

Sitting with a woman who got him, and wasn't afraid to talk about his accident, he told the truth. "Sasch, that's sweet but you know, I can't even begin to tell you how badly this sucks."

She nodded. "Must suck something awful. Worse than anything."

He was silent for a moment. "Worse than . . . losing your high-school sweetheart to your brother?" he finally said.

She raised her eyebrows, then upped the ante. "Worse than . . . my first period?"

He looked at her and she started giggling. "Okay," he conceded. "Maybe this little flesh wound is survivable." He waved the end of his arm around for effect.

"Maybe you're going to be all right after all."

"Yup. Maybe."

The door swung open. Caleb strode in.

"What's so funny?"

"Nothing like your sardonic ex to cheer me up."

Caleb planted his lips on top of Sascha's head as he passed her.

"Take it outside, lovebirds," Phoenix said irritably.

Sascha registered hurt in her eyes. *Weren't we just connecting? Aren't I on your side?*

You're not going to make me better with a simple laugh, babe, his look retorted.

Caleb sank into the chair at his bedside.

"I know the cops grilled you, but I've got some questions."

Phoenix closed his eyes. He was so tired. Not just physical fatigue or pain from the wounds. He was so damned tired of talking about himself.

"I still don't get what happened," Caleb said.

"What don't you get? It was just a stupid, senseless accident." Phoenix said.

"It wasn't senseless. You saved someone's life," Sascha interjected.

"Who says that asshole didn't plan it all along?" Caleb asked.

Phoenix sighed and opened his eyes. "He was probably out of his mind. I was just in the wrong place at the wrong time."

"You guys didn't argue, right?"

"Nope, I gave the bum money."

"A buck, right?"

"Yeah, a buck." Phoenix looked thoughtfully at his brother, a new thought penetrating his foggy mind. "You don't think he got mad because I gave him too little, do you?"

"Mad enough to try to kill himself?" Sascha coughed a little laugh. It did sound preposterous.

"Who knows what sends people over the edge," Caleb said.

"So to speak," Phoenix added dryly. No response to his gallows humor.

"What'd he do when you gave him the money?" Caleb continued.

"I wasn't looking at him. I was reading a note from Orchid." *Could it have been as simple as money? What if I gave the guy a five? A hundred? Hell, I'd give the bastard all my millions to get my limbs back.*

"Did he look suicidal to you?" Caleb continued.

Phoenix wasn't listening. His mind raced with what he could've done differently. What altered route could've changed this nightmare.

Sascha gripped Caleb's arm. "Stop already. Don't you see this isn't a good time?"

"Sorry," Caleb muttered, not making it clear whether he was apologizing to his sibling or his ex-girlfriend.

"Come on, babe. Let's go. Let the man rest."

Phoenix heard the door shut and the rhythmic clicking sound of two pairs of feet walking away down the corridor.

CHAPTER 12

LITTLE ACORNS

Phoenix

What asshole thinks I'm well enough to move to rehab?

A knock at the door announced the arrival of a trim woman, wearing a tracksuit and a cheery attitude.

"Hello, Mr. Walker." The fit young woman with the ponytail of a cheerleader took in all of him, not averting her eyes but looking straight at him, with warmth and competence. She stuck out her hand. "I'm Nadine, your lead therapist."

"You want to know how I feel about that?" Phoenix asked dryly.

"Funny one. *Physical* therapist, not a shrink."

"Well, good luck with that. Not much left to work with."

"May seem that way now." She nodded affably, as she checked him out like a side of beef at a Brazilian barbeque. "You've got the physique of a twenty-year-old athlete. Best abs I've seen in a while. So, how are you feeling?"

"Like I've been run over by a train," he answered, aiming to point out the uselessness of her question. However, there was no dampening her enthusiasm for the body that was in her charge.

"I appreciate that it's hard to see right now, but I promise, it's going to get better. First, let's talk about your goals."

"Goals? How about getting me out of this nightmare and back to my regular life?"

Her tone softened. "It may seem difficult right now, but that's exactly what we're going to work towards."

"Okay, tell me about your regular life. What do you do?" She removed a pen from behind her ear and opened up a tattered notebook.

"I run an ad agency, work out, entertain clients, travel." *In the past, anyway*.

"Running an agency is, like, a desk job, right?"

"Yeah." He could see where she was going with this: that even double amputees can sit at desks. He wanted to resist. She was so damned upbeat.

"And entertaining clients means eating at restaurants, am I right?"

"Uh, yeah."

"I don't see any problem there. What about workouts? What do you do?"

"Weights. Running, swimming, biking. I'm a triathlete—" He stopped, remembering the last time he'd competed in a triathlon. Orchid had come to cheer him on. Caleb, too. Afterwards, something sharp on the beach had sliced open the bare arch of her foot. That's when he learned that she couldn't stomach the sight of her own blood. Which meant that now, he would be the one to repulse her.

"It's a long road. You'll learn modifications. No reason you can't continue those things. Plenty of muscles left."

She was experienced at this. Overcoming every potential objection. He wasn't buying it. "On holiday, I ski, climb, do water sports." He wanted her to cringe, to see the desperation he felt mirrored on her face.

She maintained equanimity. "Sounds like fun. You'll have to adapt how you do things. Prostheses have come a long way. We should be able to set you up for the things you want to try. What questions do you have?"

Questions? How am I going to manage? When will I leave this hospital? Will I be independent? He couldn't even get out of bed on his own or make it to the john. *How am I going to go to work, run a meeting? Will I revert to being Mom's little boy?* It all seemed so overwhelming.

"Here are a few questions. Can I live on my own? Do I have to sit to pee? What about getting laid?"

She wasn't shocked. "You are going to drive, live on your own, don a prosthesis if you want to stand to pee, and have all the sex you want. We are going to work together towards all those goals—except for the last one. There, you're on your own!"

In spite of himself, he smiled as she walked out of the room.

CHAPTER 13

CONSOLER OF THE LONELY

Phoenix

"**A**gain? Don't you have a business to run?" Phoenix erupted at the sight of Caleb walking towards his table.

The rehab center's cafeteria smelled like a mix of sugar-glazed donuts and cleaning supplies.

"I'm happy to see you too," his brother said dryly, easing into the plastic chair adjacent to Phoenix.

"Seriously, isn't Saturday a big day for you?"

"Yup. That's why I've got staff to run my parlors."

"Right. You have Sascha, and she's been here, too, every other day? What happens when you're both here?"

"I've got other guys to run my shops, too."

"Who are probably pilfering your cash while you're here."

Caleb leaned forward, his face reddening. "Why the fuck are we talking about my shops? Who cares about money? What's more important than being here? I've got news for you: I'm going to keep coming every freaking day until you walk out of here."

Caleb took a breath and leaned back in his chair. "Man, I'm sorry for yelling," he said.

"I was out of line. Don't think I'm not grateful. For you being here and all." Not being in charge made Phoenix feel vulnerable and real.

"What? What do you need?"

Phoenix shook his head, his throat tightening. "Nothing." *It's just, it sucks to need help.* He grabbed the bottled Evian off the table and tucked the rounded glass under his left elbow. He twisted with his right hand. The cap didn't budge. Instead, the whole slippery surface rotated under his less-than-optimal grip.

"Let me help." Caleb took the bottle and opened it. Needing help made Phoenix feel worse.

"I can't believe it. I'm the fucked-up one. Not you, Mr. Perfect." Caleb continued, staring at the blank painted walls. "I want to find the guy who did this and fuck him up so bad."

Phoenix couldn't help himself. He dwelled on the image of Caleb's burly strength and anger pummeling the crazed guy. "You do that. 'Cause I couldn't do anything about him."

"Don't say that. It wasn't your fault. Have you talked to the therapist about that?" His leg twitched like a nervous jackrabbit.

"Humph, if I do that, I may as well ask for a straitjacket." He thought for a moment. "Except they wouldn't know where to attach it."

"Not funny," Caleb answered, his face pinched. "You should talk with her."

"Seriously, I don't want them giving me happy pills on top of all the other drugs. It's making me loopy as it is. I need to get off the pain meds."

"If you need the meds, take them. Don't try to be a superhero."

"A superhero who's able to fall down stairs with a single bound," Phoenix said.

"Don't fight the meds. You know, in Africa, they found that chimpanzees eat special leaves to rid themselves of parasites."

"What the hell are you talking about?"

"I'm just sayin' even animals self-medicate to feel better. I read it in a journal."

Phoenix gave him a patented superior brother look. "You're really somethin'. You want something to eat?"

"No, I'm good. You want anything?" Caleb peered at the uneaten burger sitting in front of his twin.

"I'll take some of those chimp leaves for parasites." Phoenix looked around the nearly empty room. "Where's Mom, anyway?"

"I ran into her in the waiting room. I said I'd take you back to your room. Let her rest."

Phoenix slumped a little. He was exhausting their mom.

"I don't mean it that way. You know she wants to be here."

"That's the part I hate," Phoenix said. "I know you guys would do this for me. Be here. Do whatever. It's like I'm an invalid."

"You're not an invalid," Caleb said quietly. "You're going to be fine. You just need a little recovery time. It's been a hell of a ride."

Phoenix sat lost in contemplation. "You know what's the worst? No one needs me. Really. My office is running just fine without me. You guys would've gone on with your lives. It wouldn't have mattered if I'd died. People'd be sad for a bit, but then they'd pick up and move on."

"Bruh, you are not thinking straight. Listen, everyone's just giving you space to breathe. Your office wants you to get better. They're not going to bog you down with whatever stupid questions they've got. We all need you, believe me."

Phoenix shook his head, his convictions so clear.

Caleb straightened as if with a new thought. "Hey, didn't you text me about Orchid? There's someone who needs you. She looks at you like you're the moon and the stars."

Phoenix wanted to laugh, a crazy derisive laugh. Then he wanted to scream over the injustice of their now-impossible relationship.

"She's on a business trip."

"Well hell, has anyone told her? Does she know what's happened?"

"No, not yet."

"Give me Orchid's number. I'll text her."

Phoenix shook his head. "There's no point."

"What do you mean? She'd want to know."

"You don't know her. Give me some time to get better first. If you tell her, she'd be on the next flight, even if she had to blackmail a nun for the last seat."

Caleb chuckled. "That sounds like her. But didn't you text that you guys are a thing?"

"It was one night. It was nothing. It's over."

Caleb scratched his chin. "But you texted that like two weeks ago. How could it be over already?"

"I've told you guys, I just don't want anyone here. Not Dex, not our cousins, no one."

"Why not?" Caleb persisted.

"I'm in no shape to see anyone. My mind's all fuzzy and my moods are all over the place."

"She might be understanding about that. Like Sascha is."

Phoenix allowed a thought of Orchid. Beautiful, sensitive Orchid was as skittish as a kitten over trauma.

"Believe me, there's no one to call."

"Okay, if you're sure."

"I'm sure." And yet, how sure was he, really?

CHAPTER 14

MY DOORBELL

Phoenix

"Christ, Mom, just tell him no," Phoenix said.

"It might make you feel better," Mom said, adjusting feather and foam pillows behind his back with experienced practice.

"Nothing is going to make me feel better," he said.

"Besides, Dex and his wife Fiona are on their way," she continued, choosing to ignore his wishes. Gliding over to the lone window, she raised the blinds. Like stupid sunshine could make an atom of difference in his ruined life.

"Aw, shit. Today?" he asked.

"Yes, any minute now," she said, glancing at her watch as if it magically tracked Dex's whereabouts.

He was pissed, at her, at Dex, at himself, at his whole awful situation. He grabbed the arm of his wheelchair, yanking it right up next to the bed. Mom hurried over, fear of him spilling onto the floor evident in the creased lines of her face. She put her arms around him to help with the transfer to the chair, making his gut clench over his predicament.

He pushed the rim of the chair forward, the action giving him the small satisfaction of translating energy into motion.

"I don't want to see anyone," he said, the refrain clearly not landing with his mother. He wheeled towards the bathroom. Mom, one step ahead of him, opened the door before he could wrestle with it.

Sledgehammer that mirror already.

He balanced his toothbrush onto the porcelain surface and squeezed a smear of toothpaste. His brain tried to find a crescent of hope to save him from impending self-pity. Running a razor over his cheeks, dragging a wet comb through his wavy mass of overlong hair, none of that changed the haggard expression that stared back at him.

Shock clenched his stomach as he recognized the dark circles haunting Caleb and his mom's features mirrored on his own face. *Damned train took more than my limbs.* It gutted his insides until he couldn't recognize what was left. Those wounded soldiers from their non-profit work had more tenacity than he could've previously appreciated.

Time was up. Through the flimsy door, a familiar booming voice greeted his mother, and a softer one followed. He looked down at the T-shirt and gym shorts emblazoned with a prestigious school logo that no longer seemed important. The outfit had been his uniform since descending into this surreal torture. The short sleeves and short pants exposed bandaged endings of limbs.

Here goes nothing. He pushed open the door. Two sets of eyes turned towards him. The few revolutions his chair took to reach them fractured into dozens of split-second judgments that passed on his friends' faces. Dex's mouth wavered at the corners, like a hairline fracture on a window about to shatter. He turned, teeth glinting white beneath a bushy beard. His narrowing eyes belied his effort to mask his emotions. Fiona, on the other hand, conveyed her shock in a silent film with no subtitles. Her mouth gaped open in a pink oval like a mewling kitten, then slammed shut in an apparent memory of manners, only to be replaced by fingers twitching uselessly at the hem of her tunic.

"Hey," Dex said with affection, taking a step to meet him before he leaned down for a one-armed hug. "I cannot believe what happened."

"Yeah, me either."

Fiona recovered enough to bend and hug his seated form. "You okay?"

Nothing was okay. The frozen horror on his friends' faces confirmed this. "I'm about as okay as I look."

Dex brought over a chair for his wife. She sank into it, eyes rimming red.

"Everyone sends their greetings," Dex said, propping a card onto Phoenix's side table. He plopped onto one side of the hospital bed.

"And they brought pastries," his mom said, indicating the white paper bag. "I'll get some coffee for us." She pushed out of the room, her cardigan floating behind her.

"They find the bum you saved?" Dex asked, bushy eyebrows knitting into one.

"Nope. Caleb's spent hours with the cops. They looked at all the surveillance tapes but the cameras down in that part of the station were busted. Not that I see the point."

"Maybe he wants to get the guy into therapy?" Dex chuckled at his own ludicrous scenario.

"I think if he ever found him, Caleb would want to finish the job."

"I'd like to find him so we can get you guys on talk shows together. Turn you into the media hero that you deserve to be," Dex said. His art-director-quirky bowtie bounced with mirth.

"I'm no hero, and I definitely don't want media," Phoenix said.

He pictured sitting on stage in his wheelchair next to the dirty bum. His stomach heaved. His eyes watered.

"You have everything you need?" Fiona asked, leaning forward to put a hand on his. Etched lines dragged the corners of her mouth towards the ground like a ventriloquist's dummy.

"Yeah, Mom's made sure I have the best of everything. She even convinced insurance to maximize my inpatient rehab." He didn't want to talk about this. *Just go.*

"Any cute nurses?" Fiona asked, running a hand through her hair.

Dex brightened. "Didn't you have something going with that L'Oreal marketer?"

Fiona turned to face his chair. "Who?"

"Orchid. She's in China," Phoenix said.

"Oh, the one you brought to the Effies?"

"Yeah, but we're not in touch anymore." The night before Orchid had left portended a future. One finger beneath his chin, she had brought his face closer to hers. She had leaned to bestow a kiss sweeter than caramel, her lips brushing his until he had lost any sense of time. What cruelty to have every memory paired with imagining her repulsion.

Phoenix nodded his chin towards the card, seeking a distraction from the focus on him. "How's everyone at the office?"

"Everyone's fine. Worried about you, of course. Liv really wants to come visit."

He didn't want Liv to see him like this. "Tell her I'm not up for company."

Dex pushed up his sleeves, looked at Phoenix and pulled them back down. "She'll be disappointed. She told me she'd feel better if she could see you."

"You sure she'd feel better?"

Dex ignored the sharpness in his buddy's tone. "You'd be proud to know Liv's really stepped up."

Phoenix nodded. "She's great. One of these days you should try her on a creative team." Phoenix suddenly flashed to a vision of the agency running smoothly without him, Liv leading creative meetings, Dex managing the company. *What can I add?*

"Do they know how long you'll be here?" Fiona asked.

"They're saying another few weeks and I can come in for outpatient rehab."

"Well, we're coming back next weekend, no excuses, you hear?"

They got up, leaving him the only one seated.

CHAPTER 15

STORE-BOUGHT BONES

Phoenix

The cool, rubber-scented physical therapy rooms represented normalcy, his workday routine. Under Nadine's tough and patient tutelage, Phoenix learned the purpose of every mat, table and set of parallel bars. He practiced over and over, his muscles memorizing new routines.

Early on, Nadine explained how Phoenix was lucky. She showed him his portion of her notebook.

"LBK—left below the knee—means you can walk with a completely normal gait. You're really just missing an ankle and a foot."

"Oh, is that all?" he asked dryly.

She liked his work ethic. "You really push yourself," she commented.

"Well, better that than to picture my mom wheeling my chair or sponge-bathing me," he deadpanned, huffing between repetitions of sit-ups to strengthen his core muscles.

After a few weeks together on a daily basis, Nadine got his vibe pretty well. He refused her encircling arms and grimaced as he stumbled while practicing on stairs, hopping with one hand on a railing. She cocked an eyebrow at him, a sure sign she was about to give advice.

"I know you're really pushing yourself towards independence, and that's great." He nodded, waiting for the *but* while forcing himself upright. "But," she continued, "if you do need help, or need to look foolish, don't let pride get in your way."

Sweat dripping, he pulled out his ready shield of sarcasm.

"Easy for you to say as you stand there on two feet, two perfectly good hands on your hips as you judge me."

"Hey," she said softly, "I like you well enough I'd give you one of mine if I could."

Damned if that genuine look of concern didn't make his chest swell with emotion.

"Nah, no donor limbs for me, with the rejection drugs and all. But you're really thoughtful, you know that?"

She rolled her eyes. "With all that sweet talk, your girlfriend better get here soon," she warned.

He looked away. "There's no girlfriend."

Even so, Phoenix thought of Orchid. She'd be returning from China the following Saturday. And expecting him at the airport. He couldn't even get himself to a Starbucks, much less JFK.

"Any woman would be crazy to turn you away," Nadine assured.

"There's some kind of crazy going around, all right," he responded.

"Speaking of crazy," she said, eyes twinkling with mischief, "can you believe all your progress in a month?"

"Yup," he shrugged, "tomorrow's the one-month anniversary of my accident."

Nadine leaned back to examine his expression. "You know, maybe a month is too early, but people sometimes celebrate the anniversary of their near-miss with death as an 'Alive Day.' It's better than mourning what was lost."

"You can ask me in a year, but you'll have to pardon me if I don't feel like celebrating right now."

The mischief effervesced higher in Nadine's eyes. "You might change your mind when I tell you what we're doing today."

"Oh yeah?" he asked, curiosity piqued. "You going to stretch me until I cry? Make me do another umpteen push-ups?"

She stood, pointing at his chair. "Not quite. Let's go get you fitted for prostheses."

"Today?"

"Right now."

Phoenix pulled the chair closer. Then he pushed to a stand and lowered himself into the seat.

"Ok," he said, placing a hand on the push rim, "where to?"

CHAPTER 16

BLUE ORCHID

Phoenix

Phoenix's phone buzzed with a familiar name.

"Hi, Tish."

"So, I have news and the news is I'm engaged," Tish said, giggling.

"Congratulations, Tom's the lucky guy, right?" Phoenix looked down at the form that would no longer be anyone's lucky guy.

"After nearly two years, he better be. We've a date set for the first week of April. It's been hell securing a venue. Anything less than a year out is a crapshoot. You know weddings in the city. Wait—no you don't! Forever the bachelor who breaks women's hearts, right?"

"Forever's a long time, but you're right, I've been fairly committed to bachelorhood." Even more so now. *No left-hand finger to even wear a ring.*

"Tell me the gossip. How's Caleb? Veronica? I want details. I've not seen you since your dad's funeral. Jesus, has it been a year already?"

"Caleb's surly as ever. My mom is hanging in there, and I'm four weeks into a multi-month staycation in rehab," he said, thinking of the two family members looking as ravaged as he was.

"Rehab? For months?"

He didn't particularly want to answer the concern ascending in her voice, so he kept to the barest details. He swallowed. "I fell onto a subway line."

"Holy shit. Are you all right?"

"Yeah, I'm okay." He thought for a moment. "What's left of me, anyway."

"What do you mean, what's left of you?"

Gripped by sadness, he pictured their jaunts to Vegas, Joshua Tree and the wine country. Another goodbye to the person he was.

"Damned train took a leg and my hand."

In the silence that followed, Phoenix pictured her hyperventilating.

"Phoenix, I'm so sorry. Your poor mother. First your father and now this. What can I do? Should I send a fruit basket?" she asked, referencing an inside joke the couple had years ago as to the protocols of whether to send a fruit basket or flowers.

If only there was something anyone could do.

Tish came by that afternoon, *Car and Driver* magazine in one hand and a bouquet of Vanda orchids and blue sea holly in the other.

"I figured you won't be driving anytime soon, but it might help with inspiration," Tish said as she her eyes skidded from Phoenix's bandaged arm to his injured leg hanging down from the seat of the wheelchair.

"This is me looking better," he promised, wanting to wipe the look of horror from her face and his memory.

She mechanically took the dozen steps from the room's doorway towards him. "Maybe I should just put these down." She placed the bouquet and magazine on his bedside table.

Orchids, really? Like I need a reminder.

He was relieved that at least she figured out not to give him anything, which would leave him with no hand for wheeling the chair.

"How are you feeling?" she asked, perched in the blue vinyl seat, finally eye level with him.

"From the expression on your face, not as bad as I must look," he replied, feeling as pained as she appeared.

"To the contrary," she denied. "You look . . . fit."

He knew what her expression meant. No sane woman would ever look at him the same again. Eligible bachelor no more. Catch no more. Player no more. Dreams, vanished. He swallowed past the ache crushing his chest.

"Thanks," he said, then turned the conversation to her. "So, how's Tom?"

"He's good. I think he's excited." She pulled up photos from her smartphone, showing pictures from their engagement party, then shared their choice of venues and details about her wedding dress.

There was no getting around it. While his life had taken a dive from which there was no recovery, others' lives would progress.

"I'm happy for you, Tish."

"Thanks. But I mean, it doesn't seem so important now, with everything you're going through."

"Don't be silly. Life goes on. That's the one thing I've learned. Hell, they even have a phrase for it—my 'new normal.' And next year in the spring, you'll walk down the aisle and you and Tom will have a new normal."

Spouting other people's crap didn't sound any better coming from him.

"In any event, I hate this is happening. Is there anything you need?"

"Nothing you can offer," he replied, squeezing his eyes as the corners of her mouth headed south.

"I'll tell you what. When you're out of here, we'll do something fun."

Fun? The concept sounded foreign.

CHAPTER 17

THERE'S NO HOME FOR YOU HERE

Orchid

Orchid's most surprising experience in Beijing was looking Asian but not being treated as a Chinese citizen. Lips loosened with wine, she confessed her confusion to her R&D colleague over dinner.

"We can see you are not Chinese from blocks away," Orchid's friend, Star, confirmed.

"Because I'm only half Chinese?" Orchid sputtered, thinking how her mother's genes had graced her with nearly black hair and deeply brown eyes.

"No," Star laughed correcting her. "Because of your dress. Your hair, *toufa*. Your mannerisms give you away like a schoolgirl."

Orchid looked down at the pleather edging her miniskirt.

"Very funny, Star. But you know what's unfair? In the US, people don't think I look American enough. In China, people don't think I'm Chinese enough. Guess I don't fit in anywhere."

"You are pretty like Chinese and western like American."

That lightened Orchid's mood. She smiled and sipped her

putaojiu, or wine, and pictured what Phoenix would say. That she fit in anywhere. Or better yet, why he liked her uniqueness.

"Tell me how your family is doing," Orchid said. She hoped her friend's grandmother was feeling better, and wanted to hear about their upcoming Autumn Festival plans.

After they'd conversed and the dishes were cleared, the talk turned towards work.

"So, how's beauty strategy coming?" Star asked. Orchid thought about the seminal document she needed to deliver in two weeks.

Orchid trusted her. Star was smart, funny and didn't hold it against her for being *waiguoren*, or foreigner.

"Honestly, I think it's rock solid. I mean, really good," Orchid said, correcting her use of slang that wouldn't be understood. She was lucky that her company conducted business in English. "The problem is Eban."

Her friend nodded. "He is very difficult."

"He was fine with my deck when I showed it to him one-on-one, but in his team meeting, he shredded me. Um, made me look bad," Orchid explained.

"You need a big dog."

Orchid laughed at the expression.

"Go tell Li Wei. Or Wang Ming."

"I need them to approve my recommendations. I can't let them think I'm having trouble with the head of sales for our biggest region," Orchid said.

Star tilted her head. The Chinese valued the idea of saving face. "Maybe American big dog."

Orchid brightened at the spark of an idea. They chatted until the check came. At the exit, Orchid bought two tins of cookies, packaged in a traditional blue and white pattern. She handed one box to her friend and hugged her goodbye. The other tin, tucked safely in her bag, joined gifts she'd purchased for friends back home. She couldn't help herself, she'd even chosen special things for Phoenix—a silk dragon tie, Chinese character cufflinks, and magazines with outrageously creative ads.

After dinner, Orchid lounged on the fainting couch in her hotel room and ruminated on the idea that she needed a *big dog*. Her network in China wasn't that deep. But back in New York she had several mentors.

Orchid grabbed her phone and touched the icon for LinkedIn. She scrolled through colleagues' updates, sending congratulatory notes for those celebrating work anniversaries and promotions. It made her happy to see familiar faces from home. Now, who among her contacts had experience in China? Specifically in the beauty industry? Each search included one person whom she'd been avoiding. She'd spent the month pushing away thoughts of Phoenix. She tried leaving an open mind on how to interpret his silence. Maybe he was giving her room to work. Maybe he was busy himself. Maybe he was just an ass.

She swigged a mouthful from her wine glass and typed Phoenix's name into a browser. The search returned pages of results. Nothing personal, of course, since he avoided all social media. Instead, old industry articles appeared. *Ad Age* had named counterAgency a "Small Agency to Watch" and praised its vision of building brands with a conscience. The articles commended this young thirty-two-year-old's accomplishments. He really was something. So impressive. It didn't hurt that his boyish grin made her heart squeeze tighter, that his habit of running fingers through his unruly hair made him handsomer than a young David Beckham, and that his presence filled whatever room he strode into.

She chose his work number from her contact list. Phoenix was her mentor, after all. It seemed quite professional to use his office line. She'd tell him about the old-school sales guy who kowtowed to her wishes one-on-one, but then mowed down her ideas in high-stakes meetings. If it came up, well, she could laugh off their romantic kiss and her attempt to talk about it at the airport.

His admin answered, an efficient presence she'd never met but whom she'd heard about during her *pro bono* work with Phoenix.

"Mr. Phoenix Walker's line. This is Liv."

"This is Orchid Paige. I'm trying to reach Phoenix. Is he in the office?"

Liv's pause, brief as it was, unfurled more unsavory stories in Orchid's mind. *He'd fallen for some sophisticate. He'd met a movie starlet, magazine editor, or travel blogger with smooth flowing locks, a haughty British accent and billionaire family.*

"He's not in. Is there someone else at counterAgency who can help you?" she replied in her clipped tone. Orchid imagined the dark-haired exec slinging one leg over the corner of his assistant's desk.

"If someone named Orchid calls, tell her I'm not in."

"No, thanks. Please ask him to call me."

Traveling a painful yet familiar path, Orchid remembered Caleb's casual stories about Phoenix's ex-girlfriend. "He was with Tish forever, and then . . . he lost interest. He dumped her. She said it was like she suddenly didn't exist. And I thought they'd get married. My brother can be a bit mercurial." His words were a warning. But they meant that he'd recognized the chemistry between them.

For days following the unsatisfying conversation with Liv, there was no return call. Orchid took matters into her own hands. The next time she met with Eban and his team, she pulled out a blue-and-white tin. "*Women xiang zhexie binggan. Fenkai danshi fangzai yiqi.*" They sat up with respect at her willingness to try speaking Mandarin, and chuckled at her sentiment. "We're like these cookies, separate, but stuck together." The icebreaker made Eban jovial. He agreed with her geographical strategy to name the Southeast as the number one priority. Over treats, they haggled an agreement to overfund his region by twenty percent in return for sky-high distribution targets. She left the meeting with handshakes, and a spring in her step that wasn't only because of her lighter bag.

The morning before her trip home, Orchid entered the executive boardroom. The women and men who ran the China division welcomed her into the room. She strode to the front and caught the gaze of their president, sitting opposite her, at the table's power spot.

"Thank you for giving me the opportunity to grow your business. You'll see in the presentation that not only can we double your sales in China, this product line is addressing unmet needs across Asia. My two-year plan has R&D tweaking the recipe for Western countries next."

They debated her assumptions. After all, she was recommending substantial investment. Tens of millions in R&D, media and agency fees. After one hour turned to two, the president leaned back in her seat and nodded. "You've done your homework. Answered every objection. Not an easy task. Congratulations, we're aligned to your recommendations." In the boardroom, the leadership team presented her with gifts of appreciation: *bai jiu,* a fiery Chinese liquor; handmade pottery from Tianjin; and a photo of their first team outing to the Great Wall.

She stepped out of the room, light with elation. The assignment was a success.

Star and her other colleagues hugged her goodbye, tears in their eyes.

"I'll be back," Orchid promised.

The next day, she boarded the plane with a sense of satisfaction.

Over the ocean, one movie into her flight, New York suddenly seemed closer than it'd been during the past month and a half.

Phoenix hadn't contacted her. Not once. After they'd spent months talking or texting several times a week.

Caleb's warning echoed, again, that Phoenix lost interest easily. Her parents. Phoenix. *Will he even remember to meet me at the airport?*

CHAPTER 18

THE DENIAL TWIST

Phoenix

An unexpected thing happened when Phoenix's phone buzzed. His heart ramped up with the thrill of seeing a text from Orchid.

"Hey Phoenix, I'm in baggage claim. Are you meeting me, or am I walking home?"

One side of his mouth quirked up, maybe for the first time in weeks. Then he shook his head, attempting to clear memories of Orchid's heated stare, the tingle of her lips against his cheek, and her rose-tinged scent. Orchid's honeyed voice filled his mind. These six weeks of therapy had worked him physically harder than any sport he'd ever played, or any triathlon. He'd fought to strengthen what remained of his muscles and learned how to manipulate prostheses.

During the lulls in therapy and exercise repetitions, he'd ruminated on solutions to an impossible problem.

The potential of their relationship, he realized, hinged on what he represented. They only made sense as a couple if he could be her protector and model of physical perfection, workout friend, dance partner, European travel guide.

At work, when he'd presented ads of injured soldiers, Orchid couldn't even bring herself to look at the images—and those survivors had injuries less egregious than his.

He could find no way around the fact that he could not be who Orchid needed. There was no way she'd accept him.

He imagined her reaction to his wounds, flaps of muscle pulled taut over abrupt endings of bone, visible stitch lines. She'd be repulsed. Maybe her kindness would obligate her to look the other way, and he'd selfishly gain comfort from her presence. Then, even if she could get past the shock of seeing him so changed, how could he ask her to live this life? *How can I hold her back from travel and beaches and everyday normalcy?*

Orchid, who loved cobblestoned Paris and dancing, wouldn't love wheelchairs and canes. Orchid, who couldn't look at a cut on her own foot, wouldn't be able to look at rows of stitches closing the blunt ends of limbs that made no sense. Maybe she'd suppress her disgust, at least at first. She'd go along, following a path out of pity for which she'd find no escape.

He'd pondered for long minutes. The phone rang. He startled at the vibrating cold steel in his hand. He answered before he could decide what he'd say.

"Hey," he said, his voice sounding surprisingly raspy.

"Hey yourself. How are you? Are you picking me up?" she got right to the point.

"Nope."

"What, did you forget about me?"

"Not exactly," he answered. Guilt washed over him. Protecting her was no longer in his capability. He thought of calling her a car service.

"Are you okay? You sound funny."

Phoenix recovered, basking in the normalcy of her sweet voice, in contrast to the sympathy and unease which tinged the calls from his office and friends.

"Funny?" he asked, delaying the response to the real questions. "You know me, I'm always funny."

"That you are. You would've found me funny in China. Like, trying to speak with taxi drivers was a hoot."

"Yeah? How was your trip?"

He really wanted to know, and to hear her talking in her bubbly, happy voice before he broke the news. He could hear her heels clicking along the tile floors of the airport.

"Good. Crazy. I called for your advice. You didn't call back," she said.

"You did?"

"You didn't get my messages?"

"Nope, I've been kind of out of touch."

"Have you been busy? What have you been up to these last six weeks?"

He paused. "You'd run away screaming if I told you," he said dryly, picturing Tish's look of horror and Orchid's amplified one from his dreams.

"Let me guess. Clients from hell? Creative teams pitching multiple accounts at once? Don't tell me you lost that coveted elixir brand."

"No, I'm happy to report we landed REBBL."

"Wow, congrats, that's a coup. I didn't keep up on the news much from over there."

"Yeah, we know how much you love watching the news," he said.

"Very funny. So, I'm all screwed up on time and desperate for a shower, but we should make plans. To catch up."

End of the idle chitchat.

"I actually wanted to talk to you about that." His throat tightened, giving away more in his tone than he intended. He heard her footsteps halt on the other end of the line.

"Orchid, you there?"

"Yeah, I'm here. What do you mean, you want to talk to me about that?"

He almost changed his mind. He didn't want to do this. He thought about telling her the truth. The truth would end up damaging her more than his evasion of it.

"Orchid, I can't be your mentor anymore."

She was quiet for a moment. "Meaning?" Her tone sounded hopeful.

"Meaning that we shouldn't work together. It's probably better if we don't see each other."

"Why?" Her confusion pained him. Then, the pain of his wounds steeled him.

"I'm really sorry. It's just not a good idea."

"Um, you know, if it's that silly thing I said at the airport, just ignore me. I hadn't really slept the night before. I was rattling off some nonsense. Like now. When I'm tired, I'm a mess. Really, I'm not expecting any—"

He could hear the hyperventilation in her machine-gunned words. He cut her off.

"It's not you. It's me. I really don't have time for anything extra. I'm all tied up with the agency and everything."

"Well, if you're going through a busy period, we could just catch up afterwards. You know, figure out our next project to work on?"

"No, I don't think that's a good idea. Better just make a clean break." His voice stumbled at the unexpected image of clean breaks where limbs had been.

"Well, I don't see what the big deal is. Like I said, it's just work."

He wavered, wanting to buy into her optimism. He pictured what she pictured. The two of them, bent over drawings, pointing at one headline or another, debating each other in his agency's board room. That was the old him. *I've been hurt*, he thought of saying now. *You're not going to like this.* Instead, he spoke different words, imparting gentleness in his tone.

"It's not you. You've been great. But best not to call anymore, okay?"

He could hear her suck air. "I should just block you from my phone."

He nodded. It had worked. "You should."

She was gone, the phone dead against his palm. In a prison where he couldn't control basic mobility, he could protect Orchid. Dreams—of a dark-haired beauty, traversing the Andes, or cradling his own child—scattered like dust.

Goodbye, Orchid.

CHAPTER 19

ALONE IN MY HOME

Orchid

I n disbelief, Orchid rode the subway to her downtown apartment. She sure scared off Phoenix. He didn't buy the "I was just babbling" claim. She didn't either.

Now what was she going to do? Forget him. Move on. Just like she had after every other heartbreak in her life.

She dragged her luggage over the dirty platform. The damned elevator was broken. The *Times* had published an exposé that two-thirds of New York subways weren't wheelchair accessible. Normally, she wouldn't notice. Today, she really needed the lift. She stomped up the stairs, huffing under the weight of two suitcases.

Her apartment felt cold after six weeks away. Nothing but condiments in the fridge. She could eat dressing, she supposed. She wasn't hungry anyway. She turned on the TV just to hear a human voice. Weird to see American personalities instead of Chinese newscasters.

Then, the shock hit her in waves.

A world devoid of Phoenix. She shouldn't have dreamed. Hadn't he hinted at other trips, after they'd returned from Cannes? Her foolish heart had hoped that France might be the romantic spot where they'd return, recapturing their first magical week there. It was too much, she couldn't think about their trip to Paris, down the shore. His dark scowl.

Maybe she shouldn't have confessed her attraction. Maybe she'd pushed too fast. What if she'd played hard-to-get? Did men like Phoenix just get bored? The stupid questions all led to the same conclusions: there was no changing this outcome. He'd avoided her for six weeks, why would he change his mind now that she was back in New York?

She'd survived the death of her parents, been independent since she was eighteen, and thrived for six weeks in a country where she was illiterate. But this was too much.

Phoenix had been kind when they were together. First, he had kept her cover when her boss had introduced them. He took her lead and didn't mention that they'd actually met the night before. When she'd stumbled into him in the men's room at a club.

After letting her save face, they'd worked together on a military campaign. At their first meeting, Phoenix had presented images of fit men and women proudly exhibiting missing limbs or gapped teeth. Orchid had stared at the scarred skin and twisted muscle. Without wanting to, she had pictured the trauma that must've caused those wounds. The possibilities unspooled memories from when she was twelve, jolted awake as locked wheels skidded over ice. Her parents' car crumpled into a tree.

Phoenix's voice had faltered then as he noticed Orchid's reaction. He had skimmed ahead until the presentation stopped on a page of logos.

"Enough about the creative. Maybe you want to talk about plans to drive awareness?"

Orchid had lowered the hand blocking her view of the screen and nodded, thankful for his thoughtfulness. His gaze had caught hers. Deep and blue and kind. "You okay?"

With him, she was more than okay. Later, he'd flown with her to Cannes, guiding her through her first creativity festival. Invited her to the Effies awards show. After which, she had cheered him on at a triathlon, met his brother, and visited their family's beach house.

She'd watched the way his mouth widened when he smiled. He'd looked at her from under his lashes.

Their heat ramped up that last week before her trip. He touched her arm while they talked. The night before her departure, they'd connected on another level. He had walked her back to her apartment, even though she didn't want the evening to end. Before she could help herself, she'd kissed him. If he wasn't going to ask her out, she'd be the provocative one. And he'd reciprocated. He had kissed her temple, then her cheek and then landed on her lips, while one hand fingered the pleather-edged sash of her dress.

Now this rejection was too much. *"Can't see each other"* . . . *"better not call."*

Her apartment echoed empty. If only she had a cat, or even a goldfish. She flung her suitcase open and threw her clothes into a dirty hamper. She knew the antidote to her foul mood.

She scooped her phone out of her bag and checked her friends' social media feeds. *Hi hon, guess who's home?* she texted Mandy.

While she waited for a response, she pulled up her email.

In her inbox, a message had arrived from a name she hadn't seen in forever. With a grimace, she clicked on it.

Hello Orchid,

I'm sorry it's been sixteen long years. Your dad would whip my ass for being a stranger (may he RIP). I married a few years ago. And now, we've had a baby. So, you have a new cousin. I've thought of you often. Please give me a call sometime, I'd really like to talk.

Uncle Zach

What? Why now? From memories of childhood, she pictured the gangly grad student who sought her out at her parents' funeral and put his arm awkwardly around her. He was a skinny version of her dad, both with dark eyes and wavy hair. She'd often thought of her dad's brother, too, his unexplained abandonment of her as an orphaned twelve-year-old. He'd left her with her mother's sister one day and never called again. She refused to think about him, a reminder of another person who'd left her.

A text. From Mandy. *You get in okay?*

Not really, she started to type. No more Phoenix. He didn't want to see her ever again. This sucked. Reality sunk in. *He doesn't want you.*

Before finishing the text to her best friend, Orchid chose Phoenix's name off her address list. There it was. In block letters, every detail from his business card. No social media links. Because he lived off the grid.

"No need for clients to see me with other clients," he had explained about his lack of online presence. So, despite living in the same city, she felt as if he'd disappeared among its eight million residents. Caleb had warned her. It hadn't even taken Phoenix three months to sway her with false charm and then leave with the flimsiest excuse, over a shorter call than she'd received from the dry cleaner.

She made up her mind. *Never again.* She swiped her phone and deleted his contact info.

CHAPTER 20

LOVE IS BLINDNESS

Veronica

Veronica Walker knew something was amiss. She'd witnessed Phoenix's grief, his denial, anger and sadness. She'd also seen him pull out of it with resilience that astonished her, faster even than she was able to stop grieving for the son that had been.

She repeated the words she had heard come readily from the rehab staff. "Prostheses are amazing now. You're lucky to have both knees and elbows. You'll be able to try whatever you want."

Maybe the encouragements helped. Or maybe it was the same stubborn determination that got him through grad school, pushed him in sports and led him to risk entrepreneurial pursuits despite everyone's warnings.

Today his silence alarmed her. He refused every activity she suggested. Shopping? Restaurant? Stroll around the park? No, no, and no.

"It's good news that you'll be discharged and ready for outpatient rehab in just another week," she said, trying again to make conversation.

"That's good. You can go then, you know," Phoenix said, striking his now familiar refrain.

"Son, there's nowhere I'd rather be," Veronica said firmly, kissing him on the cheek before he could turn away.

"I don't need you."

"I know. You don't need anyone. It's not *need*. I *want* to be here."

"Well, at least go sleep at my place. You don't need to stay here on that cot anymore." Nighttime had gotten easier. Phoenix was no longer waking too hot or too cold or frantic with bad dreams.

Leveraging the rare instance in which they agreed, she broached a new topic.

"So, what's wrong? Are you okay?"

"I hurt, Mom," he said simply.

Her gut clenched. She looked him all over, seeking signs of fluid buildup at the wound sites or some other discomfort. She suspected pain was a constant, dulled with narcotics, but not eliminated.

"More than usual?" she asked.

"No," he admitted.

"Is there something else?" she asked, tugging the sheet straight in an attempt to do something, anything, for this independent son who wanted no help from her.

With fury she didn't expect, he punched the mattress with his hand. "I'm missing half my limbs, Mom. Does there need to be something else?"

She stared at the desperation lining his face. The emotions she'd held in check nearly caved.

"What am I going to do when I'm not being coddled in rehab?" he demanded.

She'd had the same worries, especially in the early days before he'd woken. But he'd moved past the useless what-if's.

"Honey, no one's coddling you. And you're going to do whatever you want. You'll go back to your place, back to work."

"And then what?" he growled, "Who's going to want me?"

So, this is it.

His pain pained her. She tested his prickly edges.

"What about your co-worker who was maybe more than a friend?"

"You mean Orchid? I talked to her. Last week. She's back from China."

Veronica studied her son's blue eyes and dark hair as he lay back on his pillows. If she squinted a little, she could almost see hints of the little boy she had raised. She pictured the photo she'd seen on his phone. Her boys had dated all types, from perky to moody, sports-jocks to artists, raucous rebels to refined debutantes. Orchid was a stunner. The two of them, squeezed into one frame, looked like they were having fun.

She asked, hopefulness evident in the upward lilt in her tone, "So? Is she coming to visit?"

"Nope, we're not talking anymore."

"What happened?"

"She's not one to deal well with imperfections."

"You don't mean she didn't want to see you because—"

"It wasn't her. It was me, but c'mon, Mom. I'm half a guy. What woman is going to want me?"

She could barely listen to his words. Blood rushed in her ears. "I can't believe anyone would be as shallow as that."

Bile rose in her throat. In that moment, she couldn't think of another person she hated more than Orchid. "You are an amazing man. Any woman would be blind not to see that."

"There's the solution, Mom. Maybe she needs a blindfold."

CHAPTER 21

CATCH HELL BLUES

Caleb

Phoenix stirred, then groaned. Not an auspicious start to the day.

"Hey, bro. Pain meds?" Caleb offered, even though he knew the answer.

Phoenix shook his head, eyes not ready to open.

"What do you need? Just tell me," he said, anguished by the depression that had come over Phoenix the past few days.

"Kill me," Phoenix said.

Caleb's voice came out husky even though he was doing his damnedest to follow their mother's admonition not to cry. "Christ, don't say that. You're the strongest guy I know."

Phoenix forced his eyes open and grabbed his brother's arm, interrupting his babbling. "I'm kidding." His vacant eyes and grimness suggested otherwise.

Phoenix pushed up to a sitting position and yanked the arm of his chair to pull it closer. Transfers were getting smoother, but Caleb could tell from the pause between motions that the pain was intense.

"Can I do anything?" Caleb asked.

"Naw, I've got this," Phoenix said, wheeling to the bathroom. Caleb strode two steps ahead of him to fling the door open.

While Phoenix washed up, a hospital worker brought a covered breakfast tray and set it on his table.

Phoenix returned and groaned at the sight. "You don't need to kill me. That stuff will."

"Want me to run to Two Boots?"

"Naw, just eat half. Make it look like I'm doing my part."

Caleb lifted the tray cover and placed it on the brown melamine side table. "You gotta eat." He tried to upend his scowl in encouragement. It felt as if his face might crack from the effort. "You know Mom's gonna check." He lowered the tray table to chair height and stuck the spoon into the gray oatmeal.

Phoenix scooped a bite and made a face.

Caleb fought the urge to smooth the cowlick sticking out in the back of his brother's hair. "Hey, didn't Orchid come home this weekend?"

His brother swallowed. "Yeah."

"Is she coming by soon?"

Phoenix shook his head, and bit open a hard-boiled egg. The green-tinged yolk rolled desolately to the curved edge of the plastic plate. "She's not coming by."

"Why the fuck not?"

Phoenix pushed his tray away. "This is too much for her. She's not in my life anymore. I really can't talk about it." His voice cracked.

Caleb exploded into a standing position, feet wide apart, as if prepared to fight. "What?" he shouted. "Too much for *her*? That selfish bitch." He slammed a fist onto the table, making the tray jump and silverware rattle.

Phoenix doubled over, holding his side as if in pain. "It's not her fault, it's mine, but can we not talk about this?"

Caleb had held out hope that Orchid could pull Phoenix out of his funk. He pictured the punked-out beauty and felt bitterness rise into his mouth at the thought of her callousness. Caleb took a step towards his brother, intending to comfort him.

Phoenix rocked forward. "Fuckin' leave me alone," he pleaded.

Caleb left the room. The door shut to the crashing sound of a tray and dishes hitting the floor.

CHAPTER 22

CALL IT A DAY

Caleb

"Sascha?"

"Caleb?" Sascha asked, her voice full of sleep.

"You up?"

"It's two in the morning. Whadya think?"

"Sorry."

Sascha clicked a switch, probably a light. "It's all right. What's the matter?"

"I can't sleep."

"Normal people take a pill, not call their ex."

"You're funny even in the dead of night. I should let you go."

"Nah. I'm up now. How's your brother?"

Caleb sighed. "I don't know. He'd been doing better, but then lately it's gotten so damn bleak." He cringed, thinking of Phoenix's morning outburst.

"I'm sorry to hear that." She was quiet for a moment. "How 'bout you? I know you're not sleeping like you should."

He'd called in the middle of the night. He may as well let out what'd been dogging him. "I'm fucked up over my big brother. Yeah, we're twins but he's got two minutes on me. That stupid fact's the kind of thing that usually gets to me. Lately, I don't have a slug of jealousy in me. I'm torn up over what happened to him. God, I'll kill the guy who caused this, if I can find the bastard."

"I should've stayed. I shouldn't have left you guys."

"Nah, there's nothing you can do. It's just, he looks like hell. I've never seen anyone look like that. It's still him, but dammit, sometimes I can't even—it's just, hell."

"Cal, are you cryin'?"

"Aww, fuck, Sasch, it's so fucked up." Great sniveling wetness came out of nowhere. He blew loudly into stiff bunched-up tissues. He was a big guy, but his watery eyes diminished him to kindergarten days, when the rules and rote confused and chafed him.

"I'm coming back out," she pleaded.

"Nah, don't, I'm coming back to work in a couple of weeks anyway. It's just Mom says we've got to be strong. And I can see he's trying to hold it together for us. And we're all just sitting around, so fucked up, not saying what we're thinking, trying to hold it together for him. And I don't know. Docs keep saying he's going to be okay, and it's not so bad. But it looks real bad, Sasch, it looks real bad."

"Course it does, but, your brother, he's strong."

"Yeah, I hope so."

Another thought struck him. "You doin' okay?"

"Yeah . . . I'm trying to date a little."

"Yeah? I want to wish you well and I want to wring his neck, all at the same time."

Sascha's response, a sweet, tinkling sense of humor, contrasted with her tattooed body and penchant for latex wear. Maybe he should let her come this weekend.

"That's the other thing," he growled, jealousy kicking back in and then waning over the thought of his brother in his chair. "You remember Phoenix liked that woman from work? Some smart, hot thing?"

"Yeah, and?"

"You know she was away when all this happened. I wanted to call her but he says no. He'd talk to her when she was back. And now, she's back since the weekend and I ask Phoenix if she's comin'."

"What'd he say?"

"That she's not in his life."

"What do you mean?" she asked.

"I don't know. It sounded like she can't deal with his accident."

She sucked a breath, sounding wounded herself. When they were little, Phoenix balanced Caleb's wildness, by being the responsible son. Now, Caleb needed to be the reliable one . . . if he was up to it.

CHAPTER 23

LITTLE GHOST

Liv

Dex had prepared Liv for what to expect. "He's in a wheelchair. I don't know how much pain he's in. He didn't look—"

"What?"

"He didn't look like he wanted to see us."

Phoenix was an independent guy, one who walked into work every day like he'd just come from a shoot for some designer label. Of course he wouldn't want his colleagues to see him less than perfect. Liv got that. Today, she was going to be selfish. She was visiting for her sake—not his.

Heading up the high-rise that housed his rehab facility, nerves tightened her roiling stomach. She stepped into his room and met his mother, a regal woman who carried herself with enough character to have both birthed the incredible entrepreneur who was her boss and deal with an accident Liv tried not to imagine.

"Mrs. Walker, nice to meet you in person."

"Thanks for coming to visit. It's thoughtful of you," she said.

"How's he been?"

She blinked and studied the floor. "So-so."

The sound of running water ended. Veronica glared at the closed door, as if her hard stare could navigate through the space between the molecules to see into the bathroom. A squeaking rubber sound and a clink against metal seemed to ease her tension. She relaxed, then after a few minutes, excused herself.

"There's a nurse's call button if you need anything," Veronica said, pointing out the controls on the bedside table. "I'm going to get coffee so you two can talk."

Then, when he wheeled out, Liv startled for a moment before remembering to get up and go to him. It took a little adjusting to seeing him in the chair. She tried to keep her eyes on his face.

"Hi, Liv." He took her outstretched hand to pull her towards him. "Thanks for coming." Still Mr. Walker, because that emanated from within, he kissed her on the cheek. Just that one action made all well for her.

"You're welcome. I wanted to come sooner but—"

"I know. I wouldn't let you." He indicated the upholstered seats beside the round table, and then pushed his chair to follow her. "Sit."

She obeyed, his voice holding no less power than she recalled.

She rested onto one industrial orange chair, crossed her legs, glanced at him, and uncrossed them. "How are you?" she asked, because she couldn't say she'd thought of him every day, that she was afraid he'd die, or that she'd taken to praying despite having renounced her faith during college.

He struggled for an answer, and she marveled at the simple truth of the one he finally produced. "Every day is a little better."

"That's good to hear." She relaxed her frozen posture a little. She indicated the pile of white envelopes on the table in front of them. "I've brought your mail, but I've opened everything and there's nothing we can't take care of."

"I figured everything's in good hands."

"I've kept up with all your email, and voicemails, too."

"Just as I always suspected. You don't even need me," he said, not reaching for the papers. His teasing tone loosened the lock of her arms against her sides.

"Is this news?" she teased back.

"Ha, I'm so not needed, I should take up golf or something." His voice faltered as he looked down.

Can you hug a boss? She touched his arm instead, as intimate a gesture as she figured he'd take. "Is there anything I can do?"

He shook his head, eyes searching hers. He seemed to see someone else.

"Oh," she said, remembering something she'd nearly forgotten. "Orchid Paige called."

His eyes lifted to meet hers. The old Phoenix was back. "When was this?"

It was hard to recall, since time had blurred since Phoenix's accident. "A few weeks ago, maybe."

His head hung again.

"She said to tell you that she'd called. I'm sorry I forgot." She was searching for the words that would bring back his hopeful expression.

"It doesn't matter," he said, eyes focused on the ground.

"I could get in touch with her if you want."

He shook his head. "We're not talking."

"What do you mean?"

"She's not one to be able to handle me like this."

"You don't mean—" His expression stopped her. She'd understood enough from the anguish plain on his face. This woman had hurt her boss.

"I'm sorry," Liv said.

Her emotions splintered across the spectrum. She wanted to comfort him, though anything she could do seemed inconsequential compared to a betrayal of that magnitude. Anger pulsed. *That bitch.* She took the most amazing guy Liv had ever met and flung him aside? When he'd just vaulted from darling of the agency world to having so much taken away?

Liv was a small, pale pacifist, but her rage was physical. What she wouldn't do to hit Orchid square between the eyes.

CHAPTER 24

WANT AND ABLE

Phoenix

"I can transfer myself."

"I know," said Veronica hovering inches from Phoenix.

He stood from the bed and pivoted into the chair. "Nadine wants me to do as much for myself as I can."

"Sure, honey," she said, leaning to tuck a loose pocket into his shorts.

He gritted his teeth against the humiliation of having become a dependent adult-child. "You know I've built a hundred-million-dollar business, and have been on my own since college."

"You've done a great job," she said, licking a finger to slick a stray tuft of hair.

He wheeled towards the bathroom. Mom walked one step ahead, opening the door just as he arrived. He pictured Orchid helping him transfer, handling his chair. The gut-punch of her revulsion, obvious in his recurring nightmares, formed a lump in his throat. He'd made the right call.

"I'm going to shower. By myself," he said.

"Of course, dear."

Nadine said the more he accepted his new state, the faster he'd recover. But phantom sensations remained ruthless. Narcotics sepia-toned his thinking until the difference between life and death didn't seem to matter.

A one-handed yank of his T-shirt over his head was the easy part. Shrugging out of his shorts required balancing on a single foot, shoving the fabric towards the floor and then sitting back down to be finally free. *I should be figuring out communications strategies, not how to undress.*

Naked, he hopped into the shower. The bumpy surface of the institutional plastic seat sneered *disabled.*

Here, there was no ignoring the blunt ends of his missing pieces, no ignoring the one-handed shower aided by a long-handled brush. Scars wound like pale red tentacles over misshapen flesh. The sutures were gone but the raised, ropy skin stretched taut in the shape of each menacing stitch. *Living death.* Every nurse, therapist, doctor and family member had colluded in the grandiose lie that he was going to be able to do what he wanted. *What the hell are they talking about?*

This week, he couldn't unlock the foil fortress of a yogurt. Yesterday, his one-handed wheeling was felled by a door that swung out instead of in.

His mind hissed, staring at his malformed stumps. *You're the punchline to a distasteful joke. You're an attraction in an old-fashioned freak show. Little girls will gape at your deformities. Adults will avert their gaze from your gruesome form, then emasculate you with degrading pity.*

There was nothing left of him. *Half a man . . .* His ears filled with howling. The door rattled with increasing alarm. The howling keened. He realized he was the one making the horrible sound. His one whole arm swept the shampoo, brushes and soap to the ground. The violence of the sudden strike stole his balance and he tumbled, landing on one shoulder. Battling upright, he dragged himself to his wheelchair, heaving the metal junk towards the sink, rattling bottles against porcelain.

"Phoenix, open this door! Let me in!" shrieked the crazy woman who birthed him. Who cared? *This whole place is crazy.* He was the craziest of them all. Beside the faucet above his floor-bound body stood toiletries, sentinels waiting. Reaching from pained knees that felt as if both feet were still attached, he fisted the glass and hurled it against the dispassionate tile.

Its splintering amped the volume from the crazy, then all fell silent. His lungs huffed air he didn't want.

The jagged shapes of broken glass glinted in the light. He wrapped his only hand around the largest shard, curved like a scythe. He caught sight of himself in the full-length mirror, a half-finished horror. His expression crazed, eyes darting wild like a trapped animal, gaunt cheeks wet with streaked tears, body naked, hideous. In the countryside, they put wounded deer out of their misery with a shot to the head.

The edge of the glass soothed with cold detachment. Just a little more pressure and relief would wash over him. It beckoned, promising pastures beyond his prison, a place with no struggle. He could smell the flora, sense the sun and relax into the illusion of peace.

He held no more responsibilities. His agency ran without him. His family could resurrect lives that had paused mid-action for him. Now, with Orchid set free, he was truly unanchored, unneeded. Nothing made sense more than to end the pain. He pressed the razor-sharp point against the flesh of his useless arm. He raised it to slice. He craved relief.

The door flung open. A male nurse towered, two hands out, beseeching, surrendering. "Real slow, Mr. Walker, just put that down."

His mom was planted behind the nurse, open-mouthed. The nurse bent over his half-body, uncurled the claw formed around his weapon, and removed it. He righted the wheelchair and placed his arms around Phoenix's torso. "Let's get you out of all this broken glass," he said, helping him pull into the chair. And then Phoenix shattered, his life fractured into more pieces than the ruined tumbler.

He was broken.

His body.

His will.

Irreparably so.

The male nurse helped Phoenix dress. He was consigned to bed. Much later that day, his assigned psychotherapist arrived, tall and slender, in a midnight blue suit as if she'd come from an insurance commercial. She motioned to the chair by his side. He shrugged his bruised shoulder and turned away from her kindly smile. As if she needed his permission to sit.

"Hi. I was hoping we could talk."

He closed his eyes. The physical pain battled with his emotional pain. He stayed silent.

"Talk to me about how you're feeling."

What was the point? He had no energy for this. She waited, and he said nothing.

"Don't tell me you just wanted to see me twice this week."

"Humor? You came to make me laugh?" He turned to throw her a sour look.

"That'd be a start."

"And when's the finish?" He watched her keep her face even. Damned professional.

"I don't think it's your time yet, my friend. Haven't you always been a fighter?"

She crossed her knees and bent a hand to cup her chin. Her long arms and legs mocked him.

"Phoenix, how long have you been thinking about this?"

"Thinking?" He choked out derision. "I'm not thinking about anything. I'm just trying to make it through each day."

She frowned. "Do you want to talk with the doctor about increasing your meds?"

"No. I can't think straight on that stuff."

Her rigid back eased. "And how about now? Are you thinking about hurting yourself?"

"If you keep asking me questions, I might think about hurting you," he mocked. The thought of how little half a man could do to this wiry woman made him chuckle instead.

She tilted her head. "Okay, no more questions." She smiled. "Just a promise."

He groaned. *What does she know with her able hands and feet?*

She leaned towards him. "Will you call me or tell someone if you feel like hurting yourself?"

"That's another question."

"Nope, that's a request for a commitment."

"Smoke signals or carrier pigeons, you'll be the first to know."

"Cell phone works, too. You know a lot of people care about you?" She paused. He didn't answer, so she kept going. "I'm going to send your mom back in. She's going to be here with you over the next few days, and let's not discharge you to outpatient status just yet."

Great, a prolonged sentence in rehab, as if the life sentence of limb loss wasn't bad enough.

"I'll be back tomorrow," she promised. To Phoenix, it sounded like a threat.

That night, Mom's cot was put back in place, next to where he lay in bed. "I shouldn't have left," she muttered. She put an arm around him. It felt like a restraint. "I love you."

He'd been her pride and now was her burden.

She prattled on. He couldn't listen. He'd found a solution and now just needed a plan that he could execute.

CHAPTER 25

JUST ONE DRINK

Phoenix

Nadine sat on the side of Phoenix's bed, her tresses freed from the usual elastic. A knit shirt hugged her contours. Her normally smooth face puckered between the brows, mouth drawn at the corners to ripple her chin in worry, more somber than cheery.

"Hey, there."

He said nothing, twisting under the sheet to find a place of comfort.

"Are you having pain?" she asked.

She got up, headed for the amber bottle just out of reach of his bed. He shook his head, so she sat down again.

"Want to tell me what's going on?"

His therapist, his mom and now Nadine. He had no words left.

"You know you're important to me?"

He groaned. "Stop with the head games, the lies. I'm not going to get better. Nothing's going to change that."

She looked around the room, adjusting the little ruffled sleeves. "Look at all the progress you've made. Faster than most. Before you know it, you'll be back home, and back at work. You'll have accomplished all those goals we set."

"You and your stupid goals. Just go. This is your day off. Go see your boyfriend."

She read the hitch in his voice and slumped shoulders, spot on as usual.

"Phoenix, I promise it's going to get better."

She sat for a long time waiting for a response. He had none.

That afternoon, his brother barreled into Phoenix's room. Caleb's face was twisted, eyes shot through red. He ran fingers through his hair as if grappling with a hidden beast.

Mom was only willing to relinquish guard with another blocker in her place. Phoenix wasn't even allowed to use the restroom by himself.

Silence. Just the two of them. He didn't know how long Caleb sat there without talking. When Caleb finally spoke, his voice was low like he was trapped in an old church confessional. "You know, there was a time I thought the same thing."

Phoenix glanced at his brother, and then away from his devastated expression.

"I was so fucked up. Everything about me hurt. Everything was too hard. And it almost seemed like death would be better than living my hell."

"Really, when?" Phoenix struggled up onto one elbow to get a better look at his brother.

"It doesn't matter. All I know is that I wanted to end my suffering."

Good. One family member who would understand.

Caleb continued. "But then, I saw that was a lie. Because what comes after? Nothing. And nothing's worse than at least fighting. Fighting whatever demons."

Phoenix laid back and closed his eyes. Shit, he was on their side, too.

"Part of me thinks your accident was my fault. Like the universe making you save someone because someone saved me."

"Nah, stop it," Phoenix said, his voice hoarse.

"Maybe I'm wrong to tell you this. Mom probably wouldn't want me to talk about it at all. But listen, if fucked-up me can make something of myself, well, look at you, with your degrees and brains and all those badass ad ideas. You've got more going on than ninety-nine percent of the population who have their legs and arms."

Phoenix rolled over, pressing into his pillow, throat closing in on him. His mind was a jumble, the meds he needed making it even more confused. He couldn't see Caleb's perspective. He saw a wheelchair, obstacles in every staircase, rotating door, and curb, stares of pity and horror, and the pathos of not being able to look at himself.

Caleb kept talking. He persuaded. He cajoled. Phoenix couldn't listen.

In the evening, Sascha replaced Phoenix's brother. She sported flamboyant red latex Saran-wrapped around her short, curvy figure.

She sat on Phoenix's hospital bed instead of the vinyl visitor's chair which would probably adhere to her plastic-wear. The thought made him laugh. The sound, erupting with air like a choke, was rusty, unheard of in the past dark days.

"So, luv," she said, cupping his cheek to kiss it. "Sorry it's been rough." Her light touch smoothed a little part of the hurt inside.

She produced neatly folded clothes from her shiny backpack. With her head-to-toe synthetics, she'd stay dry in a monsoon.

"You'll feel better in these," she said, shaking out dress pants and a dark linen button-down. He didn't take the familiar articles from his wardrobe. "You want a hand, or do you want me to give you some privacy?"

He stared at her. "You're smarter than this. You think clothes are going to make a one-handed guy better?"

"It's not for you. It's for me. I like going out with a well-dressed man."

He turned his face away, the thought of going out anathema.

"Aw, honey, try for me, okay?"

He lay still, eyes closed, for long minutes. He tested the paths of his thinking. There was no flaw in his conclusion. No one needed him. Most days, the pain was unbearable. There was no point in pressing himself, no point in forcing others to try to do for him. He got that other people in his situation needed to keep going. They had children, responsibilities, people who counted on them. *I have no one.*

Then Sascha laid a warm hand on his. She applied a little pressure. *Hey, I'm here,* the friendly motion seemed to say. He squeezed his eyes shut tighter.

He felt his lungs fill and empty in a pattern that said in no uncertain terms that he was still alive. Even a train couldn't kill him. Little by little, Sascha's connection brought him from the dark path of his thoughts to the concrete present, into the room that was his prison.

Phoenix had always had a soft spot for Sascha. The pit in which he languished had no foothold up. Yet for her, he opened his eyes.

"Can I do anything for you?" she asked, hazel irises piercing his. Her dark gaze reminded him of Orchid.

He pushed to a sitting stance. Maybe action would erase the memories. "Help me with the buttons, okay?"

"Sure, luv. You want your leg?" she asked, pointing at the temporary prosthesis next to his bed.

She helped him with everything, from liners to leg, buttons to belt, until he felt nearly whole—only seated.

"You know I'm not allowed out? I'm on a suicide watch."

She shot him a pointed look. "Promise me not to do anything rash and I'll sneak you out the service elevator. I've got the place scoped out, and Caleb's told your mom I'm watching you." With her there, taking charge, putting him back together, his rash impulses simmered rather than raged.

"You are something," he said.

In between shifts as the nurses talked, around the corner out of their sight, Sascha guided Phoenix to the right, away from their station. The two fugitives rode down the padded elevator and wheeled out the wide revolving door.

"See? No problem, and there's no lie. I am watching you." Sascha bent to whisper in his ear, voice giddy from their successful escape.

The night air kickstarted his brain. He'd forgotten there was anything other than the repetitive struggle of rehab, living in an institution, and his family treating him like bone china in bubble wrap. Here shined the contrast of streetlights against dark skies, and yellow taxis against neon-signed storefronts. He stood and slid into the front seat of her Fiat, just as Nadine had taught him. Sascha folded up his chair and whisked it away into her trunk without any questions.

"Next time, I'm driving," he said, looking down at legs clothed in tailored pants, feeling almost like a normal guy with a better-than-normal girl.

"Promise?" she asked, not expecting an answer, looking in her side mirror to pull onto the wide avenue.

"Where are we going?" he asked. He observed drunken passersby swerving in more acute angles than he ever challenged Nadine with in their mat-lined rooms.

"Rockwood Music Hall."

"I see, it's a night out for you," he said, teasing.

"Of course it is, and I picked you over that sourpuss brother of yours." He liked that she tossed his teasing right back, no kid gloves.

Sascha had arranged nearby parking. They reversed the routine with the chair and wheeled up a ramp to enter. A hostess led them to reserved seating at a table to the far right, just in front of the stage.

A gorgeous pale waitress, golden hair piled high, making a black apron over dark leggings look good, came over. Catching sight of

Phoenix, she exhibited perfect white teeth.

"I'm Ana. Do you know what you want to drink?" she asked Sascha, not breaking eye contact with Phoenix.

"Club soda. I'm driving," Sascha yelled over the band warming up.

"How about you, doll?" The blonde leaned down, ostensibly to hear him. The tops of her breasts peeked over the v-cut of her fitted T-shirt.

"Blue Sapphire martini, dirty."

She flashed her teeth like the drink order was inspired.

"Sure thing, doll," she sang, sashaying away. A funky electronic beat started up. The band featured one guy surrounded by drums and a keyboard, and another with an electric guitar.

"You're not even my boyfriend and I'm jealous."

"I have no idea what you're talking about," he grumbled.

Sascha cocked her head with an exaggerated stare. "You didn't notice the waitress falling all over you?" she enunciated. "She may be working but she's still flesh and blood with perfectly good eyesight and libido, apparently."

"You kidding? In this chair?"

"Who cares about the freaking chair? I'm with the hottest guy in this place."

He looked around at the eclectic crowd, interspersed with beatnik, casual, punk and posh. A redhead caught his eye and winked. Something familiar tugged at his insides. He looked away. "Do you know her?" he asked, shrugging towards the pinup-styled beauty.

"Another fan," she filled him in, deadpan.

"Oh, c'mon. What is this, a set-up? Did you pay these people?" he huffed over the music, now low and moody.

The waitress glided over, tray in hand. "Club soda. Dirty martini, extra olives," she beamed. She placed small bowls of mini pretzels and nuts on the table. "A little something in case you're hungry."

"Thanks, Ana," he said, returning her smile.

"Are you always so good with names? Can I get you anything

else?" Was he imagining the innuendo in her perfectly reasonable remarks?

"No, thanks," Sascha answered for them, dismissing Ana with a scowl.

She turned to him. "You think I paid these people? They'd pay *me* to hang out with you."

"You are too clever. Taking me out to show me I'm okay, instead of all those crazies at the hospital trying to convince me through words."

He dredged up sarcasm, but did feel better. The familiar memory clicked into place. That redhead's wink was flirtation. He'd been holed up in rehab for so long, and before that, starting the agency, he'd nearly forgotten the simple interplay between strangers. And of course, that short period in between, when two professionals nearly became more, needed to be banished from his thoughts. He sipped the cool gin, face wanting to split over unexpectedly high spirits.

Sascha twisted towards him, her latex straining with the movement. "You think I'm taking you out for you? My friends know, I always said I dated the best-looking guy's brother. Now quit the questioning, it's not all about you. I'm being selfish here so let me enjoy myself."

The salty olives reminded him he'd not eaten since the morning, despite his mother's pleas. He popped a pretzel in his mouth.

"This band sounds like nothing I've ever heard before. What are they called?"

"Paris Monster." She palmed a handful of peanuts.

"You're kidding."

"Not at all. Why?" She raised an eyebrow in curiosity.

"Ha, seems ironic is all. I was in Paris in July, before my monster of an accident."

Ana returned, brushing his arm as she leaned between them to retrieve his glass, empty except for a lone olive. "Would you like another?"

"Sure, thanks."

Ana beamed.

Paris Monster's sounds wreathed and writhed, its ethereal layers welcoming Phoenix back to the dream house of the living.

CHAPTER 26

I CAN'T WAIT

Phoenix

"I don't care if the arm's going to give me more *function*, I want that damned leg," Phoenix insisted as he wheeled down a familiar corridor.

"Okay, fine. We'll do it your way," Nadine relented. She walked beside him, toting his accessories. "The occupational therapist will work with you on your arm. We need to work on your gait anyway. You're putting too much strain on your joints. You don't want to end up with a hip replacement."

"I feel crappy enough and you want to talk about hip replacements?"

"Sorry."

"It's okay. You know, the leg made me feel so much better this weekend."

"Yeah, everyone's heard about your dramatic break-out."

"Ha."

"You know they're going to really clamp down on you now, right?"

"Well, there's no need. What's wrong with a guy wanting to go out?"

They pushed through the doors to the windowed room with the parallel bars. Once inside, she arranged his "spare parts" on the ground. She bent and lifted a rounded silicone liner from the pile.

"Nothing wrong with wanting to go out. But everything wrong with wanting to hurt yourself, you hear?" She cleared her throat and straightened. "That's against the rules."

"Got it."

"If you feel that way again, you have to tell one of us. Promise?"

He nodded. He'd already promised his psychotherapist, occupational therapist, and Mom. So what was one more?

"You're going to think about the prescription too, right?" she asked, handing him the liner.

He shook his head. "No happy pills. I'm off the pain meds, I'm not going to start something new."

Phoenix leaned down and crossed his right hand over his left side, starting the awkward process of rolling the silicone sleeve up his left calf. The liner was needed to protect his skin before locking his leg into the socket and prosthesis.

Nadine watched. "So what'd you do after sneaking out?"

"Sascha, my brother's ex, you know?" He looked up and she nodded. "Took me out to see a live band. They were just two guys. Amazing what they could do. One guy played the drums with one hand, a keyboard with the other, and sang lead vocals."

"All at the same time?"

"Yeah. He made the other guy, a guitarist and sound engineer, look lazy."

"You could play an instrument too, you know. Especially if you get used to using your arm prosthesis."

"I wasn't musical before the accident, and an artificial arm sure isn't going to help matters. . . . Do you play?"

"My mom made me take piano when I was young. I wished I'd stuck with it and practiced more. I met an amputee during my physical therapy internship. He could play better with one hand than I could with two." She blushed, perhaps afraid she'd hurt his feelings.

Today, it was as if he wore Teflon. Hurt deflected right off him.

"You and your stories of people who can do more with less. As if losing a limb makes them stronger."

"Why not?"

"I'm not sure I can stand those people who think I'm a saint because I can live without an arm and a leg. It's not like I have a choice. And if I did, I know what I'd choose."

"You say that now." She looked up, holding the carbon fitting in place for him.

His back to the wall of windows, Phoenix grasped the right side of the parallel bar and hauled himself upright. He eased weight onto his prosthetic leg.

"It's going to get better. You wait and see."

Standing, Phoenix's view shifted from Nadine's waist to over her head. His return to full stature lifted his mood, too. He limped a step towards the exit. "You know what, you might be right," Phoenix said.

CHAPTER 27

SALUTE YOUR SOLUTION

Phoenix

FRIDAY SEPTEMBER 29

Something was up. "Why are you pacing, Mom?" Phoenix asked, watching her wander around the ten-by-fifteen room he called home during rehab. She opened and shut drawers and doors, looking but not finding anything.

"You sure you don't want to bring your arm?" She waved a peach-hued and metal prosthesis, then peered into the bag she'd packed with clothes and toiletries.

"You won't tell me where I'm going, so how am I supposed to know if I'll need an arm?" he goaded, not expecting an answer.

"You want me to come with you?" She rearranged the items, seeking a way to make them more easily accessible for a one-handed guy.

"You won't tell me where I'm going, so how do I know if I'll need you, Mom?"

Caleb burst through the door. "Where we're going Mom's not needed," he said, then strode over to kiss their mother.

"You trained that soldier well," Phoenix joked with his brother. "I couldn't get even a hint out of her, much less a state secret."

"You're closer than you think," Caleb said, grabbing his twin's suitcase and cane.

"Hey, I can take that," Phoenix complained, gesturing towards the bag.

"No way." Caleb stalked to the door, yanking it open without a backwards glance. "Bye, Mom."

Face lined with fatigue, Veronica leaned over Phoenix's chair and wrapped both arms around him. "Have fun."

"You do the same. You deserve a rest."

Caleb poked his head back in through the doorway.

"It's just a weekend."

His mom let go, and he wheeled through the open door to follow his brother.

Out on the street, Caleb's red pickup sat idling.

"You really weren't expecting to stay long, were you?" Phoenix said. He rolled up to the side of the extended cab and pulled open the passenger door.

"You need a hand?" Caleb asked, looking up from the driver's side, where he'd slid the suitcase into the tiny back seat, next to an oversized duffel bag.

"Literally, yes. But with getting into the car? No."

Phoenix stood, pivoted and sat on the leather bench seat, pulling his legs after him. He grabbed the cushion off the wheelchair and yanked the fabric handle straight up, folding the chair so that it would lie flat.

Caleb came around to heft the chair into the bed of the truck, securing it to the ridged surface. He plopped into the driver's seat and aimed the vehicle out of the city.

They sped down the highway with heavy metal pulsing from the speakers, amiable in their silence for miles along the turnpike.

"Heading south, I see," Phoenix observed from the highway signs.

"You sure are curious," Caleb said, his face splitting into a rare grin.

Phoenix smiled too. Beyond the mystery of their trip, trees radiated early fall glory against pale blue skies. An enormous maple tree bore orange-tipped leaves so warm he could taste the sun-kissed colors. A scarlet-tinged oak stood oblivious to the speeding cars.

Caleb tapped the bottom of the steering wheel with one hand, in syncopation with the percussive music.

Phoenix stretched, relaxing into the firm seat. "Bet you're taking me wherever the unwanted get abandoned."

"That shit isn't going to work with me," Caleb said.

"Good point. Save the pity card for Mom," Phoenix countered, unperturbed. "With you, let me guess . . . pole dancing."

"Hah, we could do that. Although I don't know why we'd go to DC for strippers when we could just stay in New York."

"Washington, as I suspected," Phoenix said, proud of himself.

Caleb frowned over the unintended reveal, and merged the truck onto Interstate 95. "Technically, we're going to Maryland."

The sun shone directly overhead. They rode in silence for miles of highway, falling into the easy rhythm of the speeding traffic.

Phoenix's thoughts wandered. He sometimes wondered what his father would say about his accident. Dad had always tried to justify circumstances. *How would he find justice in this situation?* The masterful son for whom he had high expectations was now rendered powerless. The rambunctious son over whom he and Mom had fretted through countless nights was now in charge. Dad wouldn't be focused on the flip of power. More likely, he'd be the only one to see clearly how much this accident had taken away. *He'd see my position.*

Dad excelled at divining intentions. He'd understand that the nurses and therapists had an inherent motivation to exude optimism. That was their job, to get him up and functioning. They couldn't afford to let him give up. Their job was to make him try, even when he resisted.

Dad would see through his sarcastic shield. He'd know that snug against his son's sharpness was a world of hurt and disbelief. He'd know that if Phoenix's shield of toughness slipped, he'd feel the full weight of his pain. He would not be able to survive. He'd howl until the force of the sound exploded through his body, blowing him up into more bits than the train had.

He pictured that look on Dad's face when tragedy couldn't be justified. His dad would be devastated over his son's wasted potential.

"You know, I was thinking about Dad," Phoenix said.

"God, I miss him," Caleb responded, as if feeling the same sentiments as his twin. They were south of Baltimore and crossed over tributaries of the Chesapeake Bay.

Phoenix shook away the lingering image of his father's disappointment. He stared out the window, his thoughts turning to the other devastated parent.

"How do you think Mom's holding up?" he asked.

"She's strong. She's doing okay," Caleb replied.

"I think she misses her friends."

This had been on his mind for weeks. Mom had little to do, so she was generating activity where none was needed, folding and unfolding his clothes, organizing his things, and who knew what her productivity had done to his apartment over these months. Phoenix was working on convincing her to head home once he'd been discharged to outpatient rehab.

"You've got to let go of that Catholic guilt. I think she's where she wants to be. Her Bunco group can wait."

"I'm going to encourage her to go back home soon."

"After your incident in the bathroom? Good luck with *that*."

"That's ancient history," Phoenix grumbled, but honestly, there were still days where not existing seemed preferable to his daily struggles.

They finally exited the interstate to a wide avenue that cut through neighborhoods in the suburbs of Bethesda. "You hungry?" Caleb asked, looking around as they slowed from highway velocity to city speed limits.

"Nope. You?"

"No, but Mom made me promise we'd eat regular meals."

"If you don't tell, I won't tell."

Caleb slowed through the secondary roads, checking his phone's map for directions.

"Want me to navigate?" Phoenix offered, holding out his hand.

"No need. We're here." Caleb turned into a long drive leading to a complex of white buildings. He headed for a massive guard shack manned by men built like oaks.

"IDs?" asked the first military policeman, and checked his clipboard. Another MP craned a neck thick with muscles to assess the contents of the truck bed, then bent with a flashlight to check the underside of the vehicle.

"Walter Reed National Military Medical Center," Phoenix read the overhead sign aloud. "Like they need more wounded?"

"Shut the fuck up." Caleb pulled past the guard shack, following directions to parking. "Open the glove compartment, would you?"

Phoenix pushed the button and peered into a jumble of envelopes, a flashlight and a box of bandages.

Caleb reached in and grabbed a blue and white tag off the top of the pile.

"Great, you're taking me along because you want better parking?"

"You still don't get it, do you?" Caleb shook his head. He looped the laminated permit onto his rearview mirror. Phoenix couldn't identify with the wheelchair stick figure that was supposed to represent someone like him.

They followed a curved path to the car garage. Caleb pulled into an accessible space with a matching blue and white logo.

His brother jumped out and messed around the back of the truck for what seemed like forever. As Phoenix waited, he recalled stories of this place from his military client. Impatient, he finally turned, grabbed his cane and pushed himself out of the car. Leaning against the door, he nudged it shut. As the heavy panel thunked closed, Caleb looked up. He was having trouble untying the wheelchair.

"I just need another minute."

"Never mind. Nadine says it's too early for me to be up and around on my own, but if you don't tell, I won't. Let's go in."

Caleb nodded, catching up with his twin. "MAT-C," he said, gesturing to the building ahead of them.

"Military Advanced Training Center." Phoenix remembered the acronym from his client. "This place is famous. It's one of the best amputee rehab centers in the country," he said, falling behind his brother's pace. Every divot and crack in the pavement required his concentration.

Caleb pulled on the metal handle of the door and held it open for Phoenix to hobble through.

The place smelled like a mix of sweat and disinfectant. There was a hum of activity in the corridor that stretched before them.

Caleb shrugged off his leather jacket to reveal a Harley T-shirt and muscular arms.

A woman approached them, swooping in on feet that seemed to glide. Dressed in beige scrubs and white tennis shoes, she reminded him of an amped up version of one of his therapists. She looked like she could bench press an Army jeep.

"Caleb Walker?" she boomed. She didn't shirk from the tough handshake his brother offered her. "I thought that was you driving up."

"Don't they call from the guard shack?" Caleb asked,

"Smart man. You've got our security figured out."

She turned to Phoenix and stuck out a hand. "Tara." He tucked his cane under his left arm to meet her grasp. She sported the eager grin of a therapist checking out fresh meat. He'd seen that look before. She was assessing the level of his injuries, his physical capability, how far she could push him, how motivated he would be.

"Below the knee." He answered her unspoken question, letting go of her hand and hiking up a pants leg. Not that the two inches of visible plastic and metal could verify the presence of a real knee.

"Oh, yeah? The guys are going to be jealous." Odd concept. *Someone jealous of me.* "Actually, I was just going to ask your name."

"Sorry, Tara. I'm Phoenix."

"Phoenix, your brother is persuasive. Not just anyone gets a tour of MAT-C," her eyes sparkled at his twin as if she found humor in some private joke.

"He is persuasive. Tightlipped, too. Unfortunately, I didn't know we were coming here. This was a surprise."

Tara straightened and pointed down the corridor. "Well then, let's show you."

She started down the hall, with no doubt they'd follow the command in her voice.

Phoenix looked around, curious. They passed a stocky guy in shorts and forest green T-shirt, speeding along in the opposite direction. Full-length prostheses stood on the empty footrests of his wheelchair. Phoenix realized he'd never met another amputee his age. At home, the rehab center housed mostly older residents. Many were diabetics who'd lost a lower extremity to the disease. Or, in one case, a young child born without tibias, the bones below the knee. He felt a rush of camaraderie that inspired him to try to catch the guy's eye, but the soldier was already gone.

The narrow dark hallway soon opened up to an enormous gymnasium. They looked into a gigantic matted area filled with tables and parallel bars, like the ones where he and Nadine worked, but amplified to arena size. Everywhere, wounded military worked out with or without prostheses. He'd never seen so many people missing limbs.

"We used to have twice the number of amputees when we had more troops in Iraq and Afghanistan," Tara said, as she watched him take in the sight of dozens of injured soldiers. "Once our military gear got better at protecting torsos, and medics got better at stabilizing patients, our guys were surviving their injuries. Even with the bad guys getting better at making bombs. IEDs started out as a joke, a soda can that would just pop. Now, they're blowing up Humvees, but still, more guys are coming home."

Caleb surveyed the sight of patients and therapists hard at work with pride as if he'd invented the place.

It struck Phoenix how much his brother must care to go to all this trouble. "How *did* you get us in here?" Phoenix asked his twin with newfound respect for his abilities.

Caleb shrugged. "Your business partner, Dex, helped. He said you guys have some military account. Plus, I signed away our firstborn kids."

"You're not having children," Phoenix reminded him. "And me, either," he added, upon further reflection of his sorry state.

"You signed a liability form," Tara explained to Caleb, leading the way onto the main floor. "It just says you won't sue us if you get hurt."

Phoenix navigated between clients and their therapists stretching hip flexors, working out with weights and running on one or two prostheses.

"Watch it!" called a man catching a medicine ball, nearly stumbling into Phoenix.

"Sorry," he said, swerving out of the way with a sidestep that made him stumble. Phoenix's cane prevented him from falling.

As they traversed the aisle between padded tables, they passed young guy after young guy, one with a metal frame around a bare leg, squatting with a heavy ball, another solid on a real leg and a prosthetic one, shooting hoops. The sight of men and women missing an arm, with bandaged residual limbs, wheelchairs and prostheses took on a new sense of ordinary.

Here he fit right in. He grinned at nothing in particular.

"I have someone I want to introduce you to," Tara said.

She led the way to a soldier on a mat. The blond-haired guy, fair in complexion, repeatedly sat up to count each repetition for the therapist holding his prosthetic legs. When he noticed the approaching visitors, he stopped and pushed up to a standing position.

"I'm Aaron. Welcome to Walter Reed," he said, offering his only hand, his left one, to Phoenix, then Caleb.

"Thanks," Phoenix said, managing the right-hand-to-left-hand greeting.

Another guy nearby, practicing lunges, stopped and introduced himself to Caleb. "Hey, man, those tats are sick," he said, mopping sweat off a ginger-hued crew cut.

"Thanks, yours too," Caleb said and turned to admire the flame-licked dragon down one calf and matching design on his prosthesis. They became engrossed comparing tattoos.

"First time here?" Aaron asked Phoenix.

"Yup, looks like an amazing place," Phoenix said, surveying the equipment, therapists and rock-climbing wall which hulked conspicuously in the center. "How long you been here?"

"Nine months."

Phoenix exploded with disbelief. "Nine months! I'm complaining after just two."

"In the military, we get great benefits," he replied.

Tara explained. "These guys come in with shrapnel, burns, traumatic brain injuries and all kinds of complications. Some of them have been through dozens of surgeries. That's part of why it takes longer."

"I stepped on an IED. I saw my legs get blown right off. I didn't know about my arm until later. My guys got tourniquets on me and saved my life."

He looked at Phoenix expectantly. "What happened to you?" Apparently, sharing injury stories was a *de rigueur* form of greeting.

"Mine's not really patriotic. I got run over by a train."

"Ouch. How'd you end up under a train?"

"I saved a guy who was trying to jump onto the tracks."

"You rock," Aaron said.

Stoic Tara winced. "But you ended up there instead?"

"Yup."

"That *succkks*."

"The important thing is you lived to tell about it." The blond warrior whistled.

There was perspective. Yep, Phoenix lived to tell about it.

"At least the train gave you a good-looking stump." He pointed at Phoenix's bare arm, visible beneath the pushed-up sleeves of his shirt.

"Good-looking stump? Is there such a thing?" Phoenix asked.

"Yeah, instead of an ugly stump," he explained, lifting his elbow to show the bumpy, misshapen flesh and angry purple scars running up the back of his humerus. "They put metal and junk in IEDs. Does a number on you."

Tara observed one then the other, not a whit of disgust at either of them. "This guy's *below* the knee," Tara added, gesturing towards Phoenix with a nod of approval.

Aaron appraised Phoenix processing all of this. "Below the knee is like a scratch," he said. "That's what we call a paper cut. You're lucky. Left leg, too. You'll be able to drive a normal car. Wait'll you don't even need that cane."

Lucky? Not needing a cane?

This guy had the experience to know what he was talking about, and he verified the tall tales Nadine had spun. Phoenix felt hope resist stubbornly then rise a little. He wasn't alone. He was part of a community of tough guys who were fighting—not just to subsist, but to thrive.

"There are below-the-knee amputees going back into active combat," the soldier bragged.

Phoenix nodded, absorbing a new sense of possibility.

Caleb's murmured conversation with the other veteran turned towards motorcycles.

"I can't wait to get back on my bike," the ginger-headed guy said.

"I'm going to rock climb. You want to come?" Aaron asked, pointing towards the artificial tower covered in multicolored hand and foot holds.

"There's a first time for everything. Sure." Phoenix shrugged, assessing the wall's height.

"When you try it, you might find it almost easier if you've never done it before," Tara assured him. "You won't have to unlearn how you used to climb."

"It's all about shifting your center of gravity, and now your center of gravity's different," Aaron explained.

Tara led them towards the rock-climbing wall while Caleb hung back.

Along the way across the massive hall, Phoenix observed men and women working on balance and strength. One guy with no legs was strapped into a bowl-like bucket, and he moved forward with two crutches.

"Hip disarticulation," Tara explained, noticing Phoenix's glance. "The higher the loss, the harder it is. In his case, he's lost ankles, like you, but also knees and hips."

"Oh," Phoenix murmured.

Aaron strode along next to Phoenix. "You see me? Double above the knee? It takes me at least ten times the exertion it takes you to do the same thing."

"Geez, sorry," Phoenix offered.

He shrugged. "It's not that bad. I don't even consider myself disabled. I can do whatever I want, so it's not a big deal."

Phoenix was floored. This was a new concept. He'd simply assumed that without his leg and his hand, he was *disabled*, or at least *differently abled*. Depending on the day and on the struggle, he perceived himself as more disabled or less disabled. *But not disabled?* The possibility felt good.

"There's always someone worse off," his new friend said, nodding towards a guy with no arms or legs, seated on a padded table, wearing one prosthetic hand. A duo of therapists tossed buoyant plastic balls towards him and he practiced batting each one back, shifting and balancing on legs only a few inches in length. "Quadruple amputee."

Phoenix glanced away, not wanting to stare. From what he'd seen, though, the young warrior looked focused, not bitter or frustrated. A fresh-faced woman, who also appeared to be in her early twenties, looked on with pride.

"He doesn't look too bad off," Phoenix commented.

"You're right. He's doing really well," Tara confirmed, continuing towards the rock-climbing wall, which now loomed larger as they drew closer.

"He's got his own cheering squad," Phoenix noted.

"Huh, some guys have all the luck," Aaron said, his face twisting. Phoenix wondered if the effort of traipsing across the enormous gym was physically too much for him.

"His woman left him," Tara said, explaining his new buddy's sudden sourness.

"Of course," Phoenix said before he could stop his sarcastic tone.

"She said it wasn't working out anyway, even before I came back all blown up," Aaron said. "Yeah, right. Nothing to do with the missing parts."

Tara threw him a glance. "It happens. People react all different ways."

"That quad's girlfriend is a saint. She's here every day," the guy added, nodding back towards the spot where the batting exercise continued. "You married?" he asked, curious.

Phoenix shook his head, keeping pace with the group. "I'm single. There was someone. But this is too much for her," he shrugged his arm as evidence. *Dark hair, charcoal-shadowed eyes, lips like velvet, a husky laugh, arms thrown around him with abandon.* The memories swamped him.

"Boom," Aaron said, cheered despite Phoenix's somberness. "There you go. Some girls just can't deal. We're like soulmates, you and I. After the climb, we should go grab a beer or grub or something."

Yup, soulmates with this dumped triple-amputee, who confirmed the truth Phoenix already knew. *Some women just can't deal.* He was smart to nip it in the bud before Orchid broke his heart.

"Sure, a beer sounds good."

CHAPTER 28

I'M SHAKIN'

Phoenix

D-Day. Done-Day. Final day of inpatient rehab.

"Jailbreak!" Phoenix joked, standing among staff members bidding him farewell.

"Are we diggin' a tunnel, crawling through ducts or shooting our way out?" Caleb asked, heaving two bags onto the wheelchair.

"Nah, nothing as hard as all that. Insurance has run out of money, so makes it easy to give me the boot."

He pulled each nurse and then his therapist into an embrace. "Nadine, you taught me everything, and I would've never guessed I'd be standing here, leaving for home if you'd asked me all those months ago."

"You deserve the best, really. Never saw someone work so hard to get out of here."

"Stubborn, isn't he?" Caleb asked.

"Compliments, compliments," Phoenix interjected.

Nadine held out a wrapped parcel. "We put together some pictures of your time here. We thought you might want to remember how far you've come."

Phoenix looked at the square package with skepticism. "Doesn't sound like something I really want to remember."

Caleb grabbed the gift. "Thanks," he said gruffly. He shoved the album into an empty space in one bag.

Outside, Phoenix's cane found steady ground in the shoveled pavement wet from a winter nor'easter. He'd convinced his mom to leave before the weather turned bitter. She'd be back soon enough for Thanksgiving.

Caleb loaded Phoenix's car with his bags and chair, and Phoenix drove with one hand.

Directing the vehicle's movement imparted a surprising feeling of possibility. The freedom to go anywhere at any time rolled ahead of them.

"Well, look at you," Caleb said.

"You're surprised I'm driving? Didn't you tell me I could do anything I wanted?"

"Usually you're too stubborn to listen to me."

"I'll work on that," Phoenix said.

"Good," Caleb said, ignoring the sarcasm, "because I've got a favor to ask."

"Yeah?"

Caleb looked at him, one hand rubbing the snake imprinted on his thick neck. "I need you to come down to the station with me and show me what happened."

"What?" The car swerved as his head jerked to glare at his twin, then he quickly adjusted the vehicle's direction. "You want to go back to the station where my accident happened?"

"It's on the way to your place anyway."

"You want to go right now?"

"Why not?" He shrugged. "It might be good for you."

"Good for me? You think reliving the worst thing that's ever happened to me could be good for me?"

"Sorry." Caleb glared through the windshield as Phoenix's internal debate took another turn.

"Actually, there's some crazy part of me that's obsessed with going back. I see that guy, you know. In my dreams."

"You know a guy called Peter Levine?" Caleb asked.

"No. Who's he?"

"Some PhD who's studied how wild animals get over trauma."

"You're kidding me, right?"

"No, listen. Young cubs and stuff, if they get threatened by another animal, then later on when they're safe, they go back and re-enact the trauma to get it out of their system. You never hear of animals in therapy, right?"

"We're a block from the subway stop. You want to do this?"

"Yeah."

"Crazy thing is, me too."

Phoenix pulled over to the curb. He swiveled out of the car and met his sibling on the sidewalk. As they walked, Phoenix caught their reflection in the clear expanse of a bakery window, two dark-haired men ghosted onto the image of people clustered around café tables. One burly with a scowl, one pitiful with a cane. He turned away from the truth in the glass and towards his brother.

"How's Sascha?"

"She's dating some divorced dude."

"Doesn't sound like you approve."

"He could be a saint and I wouldn't approve."

"So, go fight for her."

"I can't give her what she wants."

Phoenix ducked his chin, in more agreement than Caleb could know. "If you love someone, set them free."

"Can't set a free spirit like Sascha any freer."

Phoenix grew pensive. "I owe Sascha. She gave me perspective just when I needed it. Seeing life outside of rehab gave me something to work towards."

"Good thing it worked. Mom almost had a coronary when she heard where you were."

"Yeah, Mom watched me like a hawk for days after that."

They entered the west entrance for the 4, 5 and 6 trains. The stark black and white sign, *86 Street Station Downtown and Brooklyn*, produced a shudder. Last time here, Phoenix had relished the summer sun and taken the steps two at a time.

Tucking his cane under his left elbow, Phoenix picked his way down the stairs. "What if he's here?" His eyes closed for a moment, despite needing to be able to see every step to navigate them.

"I've been here a few times since the accident. I've never seen any homeless guy, but if he's here, he better kiss your feet and thank you," Caleb said.

"Foot," Phoenix corrected.

"You still have two. You're cyborg."

At the bottom landing, cold dankness emanated from the grayed tiles. Caleb pulled a Metro card from a worn black wallet. He swiped it twice, allowing Phoenix to push through the turnstile first.

"He was there," Phoenix said, limping over to a discolored spot marked in old-world tile. "He was sitting here, on a piece of cardboard, wearing crazy amounts of clothes for the weather."

The words came out of some foreign place he didn't recognize as his vision narrowed to a wild grimace and face full of rage.

"You okay?"

"As good as a cub re-enacting trauma."

Phoenix caned deeper towards the darkened tunnel. He transfixed on the columns of dull green I-beams receding to the end of the platform.

"I gave him a buck," he said, "and found a note Orchid must've slipped into my pocket."

"Damn, look how fuckin' narrow the platform is here," Caleb noted, hands on hips, looking back and forth at the span that, if he lay down, would nearly force his feet to hang over the edge.

Phoenix stepped over to the start of the yellow warning strip, almost at the mouth of the tunnel, his plastic foot unable to feel the nubby raised grommets. His cane wobbled on the uneven surface.

"I was listening to music, a song from Orchid's playlist."

"Orchid this, Orchid that. Fuck Orchid."

Phoenix didn't pay heed to his brother's muttering. "I didn't see him until I heard the train coming. All I knew was this guy was going to jump. I wasn't even thinking. I just grabbed him. To save him. But—"

Caleb cupped his elbow. "It's okay," he said, voice low. Phoenix looked at his brother. Uncontrollable tremors came from within him. All moisture evaporated from his mouth, leaving it as dry as the dusty space between the tracks.

"But then *he* pulled back. And *I* fell over the edge."

Phoenix stared at the rusty rails and dirt-brown floor littered with cellophane and crumpled napkins. "I fell right onto the tracks. I couldn't catch myself. I could hear the train coming. I couldn't move fast enough."

"Christ."

"I knew I needed help, but I couldn't move."

"Of course."

"I heard screaming or something, so I figured someone knew I was there."

"They said the train guys were lightning fast. They called 911 and got tourniquets on you right away. Saved your life."

Caleb dropped his brother's arm and turned to face the track. He appeared lost in thought, probably formed from hours spent with the police on eyewitness testimony and watching videos from the few functioning cameras at the entrance of the station.

"You know fifty people died on the subway tracks this year?" Phoenix said. "I don't know how many were accidents."

"What the hell is wrong with this world?"

"Yeah," Phoenix said, straightening. "You know what? I'm one of the lucky ones."

Caleb eyed him, lost for words.

"We should go. You wanna go to my place? See what contraptions Mom's had installed?" Phoenix said.

When they arrived, Caleb removed his brother's belongings as Phoenix hobbled towards his neighbor, Mrs. V.

"Oh, hi Phoenix." Her smile ebbed as her gaze traveled down the length of Phoenix's cane.

"I've been away for a while. How've you been? How's Elton?" he asked about her dog.

She forced her attention up to Phoenix's face. "Sorry to hear about . . . Do you need—"

Well crap, even his normally loquacious neighbor couldn't find words. Phoenix shook his head, trying to erase her consternation, and in the act, feeling the confidence he'd built erode.

Caleb pushed the wheelchair past the two of them. "Eleventh floor, right?"

The diversion refocused their attention. "It's nice having you back," she finally said.

"Thank you." Phoenix followed his brother's broad shoulders.

Once they reached his hallway, grief simmered in his chest. He limped down the hall whose shortcomings seemed oddly as glaring as his own. He noted spots where paint had flaked from the corners of the wall, a scuff along the baseboard and the dated print of Central Park in watercolor. He flashed to how he must look, with his uneven gait, clinical cane, fumbling for keys, an echo of his former self. The essence was there, like watercolors that captured the main features and colors, just not the details.

Opening his door, he saw his mother's handiwork. Throw rugs no longer graced the floors. The furniture seemed sparser, pushed apart with a chair-width between tables and sofas. He caned by the living area and towards his bedroom, passing the square table for casual meals that normally had four chairs around it, now with just three.

Caleb followed him into his master bedroom, pushing the wheelchair and bags. A scent of paint hung in the air. *Ah, that's why.* The bathroom and closet doors had been widened. Here was the start of the rest of his life. If he made it to old age, two-thirds of his years would be hampered by his injuries.

Wish I had appreciated my agility when I had all four limbs.

Caleb stood behind his brother, scowling again. Phoenix turned. "Hey, welcome to my wheel-in closet."

The stupid play on words was the first thing that popped into his mind. His brother stored the bulky bag in the back of the closet and parked the wheelchair there.

"Want me to stay?"

"Nah, go. Thanks for coming for this."

"Well, call if you need anything."

With Caleb gone, reacquainting himself with the apartment took just minutes. His thoughts turned to Orchid. *Hope she's happy.*

He typed her a text. "How are you—"

His thumb paused, poised over the keys. He pictured her arriving at his door as she had several times in the past, then her open-mouthed shock, and his quiet explanations trying to calm her.

"Listen, there was an accident, I didn't want to tell you. But now I'm better and—"

The words died in his mind. His injuries had rendered Mrs. V mute. What could he say to comfort the fear in Orchid's eyes when he was the one causing it? *Better for her to remember me as I was.*

Reminding himself of all the reasons it couldn't work with this particular woman, he deleted the text.

CHAPTER 29

THE WORLD

Phoenix

naugural day at work. Phoenix rode the elevator, glad for a few minutes of not seeing anyone he knew before he faced the office. Leaning on his cane, Phoenix exited the lift to counterAgency's floor. The refreshingly light space elevated his thoughts. The design spurred ideas. *What if hospital rooms sported the same individuality and airy, who-cares architecture?* That was a relief; the train hadn't stolen his creativity.

"Look who's here!" the receptionist called as he entered the agency. Co-workers turned from a table laden with food and broke into applause. The sign above the breakfast platters proclaimed *Welcome Back!* Colleagues trailed closer to greet him with hugs and hellos. A producer reached out, then froze as he fixated on Phoenix's occupied grip. Phoenix shifted the cane under his left elbow and clasped the guy's hand. "Great to see you," Phoenix said with affection. It struck him that he'd need to help people feel comfortable with the changes in him.

"So much for flying under the radar," he quipped to the growing crowd, transferring the cane back to its supporting position. "Come to think of it, so much for flying at all." The hubbub echoed through the industrial space of painted ductwork and whitewashed brick walls, bringing more staff into the open foyer.

"You look great," said a copywriter with a sleek blond 'do and black suit. Her urbane get-up made him feel disheveled in comparison. The feeling had nothing to do with the crisp suit he'd donned, and everything to do with the jacket sleeve cuffed halfway up his forearm and the crutch he leaned upon.

"We're so happy to see you!" A bubbly producer threw her arms around his neck. Her enthusiastic embrace caused him to wobble and adjust his stance. He cupped an arm around her and then let go.

"Thanks. I appreciate all the cards and flowers. How are you?" He looked around at his staff, nodding and murmuring affirmations. Their care warmed him, yet wide-smiled stares were tinged with tightness. A young copywriter broke away from the huddle, but not before he glimpsed her crumpled chin and wet eyes. He'd exerted monumental effort to go from immobile in a hospital bed to walking. In his own assessment, he was doing much better. But this employee and her colleagues had last seen him as a capable, whole man.

He straightened, an attempt to regain the feeling of stature his physicality had lost. The group quieted, waiting for his words.

"It's really great to be back. I'm proud of the bang-up job you guys are doing. Congrats on winning REBBL. I know how you really pulled together these last few months. So many of you reached out to me. I'm sorry I wasn't in any shape to see all of you. It's been . . . hard." His throat tightened.

He glanced away, seeking to regain composure. Here he was, at the center of the business he'd built. Where everything was the same—maybe even better—except him.

"Now that Phoenix's here, we are really going to kick some butt," came a jovial voice. The crowd cheered. Dex stepped around the back of the group to join Phoenix at the center of the ragged circle. "Who are we going to win next?"

People called out names of pitches and accounts under review.

Dex's familiar grin was just what Phoenix needed to pull himself together. He turned towards his buddy. "Thanks to you, and Liv and everyone for helping out these last few months."

"You would've done the same for any of us," Dex said. He faced their employees. "This team's really the best in the business. Now go scarf some pastries."

The crowd dissipated, most heading towards the buffet. Some art directors and copywriters pressed nearer. "Hey, can I set up time to bounce an idea off you?" "Do you have time to meet my new hire later today?"

Liv parted the crowd with one sharp shoulder and took her place at Phoenix's side with a tilt of her chin. "Mr. Walker, we need to prep before your ten a.m.," she said, looking up at him through glinting glasses.

"Sure, thanks. Excuse me, everyone." He followed Liv down the long corridor to his office overlooking Midtown.

"Do I really have a ten a.m.?" he asked, out of earshot of the others.

"Yes, you're scheduled for a rendezvous with a double espresso," she said, indicating the miniature handled mug on his desk.

"Brilliant. Thanks."

Relieved to have a moment off feet untested for marathon workdays, he sank into his chair and stared at the cool white expanse of his desk. Liv's neat efficiency kept the objects to a minimum. His Mac sat open, logged into an email account showcasing no unread messages. A picture of his parents with him and Caleb at their last birthday celebration stood in one corner. Which reminded him of the photo with Orchid that she'd framed from their sunny day in Cannes.

No time to contemplate where that picture had gone, as a steady stream of co-workers came by to welcome him back and inform him of business dynamics.

By two p.m., Phoenix still hadn't had time to eat the roast beef panini Liv had brought back during her lunch break.

She knocked, and pushed through the glass door to interrupt his conversation with Dex. "Five minutes," she told the big guy, "and then Mr. Walker has to leave for an appointment."

The barrel-chested executive leaned back, chair groaning in protest. "With whom?" he boomed.

"It's a private meeting, but I think he's interviewing replacement executive creative directors," she snarked, allowing the door to swing shut on the appreciative audience behind her.

Ten minutes later, Dex got up to leave. "It's not been the same without you, buddy. You let me know anything you need."

"Sure, thanks. I appreciate you and Fiona coming to see me in rehab."

"You're looking good."

"Maybe better than right after I was run over by a train, but I doubt that I qualify for *good*."

Liv peeked into the office, her brown-slicked hair and cat eyeglasses sending enough of a message without saying anything.

"Okay, okay." Dex ambled out as she entered.

Phoenix looked up at his administrative assistant. "I don't have an appointment, do I?" Suddenly, he realized how tired he felt.

"You are on half days until further notice. Dr. Liv's orders," she said, picking up his uneaten sandwich and placing it into an oil-spotted paper bag already heavy with other contents. "I'm taking you home."

"You don't have to do that," he said.

She walked out with him, matching her pace to his, carrying her rigid, structured purse in one hand and his bagged lunch in the other.

At the street, she put up a hand for a cab and one pulled over within minutes as if no one dare ignore the efficiency she embodied. He caned down the curb to the door she opened for him, grateful to sink onto the seat. She shut his door and then, surprising him, slid in on the other side, behind the driver.

"East Eighty-Fifth at York," she told the bearded man, pulling the door shut behind her.

"You don't have to come with me," Phoenix said, resting his cane against the side of the door.

"When else am I going to get an excuse to sneak out of work early?"

"You must have an ogre of a boss."

"Yup. The worst."

"You probably won't even get Thanksgiving off."

"Never," she agreed, lips stretching across her tiny face.

He turned forward, facing right into the cabbie's ID picture. The swarthy fellow overflowing with facial hair didn't have the doughy bulbous nose or bushy eyebrows of the homeless man. But there was no telling that to the images suddenly racing through his mind. He shut his eyes to stop picturing the bearded guy with crazed eyes leaping for the tracks.

When he forced them open again, Liv was staring at him. "You okay?"

"No," he admitted.

"I was just kidding about the bad boss." She put a tentative hand on his arm.

"I've got to get out of here."

"Pull over," she demanded through the opening in the clear plastic partition.

Liv tossed a twenty-dollar bill up front as the car slowed. She jumped out and stalked around to his side. Yanking open his door, he tumbled out and leaned on his cane to get up onto the curb.

"What's wrong?" she pleaded.

His knees didn't feel strong enough to hold him up. "The homeless guy . . . from the subway."

Liv's mouth fell open in horror, shooting a useless stare at the already departed cab. "That was him?"

He shook his head. "Just looked like him."

Liv's brows knitted behind semi-circular spectacles. "What can I do?"

"Nothing. I'll just walk home. You go."

"No way. I'm not leaving you."

He glared at her.

"It's only a few blocks," Liv reasoned. "We can either call an uber, or I'll walk with you."

"Let's walk." He found he could take steps, each steadier than the prior one.

As they made their way to his apartment, she pressed. "Is there someone I can call?"

"No, I'll be fine."

"What about Caleb?"

"I'm not calling my brother."

"Anyone else?"

He shook his head with a nonchalance he didn't feel.

"Well, I'm always here," she said.

His loneliness was not a subject he wanted to discuss; he was glad they'd arrived.

"Thanks again," he said, entering the foyer and passing the guard's desk.

"There's enough for lunch and dinner in here," she said, holding up the white paper bag as she accompanied him to the elevator. He'd forgotten about the need for meals. Liv hadn't.

"That's really thoughtful," he said, tucking the bag into the crook of his left elbow. An appetite for food seemed as foreign as cactus in a rainforest.

"Do you want me to stay with you?"

"Thanks, but there's no need."

She looked up at him, cocking an eyebrow as she formulated a smarmy remark. "Even though you're a terrible boss, you know I'd do anything for you."

"I don't doubt that for a minute," he said, turning toward the elevator.

The next morning, Phoenix groaned upon seeing Liv in his lobby.

"If you didn't have new clothes on, I'd guess you'd been here all night," he said dryly to the pert brunette.

"Who else is going to introduce your new driver?" she asked, accompanying him outside.

"New driver?" Sure enough, a dark sedan livery service stood at the curbside. Inside sat an elderly gentleman with hair the same color and density as a dandelion gone to bloom.

"Don't worry. I negotiated. Once we arrange the pickup and drop-off times, it's not much more than an uber." She welled with pride.

Phoenix introduced himself to the elderly gentleman and shook his hand. "Nice to meet you."

"Am I that bad off, that I need a babysitter?" he asked Liv, maneuvering into the back seat.

"You're not the only agency head to have a driver, you know."

"Thanks, Liv," he managed. From the back seat, he stared at the blue accessible parking tag she must've ordered. Above the seated figure in a wheelchair, the placard was stamped in capital letters: *PERMANENT.*

Like I need a reminder that this isn't temporary?

As they merged into traffic, the hangcard swung from the rearview mirror like a noose.

CHAPTER 30

ONE MORE CUP OF COFFEE

Phoenix

SUNDAY NOVEMBER 18

The loneliness of being home propelled Phoenix outdoors. He turned towards the Starbucks near his building. A tall woman with golden-brown hair in a long bob arrived before him. She was dressed professionally for a weekend. She wore a belted coat over dress slacks.

She eyed his cane and swung the door open for him.

"Thank you," he said.

"You're welcome." She stepped in behind him.

"Please," he gestured, "you were here first."

"I'd prefer to have an excuse to delay getting to my office. You go ahead. And if you could linger over the ordering, you'd be doing me a favor."

Phoenix tried not to be intrigued. The granite slab of her back, like an I.M. Pei monument, was antithesis of the soft, sensual one he missed. "What horror are you trying to delay?"

"Corporate tax review."

"Are you an accountant?"

"Actuary."

He snickered.

"I'm not joking."

He couldn't help it, he laughed harder.

"I'm a CFP," she added, seeming proud of her certified financial planner status.

Phoenix tried to control his clenching stomach muscles. The queue moved ahead, and though he was next in line, he couldn't gain enough self-control to close the gap between him and the cashier. He waved the woman forward, "Please—"

She looked at him askance and turned to the barista. "Caffe Americano, two Splendas."

Phoenix composed himself enough to join her. "Double espresso, black." He pulled out his credit card, "I've got these," he said.

"You paying for laughing at me?"

"I'm sorry. I wasn't laughing at you. But I would like to pay."

They waited at the counter for their brews. He didn't know what overcame him. "Would you like to sit for a moment and delay the tax filing further? I'll try to explain my jocularity."

She nodded with such conservation of motion that he wasn't sure it was assent.

When their drinks arrived, she double-fisted them and followed him to a small round table.

She sat and put out her hand. "Catarina Dubrovski; friends call me Rina."

The last time he'd laughed this much was with a woman who couldn't be part of his life. Phoenix grimaced. He rested his cane against the wall to shake her hand. "Phoenix Walker." He settled into a chair and tried to get serious.

"Ms. Dubrovski, I hope I've not offended you. I work in advertising, and we had a creative idea about bots replacing actuaries. It was hysterical but too offensive to be produced."

"Well, Mr. Walker, there's nothing funny about actuaries."

He took a sip of the scalding espresso and used the pain to still his mirth. "Well, Ms. Dubrovski, I've laughed more just now than I have in a month."

"If the idea of actuaries cracks you up, it must've been some serious month."

"Yea, it's not been a great few months."

She nodded and pulled out a business card. "If you ever need an actuary here's my number." She wrote her personal contact information on the back of the card.

He peered down at it. "Your office isn't far from mine."

"I'm here on assignment from Toronto, and I've picked up some tips, like don't try to find an uber on a rainy day, and don't buy the homeless a sandwich 'cause they just want the money."

He was suddenly inspired by the idea of her being a welcome diversion at an upcoming family commitment. "Have you ever experienced Thanksgiving in America?"

"Not yet, but call me. It'd be fun to spend Thanksgiving being laughed at."

CHAPTER 31

SIXTEEN SALTINES

Phoenix

Caleb and Rina accompanied Phoenix to Uncle George and Aunt Betsy's brownstone. Mom embraced her boys. Phoenix turned to introduce the woman behind him in the foyer, clothed in a metal-gray interview-ready suit. "Rina is on assignment in New York from Canada."

The large-framed woman offered a handshake.

Mom took it, and eyed Rina with an appraising expression like a physician discovering a pernicious infection. Aunt Betsy hurried over and hugged her sister's boys. "You two get better-looking every time I see you!"

Too polite to say so out loud, Phoenix leaned on his cane towards Rina. "Not sure how I should take that. Last time she'd seen me, I'd just been run over by a train."

"She didn't say anything about my appearance. Does that mean I look worse than someone who's been run over by a train?"

Phoenix nearly choked laughing. That's what he needed, someone to wisecrack over his accident. He caught sight of Caleb's scowl.

"You okay?" Phoenix asked.

Caleb tried to straighten his face and brightened from scowl into grimace. "Yeah. You?"

"Sure."

"It's good to see you happy," Caleb said.

Phoenix had a mix of feelings. Being in this place reminded him of Dad, and how the last time he'd been there, he'd been solid on his own two feet. The contrast pained him. Yet something about this no-nonsense woman reminded him how to laugh again.

They trailed their hostess and Mom, who were walking arm-in-arm.

Phoenix leaned on his cane to whisper to Rina, "My Uncle George has a heavy hand at the bar. He needs one for his own sanity."

"I don't drink," she whispered back.

This serious woman appeared to need a drink as much as any of them.

"I'm not joking," she said.

He couldn't help it and cracked up.

"Are you laughing at me again?"

In the kitchen, George was already plunking hand-cut ice into tumblers and rimming the glasses with lemon wedges. He stopped when he spotted his guests.

He pulled each boy into a hug. He looked appraisingly at Phoenix all the way to the ground. "Well, look at you. As good as new."

"Hardly," Phoenix replied. At least Rina chuckled at his dry tone.

Mom turned. "Thanks, George. Phoenix worked so hard at physical therapy and is doing really well. He's back at work. You'd hardly know what he's been through."

Is my family daft? His left sleeve was half-empty. His upright stance was only possible with a crutch.

Their hosts ushered them into the sitting room. Every surface appeared covered in fine fabric, from the windows framed with damask curtains to the overstuffed camelback sofas strewn with tasseled pillows. His cousins Stew and Harry stood to greet them. Caleb joined the guys around a chess table, perching his broad mass on a delicate upholstered chair.

Mom, George and Betsy gathered on loveseats nearest the mantled fireplace, settling drinks onto side tables.

Phoenix rested his cane against the camelback to place a hand on the sofa before easing into the seat.

"Can I get you a drink?" he offered Rina. He realized too late that he probably couldn't deliver if she assented.

"I still don't drink, same as five minutes ago. But I can get you one." She stood and insisted. "Seriously, this one's on me."

Mom joined Rina at the oval serving table cluttered with decanters and crystal-cut bottles. As Rina prepared two tumblers of ice-cooled liquid, Phoenix could overhear parts of his mother's cross-examination.

"How did you meet Phoenix?"

"In a coffee shop."

"How long ago was that?"

"Sunday."

"This week?"

After a longer conversation that Phoenix couldn't hear, Rina returned, handing Phoenix an amber colored liquid.

"Chivas," she said, pointing to his beverage. "Water," she explained, lifting hers. She sat and touched her glass to his. "Do all your dates get the third degree?" she asked.

"It must be a new hobby of Mom's," he said, noting the frequency with which his mom glanced at them. Then, making the connection, he added, "She's been hyper-protective since my accident."

"Yeah, she told me a little about it. Well, Happy Thanksgiving."

The reference to the occasion again reminded Phoenix of his father. This was the second Thanksgiving without Dad. *I wonder what Orchid is doing for the holiday.*

She had confessed that holidays without family were hard for her, too. There'd been no calls or contact with her in the two and a half months since they last spoke. He doused the dull ache with a mouthful of Scotch.

"Dinner is served," Betsy announced.

Seated between Rina and Caleb, Phoenix swigged some wine.

He tried cutting his meat with his fork. "So how long will you be in New York?" he asked Rina.

"Um, I'm on a six-month leadership assignment." She stared at his plate. "Do you want a hand with that?"

"No, thanks," he blurted, his automatic reply.

"Don't they make artificial arms?" Rina asked.

"Yeah, they do."

"And if you had one, you'd be able to cut your own food?"

"Yeah, I would."

"So why don't you have one?"

"What's left still hurts. And I seem to be able to get by without one. Mostly."

She nodded at the logic. "So, what do you think I should see while I'm on assignment here?"

"Hmm, what do you like?"

"Watching sports, hockey, live country music."

"There you go. Check out the Rangers, sports bars and Madison Square Garden."

"You're the first person *not* to tell me to go to the opera and Broadway shows."

"Those are super, but I didn't hear fine arts on your list."

"I might like them. I've just never tried them."

"Would you like to go to a show? I can get tickets. We just need to head there soon or after the holidays. Everything's booked mid-December through New Year's."

She smoothed her silken bob. "I'll tell you what, you bring me to a fancy show and I'll take you to a Canadian hockey game."

CHAPTER 32

FREEDOM AT 21

Orchid

The chaos in Mandy's apartment assaulted every sense. At least Orchid felt at home.

Mandy's son Matty shrieked and brought tiny pea-smeared fists to his hair.

A small dog twisted beneath the highchair, catching food as it fell.

Mandy aimed another spoon of mush toward her son while directing her husband.

"There's no need to baste. That's what the oven bag does," she explained to her apron-and hot-mitt-outfitted spouse.

Then Mandy swiveled back toward Matty, whose rigidity surpassed comical. Stiff legged, he used the leverage of the tray to press one cheek against the cushioned back, avoiding the contents of the spoon.

"Now that it's calm, tell me again about this uncle of yours?"

"This is calm?" Orchid registered the explosion of cranberry red on the stove's backsplash, and crowded dishes on top of the microwave and toaster oven.

"'Bout as good as it gets in a household with a one-year-old!"

Orchid pulled out her phone. "Okay, so you know my dad's brother messaged me months ago, all 'sorry I've been lax' and 'oh by the way, you have a new baby cousin, aren't you happy for me?' Well, today, he sends me this.

Dear Orchid,

Just wanted to let you know we're thinking of you on Thanksgiving. Hope we can see you soon.

Love, Uncle Zach, Aunt Esty
and Baby Quentin

What do you think he wants?"

"I don't know. What do you know about him?"

Orchid shrugged. "My dad always seemed fond of his little brother. We didn't see each other much, because he went to school in LA. Uncle Zach seems really excited about being a new father. But don't forget, after my parents died, I didn't hear from my uncle for sixteen years."

"Well, you know I think that totally stinks. You don't owe him anything. But maybe he's okay. He sounds like he's trying to be nice. What does it hurt to call him?"

"I don't know. I don't trust him."

"You don't trust any guys," Mandy reminded her.

"I trust Matty."

"Babies don't count. Name another."

"Well, I trusted Phoenix. And look where it got me."

"Aww, honey. Don't."

Orchid sat on Mandy's couch. The space between the cushions revealed crumbs where her weight compressed the sofa. Her dad would want her to give him a chance. Zach was his only brother, after all, and had suffered his own grief at the loss of family at a young age.

"Uncle Zach?"

"Orchid! Hang on a sec. Let me get to a quiet spot."

"Okay."

His voice sounded the same, its warm timbre suffusing her with a feeling of familiarity.

"Sorry about that. It's a zoo here."

"If this isn't a good time—"

"Oh no, that's not what I meant. Don't go. How was your Thanksgiving?"

"Uh, good I guess. How was yours?"

"Esty made the best tofu turkey this side of LA. Listen, I'm really glad you called. I feel terrible that we haven't talked in so long. It's totally my fault. What a terrible uncle. Your dad would kill me, he really would."

"Hey, no sweat," she interrupted. "Congratulations on your little boy."

"Thanks! You should meet him. Especially since he brought us together and all."

"What?"

"I guess, more accurately, it was Esty. You know, my wife?"

"Yeah?"

"She just couldn't get over that I had this niece I never spoke to. And I'd thought about you, really. It's just after a while, so much time passed, and I didn't know how to just call out of the blue anymore."

"Guess you figured out a way."

"Ha. Well, once we got pregnant, Esty was like, 'you see how important family is?'"

"Uh-huh."

"Seriously. Then he came. And he was so perfect. We were so proud. Just like your parents were so proud when you were born."

He waited a beat then nailed her exact thought. "I feel terrible I haven't been around to tell you things like that about your parents."

She exhaled slowly as if meditating. "Right."

"So, um, are you doing well? Tell me all about you." His tone indicated that he found it as awkward as she did, being family and strangers all at the same time.

"I don't know what to tell you. I got my MBA and ended up working in marketing, which I love. I'm at Estée Lauder working on a global project."

"Wow, I'm impressed. Does global mean you travel?"

"Sometimes, though we hold a lot of video conferences too."

"Well, if you're ever in L.A, you've got to call me."

Quentin sounded a shriek in the background.

"Are you married? Do you have kids?"

"Nope," she said.

"Well, you have plenty of time."

Orchid puffed up her cheeks. "I know. It's just . . . it's just that I fell for a guy who wants nothing to do with me."

"Aw, I'm sorry. Want me to come kill him for you?"

The ridiculous offer cheered her. "Yeah, actually, that'd be great. We were getting along super. Then I came back after a month and a half to China and *boom*. He says we shouldn't see each other anymore."

"Ouch. Guy's got no taste. He's not good enough for you."

Orchid stared at the ceiling. Entrepreneur, model-ready dance fiend with a touch of European. That's what family's for, to boost spirits by saying the opposite of the truth.

CHAPTER 33

STEADY AS SHE GOES

Phoenix

SATURDAY DECEMBER 1—DECEMBER 8

"Do you want me to calculate the chances of you laughing at me before we arrive at the Marquis?" Rina asked from the back of the car.

"One hundred percent?" Phoenix said.

She followed him into the theater. First time in a crowd on a custom-made stilt made him feel vulnerable. "Think I need a second crutch," he said, putting his left arm around her.

"Would you like sparkling water or something?" he asked at the concessions stand.

She shook her head. "I don't want to have to go to the bathroom during the performance."

Which, of course, elicited guffaws of laughter from Phoenix.

Clutching both *Playbill* programs, Rina followed Phoenix to their seats, located stage right. A young couple slouched in two seats adjacent to theirs. The woman looked at Phoenix's cane and stepped into the aisle, pulling the guy with her.

"Sorry," she said. Phoenix followed her stare down toward his feet.

"It's okay," he mumbled. *When did the aisles get so damn narrow?* And he had never noticed the slant before.

He managed to land in the upholstery, not on the ground. The older gentleman on the other side touched his elbow.

"Thank you for your service. Were you in Iraq? Or Afghanistan?"

"Neither. This was just a bad accident."

The man's wife craned her neck towards them. "Frank served in Vietnam. He always wants to make sure our military are appreciated, unlike the Vietnam vets."

"Well, then, thank *you* for your service." Phoenix leaned forward to lay his cane beneath his and Rina's seats.

"What happened? If I may ask?"

"You know that exhibition of mechanical dinosaurs they've built over in Jersey?" he asked the couple.

The wife put a hand over her mouth. "You don't mean?" her voice trailed off, her expression reflecting some imagined horror.

Rina smacked his arm.

The theater dimmed. Phoenix turned to face front. The stage lights shone to reveal a minimalist set: a blood-red sofa, plain table with hard-backed chairs and a Ming dynasty porcelain dog. Three characters played out a love triangle, where each party pined for an impossible relationship. The girl's heart belonged to her best guy friend, who mainly hung around to be with her roommate. The roommate, in turn, was in love with the girl.

"Unrequited love. That sucked," Phoenix joked as the final curtain fell. He pushed to a standing position.

The Vietnam vet extended a hand, forcing Phoenix to tuck his cane under his left elbow to grasp it.

"You're a nice-looking couple." The veteran's wife twisted around the guys to tell Rina.

"Thanks," she returned, smoothing her ash-shaded suit.

They shuffled out into the street with the crowd, his left arm around her. The driver awaited them curbside, as planned.

In the back of the car, Rina leaned against him.

"So, how'd you like your first show?"

"It was an experience. Artsy. Live theater is definitely different than a movie."

They arrived at her rented brownstone on a quiet street. Phoenix pulled himself out of the car to accompany Rina to the door and kissed her cheek.

"Wouldn't things be easier without that cane?" she asked.

"Yeah, that'd be great."

She turned to him. "Next time, it's my turn to take you to a hockey game."

The next weekend, they sat bundled in coats just behind the protective glass at Madison Square Garden's ice rink. Phoenix swigged beer from a plastic cup.

"This place is packed," Rina noted, swiveling her head to take in the crowd of thousands in the arena.

"Did you know the Knicks play basketball here?"

"On ice?"

"That'd be a sight, but no. Stadiums have some high-tech floor that they disassemble between sports. Sometimes they get a double header and have to change right from one to the other."

"That's inventive."

After a particularly vicious goal and a loud shout of approval from Rina, Phoenix turned to her. "This is fun."

"Yup, Canadian actuaries are a laugh a minute."

He downed the rest of the beer and put his hand up for another one, then turned to her. "You know, it's only fair to let you know that it's not just my arm that was injured—I'm a double-amputee."

Despite the alcohol-induced buzz, Phoenix was gripped by a sudden reluctance to see her reaction.

"No shit, Sherlock."

"You mean you already knew?"

"Yeah. Your mom filled me in pretty good. Why?"

"Well, doesn't it matter to you?"

"Nope." She stood to shout at the referee then sat and turned to Phoenix. "Did you see how unfair that call was?"

"Yeah, totally unfair."

"You're not even watching the game."

"And you don't even care about my leg."

"Um, you know, actuaries don't make great therapists. Are you having a PTSD moment or something?"

He nearly choked laughing, floored by her lack of compunction over the thing he thought would be deal-breaking for any woman.

"This game is totally wasted on you," Rina said.

They shared an uber home that night. He told her about his new account. "So, the VP says that he's choosing between us and one of the Big Four ad agencies. And I tell him that going boutique gives you individualized service, fresh thinking and breakthrough creativity."

Rina nodded.

"What are you thinking?" he asked her.

"I cannot believe we lost. That was brutal."

"Yea, brutal," he echoed. "So, we find out next week if we won the pitch."

"Who wouldn't hire you?"

"Thanks for the vote of confidence."

She stared out the window. "Did you want to talk about your leg or something?" she asked.

"Nah, I'm fine."

She said goodbye with an admonition that he'd have to try harder to take the game seriously if he wanted to attend more hockey matches. Then, she put a hand on his forearm, before exiting the car. "Next time, you'll have to come up to my place."

At home, as Phoenix contemplated Rina, his mind drifted to Orchid. He shook his head. If only Orchid could be as nonchalant over his injuries. . . .

CHAPTER 34

YOU DON'T KNOW WHAT LOVE IS

Orchid

THURSDAY DECEMBER 20

A gency holiday shindig. Just my cup of hell.

Orchid removed her faux-fur shrug to reveal a rhinestone and pleather dress with geometric cutouts at the collarbone, nape of the neck and one downward-pointing triangle just above her cleavage.

"Wh-oa," admired her co-worker.

She dodged his undeservedly possessive hand in the small of her back, and steered towards the bartender. "Shall we get a drink?" she asked.

The media agency event filled the oak wood bar of the upscale Midtown hotel, every group speaking louder to hear the other until the whole area echoed with their din.

Burgundy-clad waitstaff squeezed between narrow alleyways of space to offer silver trays of small bites: fresh figs with a triangle of brie, curry samosas, beef Wellington in puff pastry, tuna tartare on cucumber rounds. She swiped a vegetarian mini quiche from a passing tray. Dimly lit, the bar area melded together in dark shades, neutrals and an occasional splash of holiday red of the guests' attire.

Before Orchid could navigate a path to the guests milling around the tap, she felt the burn of familiar eyes.

"Phoenix."

The name she'd often thought, yet had no occasion to speak, formed with reverence.

He stepped forwards, the corners of his eyes crinkling in that way she loved. In her platform boots, they were nearly eye-to-eye.

"Orchid." Her name sounded lyrical in his deep rumble.

She studied the familiar features, drinking in his refined cheekbones, chiseled jawbone and dark brows. He leaned in to brush her cheek with his lips and she caught his scent of clean soap swirled with spiced cologne.

"Hey there," she murmured, losing herself in blue irises that had the power to transport her.

When he moved his arm to shake hands with her co-worker, she gaped at a petite woman tucked at his side. As introductions were made, jealousy replaced her delight in seeing him. *What does she have that I don't?*

The pretty brunette was young, *really young,* barely legal to drink. She was birdlike with smooth hair slicked back into a bun. Stylish glasses perched on the bridge of her nose. Her eyes narrowed as she reached out to take Orchid's outstretched hand. "Liv," came the clipped voice with a decided edge. A pang pierced Orchid as Liv tightened her left arm around Phoenix's waist when they shook hands.

Phoenix looked right at her. "How've you been?" he asked, sounding like he really cared.

"I'm good," she said. Her face flushed with the shame of rejection. She looked down, blinking to clear the unexpected emotion.

Politely, he turned to ask her co-worker about his position. While the minion spouted crap about the importance of his role,

Orchid stared unseeing at Phoenix's dark wool coat, draped over his left arm, trying to regain control of her emotions, praying her chin wasn't quivering as badly as the rest of her.

"Well, happy holidays," Phoenix said.

She looked up. "You're doing well?" she asked, beginning a conversation even though he was ending his.

"I'm okay," he said, radiating exuberance that comes from being in love. The thought struck her. *He's in love with Liv.*

"Glad you're well. Good, that's good," she replied.

"You too. Bye, Orchid." He wrapped his arm around Liv. They made their way, slowly picking their way through the crowd.

Orchid felt discarded, deserted again, cast off like last-season's salt-stained boots.

Jerk.

Orchid watched them step away, tentative in their movement as if so wrapped up in each other, they weren't focused on the task of leaving the party. Phoenix whispered into Liv's ear and she looked up at him with tenderness. Pain vacuumed air out of her.

At the bar, Orchid changed her mind.

"White wi-ne?" her co-worker asked.

"Double vodka on the rocks," she ordered, then pushed her way to the bathroom.

CHAPTER 35

YOU DON'T UNDERSTAND ME

Phoenix

W *ell, that sucked.*

Orchid was both at the top and bottom of the list of people Phoenix hoped to see. In some ways, it shouldn't have been a surprise to see her at an event hosted by the media agency for her brands. And she looked beautiful, except for the loser she was with.

Rina had recently convinced Phoenix to work toward giving up his cane, which was not a problem in most places. He'd been proud that at this point he barely had a limp. However, when they arrived, Phoenix took one look at the dense, jostling crowd and pictured an inebriated guest sprawling him on his ass.

"Good thing you're here," Phoenix said to Liv.

"Oh yeah?" she asked, lifting a brow. "Emergency email? Need a deck sent to a client?"

"Nope, has more to do with your boss' limitations." She shot him a look.

"Listen, I'm not so good without my cane in crowds. Even without a drink. I don't want to end up on the floor in there."

She wiped all attitude off her face. "Sure, Mr. Walker, what do you need?" She looked him up and down with concern.

He swallowed, hating to break his hardheaded promise of complete independence. "I don't want any calls to HR on Monday about harassment," he instructed. "I'm just going to put my arm around you for support, okay?"

"Of course, sure," she agreed. He leaned on her, and she gingerly slipped her arm around his waist.

"I just need to find my digital director. Then I'm leaving, but you can stay to network if you want," he said. After all, that's why he'd brought Liv instead of Rina.

"This is not really my scene," Liv admitted, after they'd chatted with his media guy.

On their way out, he spotted Orchid in the crowd in an instant. He saw her ebony hair, kohl rimmed eyes and punk-vibe attire with clarity against the whirl of activity around her. As he leaned in to kiss her hello, he could smell her rose soap. His name fell from her lips as if it were only the two of them in that raucous hall. She looked at him with love. Sweet protectiveness, longing and lust slapped him as hard as if no time had passed since the last time they'd seen each other.

His resolve nearly became untethered because, after all, he was doing better. Nadine was right; his life was coming back together. Rina showed him that maybe his injuries weren't a big deal. They didn't hold him back from doing the things couples do. And though he wouldn't want to disappoint Rina, their easy courtship fell in a different sphere than the lush feelings that Orchid evoked. His jumbled thoughts arced along a hopeful trajectory.

That is, until he saw Orchid's expression as she stared at the spot where his left hand should be.

She looked like she'd be sick, just as he expected. She stared so long, she looked like she might cry. Her expression punched him in the gut. His dreams mocked. She'd flee in horror at the full truth of his missing pieces.

Wanting this to work was as foolhardy as finding a drop of hope in an ocean of sadness.

CHAPTER 36

YOU'VE GOT HER IN YOUR POCKET

Phoenix

SUNDAY DECEMBER 23

A few nights later, the sting of Orchid's repulsion had dulled but not dissipated.

"Wanna come up?" Rina asked, one hand on the door to her brownstone. Phoenix had swilled enough wine over the evening that he paused before uttering his customary, "Not tonight."

"Come see my tree," she said, interrupting his hesitation.

"Is that a euphemism for—?"

"No," she said dryly, turning her key in the lock, "That'd be, I want to see your tree."

"Very funny." He put up a finger to indicate that his driver should wait for him, and then followed Rina.

"You're the ad guy, but you seem to find me funny."

"Always have," he agreed.

They traversed a narrow hallway. Rina unlocked a beige door with a jangle of keys and led him into her apartment. The flicker of multi-colored holiday bulbs and electric candles in the street-facing windows lit the tiny living area. A wall of warm air met them. She flooded the room with light from a standing lamp, which reduced any chance for her décor to charm.

"That's your Christmas tree?" he asked, not trying to hide the skepticism in his squint.

"Yup. The upstairs neighbors lent me their old artificial tree. Lights are theirs, too," she explained, closing the door behind them and hanging her jacket up.

"Old is the operative word there. They doing you a favor, or are you doing them a favor?" he asked, looking around. The furnishings were spare. He shrugged out of his overcoat and handed it to her.

"What am I going to do? My stuff's all in Canada. I'm lucky I got three suitcases on the plane," she said, placing his coat onto a hanger and smoothing it with one hand, in a gesture both tender and possessive. "Would you like a drink?"

"Sure, what do you have?"

"Some of those first-class airline bottles." She took the handful of steps to rummage around a kitchen drawer. "Will this do?" She held up a curvy green glass, a miniature version of a full-size liquor bottle.

"Crème de menthe? Sure, if we're going to throw an ice cream social."

She threw him a sour look.

"Don't worry about it. I'll take a tour instead."

"That should take all of two minutes," she said, waving a hand around the narrow room. "Living room, dining room, kitchen combo. Manhattan special."

"I'll bet the place came furnished," he noted. "Except for the tree, of course."

"You betcha. Next, you're going to tell me your tree is better than mine."

"Euphemisms again."

When she faced him, he bent towards her. Soft lips brushed his. She smelled earthy, like musk mingled with brown sugar.

"Okay, we won't talk in code. Come with me." She led him by the hand to the back of the apartment where a small room housed a bed, side table and closet. Streetlights shone through the bare window.

She let go of him to pad through the dark room and flip on a soft light next to her bed. She returned with a wrapped box. "Merry Christmas," she said.

"I thought we already exchanged gifts."

She touched a hand to the chain around her neck. "We have, and I absolutely love my gift. This is just a little something more."

He tucked the parcel under his left elbow and loosened the tape at the edges.

"Want help with that?"

"No, thanks." The offer irritated him. He tore at the surface one-handed. Then, the holly-covered paper ripped to reveal a logo. Rina blushed.

"Condoms? Is this a present for you?" He held up the box for inspection.

"Hope so," she smiled up at him.

He caught her wrist to prevent her from flipping on the overhead light switch. He didn't want to see his body. Why would anyone else? Yet, desire tussled with self-protection and its resulting abstinence.

He leaned down to touch lips to hers. "I haven't been with anyone since the accident," he murmured between kisses. He kept his voice even but he could feel the tightening of fear in his throat. *Where will this lead? Rejection? Repulsion?*

"Sounds like it's about time then." Rina wriggled free and stepped farther into the room, looking back to watch him following her. She peeled off her slate-gray jacket. "Your driver okay?" She slung the jacket over a chair.

"Yeah, I'm sure he can wait." He watched Rina unfastening the pearl orbs holding her silk blouse together.

"You joining me?" she asked, as she revealed pale skin against a petal pink bra. She placed the top over the blazer. Her pants followed.

She's really very pretty.

Phoenix walked over to the side table and placed the condoms onto a pile of business books. "Are you sure about this?"

She slipped over to face him and reached out, grasping his arm and his hand. "Why wouldn't I be?"

Why not? I can give her reasons. Two, to be exact.

"Of course, my trained actuary, you're pretty sure about everything, aren't you?" He stepped forwards and wrapped his arms around her naked waist, one side not reaching all the way around.

"I'm going with fifty-fifty odds on that," she retorted, slipping his buttons out of their openings until she reached his waistband and stripped away his shirt. He avoided his reflection in her bureau mirror.

He buried his face into her hair. "You smell great," he said. He kissed her, and threaded fingers through his hair. He let the silky strands flow through his grasp.

"You smell amazing, too," she confessed, her expression softer than it seemed in her business attire.

He stepped back to loosen his pants and let them fall to the floor. Rina's gaze slid down his body to the carbon fitting holding him up. He pictured what she was seeing. The stretchy fabric of his liner reached up his thigh. Below his knee, a tapered metal cylinder attached to a metal pole.

He felt shame flame his cheeks and threw a glance at the bedspread, seeking a way to cover himself. *Aw, shit. Abort mission.*

"Maybe I should take you up on that crème de menthe after all. Any booze will do."

She closed the small distance between them. "Hey, Walker, did I ever tell you that you're the hottest guy I know?" She touched a finger to one shoulder and sprang back with a smile. "Ouch!"

She ran a finger down his truncated arm. "You let me know if you need me to do something or not do something, okay?"

"I would, except I have to tell you, I don't know what the hell I'm doing."

"Me either. I'm a virgin."

"Really?" His mind backed up, how was he going to figure out how to move his unbalanced form and teach her at the same time?

"I'm kidding."

"That's a relief. I wish I was joking about not knowing what I'm doing."

She pointed at the bed. "You want to give it a try?"

"Um, you know walking with a prosthesis has given me a really strong butt?"

"I'm already sold." She glared at him.

He sat and tugged off his artificial leg and prosthetic sock, avoiding her gaze. What the hell could any sane woman be thinking, seeing his body, malformed like an unfinished painting?

Screw it. He pulled them both onto the soft expanse of the mattress.

In one hasty motion, Rina stripped off her petal-pink panties. His body responded to the satin of her flesh. He leaned on an elbow and rolled on a condom, slowed by the awkwardness of performing a new task one-handed.

"You want me on the bottom?" she asked.

"Let's try it." He maneuvered over her and threw the blanket over his leg. He tried balancing on the end of his arm. "Ouch."

"You okay?"

"Mm-hmm," he lied. He lowered himself onto his elbows and entered her warmth. She wrapped her legs around his. *What does she make of the blank space below my left knee?*

He kissed the corner of her mouth. She shifted with him languidly, then with more urgency. The sensations triggered his hips to rock against hers of their own volition. She bucked and pushed, urging him to pound faster. He tried to comply, slipping on the leg that could find no purchase. He ignored the cramp in his thigh holding an unaccustomed position. Then, they found their rhythm and he lost himself in their movement with no sense of time passing.

Her tension ascended into a crescendo. She threw her head back, arched up and cried out. He could feel her tighten around him. Before she descended from her high, he came with a shudder that ran the length of his body. His lungs expelled with a release like no other.

Their panting slowed until their breathing was in sync.

"What's so funny?" He lay on her, heavy and unmoving. Not his best performance.

She pressed her mouth into his shoulder, trying to control herself. She shook her head. "It's not you. I'm a bad girl."

"I'm getting a complex here. How was that?"

"Better than I could've imagined. You?" She rubbed his back and kissed one shoulder.

He leaned up on an elbow to look at her. "I'm good." He studied her for a few moments more, brushing hair back from her face. *What the hell was she thinking?*

"I hate to do this to you, but I have to go. You okay if I don't stay?"

She nodded and mumbled, her ability to speak as relaxed as the rest of her body. "Yeah, I'm okay. Your driver is waiting."

He pulled on his briefs, leg and pants, and stood to zip them. Then he shrugged into his shirt.

She watched him slip on his shoes. "Thanks for my Christmas present, hot stuff."

He grabbed his belt and leaned over to nuzzle Rina's cheek. "Thank you. I like your tree."

He paused at the bedroom door. She waved a hand, energy apparently sapped.

"See you next weekend," she called, blowing a kiss.

"Hockey, right?"

He wasn't really asking for confirmation. He'd teased her about arranging tickets for something in which he was barely interested. As he turned to go, he caught the reflection of his asymmetry in her mirrored bureau.

He winced.

CHAPTER 37

WOULD YOU FIGHT
FOR MY LOVE?

Orchid

During a break in their media agency meeting, a junior planner hugged Orchid hello, then plunked ice into a glass. Even with fist-high heels, she only came to Orchid's shoulder.

"So, how were your holidays?"

Orchid twisted open a sparkling water. "Not bad. I hung out with friends. How about you?"

"I stayed local. Went to a bunch of Christmas parties. Drunkfests." She rolled her eyes, which made Orchid chuckle.

"Come to think of it, wasn't the last time we saw each other at the agency holiday party?" Orchid said.

"That's right, that was some night. Did you have fun?"

"Yeah, it was good."

"Weren't you talking with one of the agency presidents? I forget his name," she continued. She poured water from a pitcher into her glass.

"You mean Phoenix Walker, from counterAgency?" Orchid asked, startled. She'd been so immersed in the intensity of her feelings, first of hope then fury, it'd escaped her that the party was a public forum.

"Yeah, that's his name." The petite woman brightened. "How do you know him?"

"We worked on some *pro bono* accounts, a long time ago."

"Oh, wow. You're lucky."

"Yeah, it was good while it lasted."

"That was before his accident?"

Orchid blinked. "Accident? What accident?"

She looked confused. "Maybe I'm thinking of someone else. I get mixed up between all those boutique agencies. Maybe it was the guy at Z—"

Orchid interrupted her pondering. "When was the accident?"

"In the summer, I think. Really scary. I didn't ride the subway for weeks after that. Some homeless guy tripped one of the agency heads onto the subway tracks. Amazing that the guy survived. The train did a number on him, I heard."

"Really? Then it wasn't Phoenix, because he looked incredible. Like he always does." She felt herself blushing.

Her friend shrugged.

A co-worker stepped over and saved her from further embarrassment. "La-dies, meeting's star-ting," he pronounced.

That night, Google yielded a small sensational blurb on the perils of riding New York City subways. A picture of the empty station accompanied the article dated August 1. There was no name of the victim and his or her condition was never updated. Nor was the perpetrator found.

Searching Phoenix's name as she'd done many times these last months returned the expected pages of interviews, press releases, bios and news of the agency's accolades.

Nothing connected the two, yet Orchid went to bed with strange new questions swirling.

February in the city, the frigid temperatures unforgiving, Orchid pulled her coat closer for the trudge home from work. She glanced into windows as she walked. As she passed one eatery, the back of a familiar head caught her eye.

Orchid entered the restaurant and wandered towards the bar where she'd seen the mirage. She rounded the corner to familiar features. She drank in the refined cheekbones, chiseled jawbone and dark brows. As she looked up, she was met with a cold glare. Caleb locked eyes with Orchid. He was dressed in a crisp white shirt, collar open to reveal the black leather cord and horn pendant, and tailored black pants. No wonder Orchid had thought it was Phoenix; Caleb was clothed like a stylish ad man tonight.

Orchid asked what she'd tried to forget for the last five months. "How are you? How's Phoenix?"

Caleb narrowed his eyes. "What do you care?" he asked.

He turned away from her and Orchid caught him by the arm. "Is he still with that girl?"

He glared at her. "Like I said, what do you care?"

"What do I care? Yeah, why should I care?" she asked, jealousy welling as she pictured Phoenix with the slender birdlike woman at the agency holiday party.

This seemed to fuel Caleb's fury. "That's right, you don't care. You left a guy while he was in the hospital. When he could've died. You didn't even come in person. I hope you rot," he spat, pushing his face inches from hers.

"Hey! I didn't do anything. I don't know what you're talking about." She stepped back, shaken. "Wait, what do you mean, hospital? What do you mean, he could've died?"

"Don't play dumb with me."

"Is he okay? Is he hurt?" she asked.

"Oh, you are a piece of work," Caleb spat and turned heel. He stormed out of the restaurant, slamming the door outwards as if a force of nature had flung it open.

She walked home, thinking. First, her junior media planner. Now Caleb. *What happened?*

Crazy possibilities ran through her imagination. Caleb spoke in the past tense, yet his rage was viscerally present. For the first time in months, uncertainty mingled with the bitter taste in her mouth when she thought of Phoenix.

The image of his business card, stark and white, came into focus. Her thumbs flew over her screen, as she texted a number her subconscious hadn't forgotten. "Phoenix, I saw Caleb tonight. Are you okay?"

The same silence that marked the prior five months stretched over the next day.

Spurred by a growing uneasiness, she called Phoenix's office. A woman answered, her tone tight and efficient, explaining that she could transfer Orchid to voicemail. There, his recorded baritone reminded her of his easy laugh, late nights together at his agency, and his ever-present kindness.

A feeling swept over her. One she didn't want to admit to herself. *Still?* She hung up the phone.

Snowdrifts sealed Phoenix in his building as tight as his misconceptions sealed his thinking into the same derailed track. *Hell of a winter.*

"Did you see Orchid?" Phoenix asked without preamble when his brother answered his call. Seeing her name appear on his phone had tightened his chest, as if it'd only been last week since they'd kissed and said goodbye at the airport.

"Yeah. Seems to have amnesia. Played dumb over your accident."

"How'd she look?"

Saying Orchid's name nudged him off-kilter so he couldn't even react to the hard edge in Caleb's voice.

"Fine, I guess. What do you care?"

"I don't."

"I mean, that bitch never even came to see you in the hospital."

"Yeah, because I never *told her* I was in the hospital."

"What? Why not?"

"Aw, c'mon, there was no way we were going to work. She can't even look at a scratch, and I've got a little more than a scratch," he said, glancing at the blunt end of his arm and picturing her look of disgust as his coat slipped off where his hand should be. He felt as sick at her reaction as she seemed to feel about his injury.

Caleb grunted, his fury dissipating. "Is that really your call to make?"

"Maybe not. But I saw her over the holidays and she was pretty repulsed by me so, yeah, there's no way this could've worked. Now she keeps trying to reach me. First time in five months."

"So, what're you gonna do?"

"I dunno. What would you do?"

"You gotta decide."

He thought of solid, dependable Rina. And her complete acceptance of him.

"What's to decide? I'm not even single."

One message from a woman, even someone as talented, smart and beautiful as Orchid, had no power to change that.

CHAPTER 38

DEATH LETTER

Liv

TUESDAY FEBRUARY 5

Following the months of managing Phoenix's correspondence after his accident, Liv continued the job once he'd returned to work. She read his emails and letters and listened to his voicemails, saving only those that required his personal attention. The rest, she'd summarize during their weekly one-on-one meetings.

The first inkling Liv had that Orchid was trying to reach him was when she borrowed Phoenix's cell phone while he was in a meeting, intending to download the most recent security updates.

A text? It was cryptic and short.

Liv's eyes narrow with suspicion. *What good could come of this woman who had abandoned Phoenix? He deserves better.* In line with hiding Orchid's photo, filled with a sense of justice, Liv blocked all calls and messages from a certain Orchid Paige.

When Phoenix stopped by to retrieve his phone, he mentioned the message to Liv with a wry twist of his mouth. "Orchid texted me last night," he said, slipping the slender device into his shirt pocket.

"What do you think she wants?" Liv asked, nonchalantly continuing her task of zipping open envelopes.

"I don't know. I'm not planning to reply to her."

Liv nodded, feeling vindicated.

A day later, an email arrived from Orchid Paige.

Liv's finger jabbed *enter* to open the email, then sprang back as if the keyboard were sullied by the vicious woman who dared contact her boss.

> *Phoenix,*
> *I saw Caleb. Please call me.*

She jammed *delete* with satisfaction. A quick search yielded the steps to block emails from a specific address. He'd do the same thing if he only thought to protect himself.

CHAPTER 39

TWO AGAINST ONE

Orchid

THURSDAY FEBRUARY 7

Navigating the tents at Lincoln Center during Fashion Week was akin to getting through an international airport, security and all. Cavernous white spaces led hordes of showgoers through metal screens and ID checks to arrive to the runway location. Only Orchid's glossy paperboard ticket printed with the right words allowed her this far. Dolce & Gabbana made Orchid's love of leather and faux fur look good, even when worn together in a seemingly unplanned flurry.

Crowded into the vestibule to await seating, Orchid studied the varied looks of the fashion editors, bloggers and others. The attendees swirled with a mix of colors, prints, naked shoulders, and high heels. Orchid paid homage to the designers, layering a pleather minidress pressed into a subtle reptilian pattern over monochrome tights and platforms that bolstered her to six feet. A simple stack of metal and crystal around her wrists completed the look.

Cool tonal music pulsed in over the speakers, setting the mood for a breezy, effortless show.

The hubbub generated by hundreds chatting seemed to mute as she caught sight of a crisp white shirt, tailored slacks and wavy-haired guy better-looking than the models shown on the screens around the tent. Phoenix's head tilted toward the woman with whom he was conversing.

Orchid weaved through the crowd, unable to stop drinking in the mirage of Phoenix, even as every sip fed her longing and the requisite stab of rejection that accompanied it.

Closer now, she could see that the athletic platinum blonde woman's arm was clearly wrapped around him, as was his around her. The tight embrace was even more intimate than the one she'd witnessed with Liv a month and a half earlier. Her blonde head leaned against his chest as the two enjoyed their private bubble. *Shit, this guy gets around.* With his looks and smarts, no surprise.

Sensing her approach, he pivoted his eyes up without moving another muscle. The look he gave her hitched in her throat. She'd seen that expression before. After the initial surprise, his eyes stormed. She was uncertain if it was with desire, tenderness or regret. Which parts were for her, and which parts resulted from the rendezvous with his flaxen-haired companion?

"Hey there," she said.

"Hey, Orchid, what are you doing here?"

She gestured towards the echoing space up high in the tent. "Same as you, I guess . . . ditching work?"

"C'mon, in our industries? This *is* work."

She took a step closer. "I've been calling and emailing. I was worried about you. Your brother said something happened. Are you okay?"

He unlocked their tight stare and licked his lips. "Yeah, I'm okay." He turned toward the blonde, who was staring back and forth between them. "Tish, this is Orchid. Orchid, this is Tish, my ex."

Tish? Oh crap, THE Tish? The Tish who Caleb used as a warning story?

The couple unhooked their arms around each other long enough for Tish to shake hands with Orchid.

"What happened with Liv?" Orchid asked, jealousy spiking her tone.

"Liv?" he repeated, confused. "My admin?"

"Admin? Isn't it unethical to date a subordinate?"

"Date?" Phoenix asked. "I'm not dating Liv." He looked down at Tish for affirmation.

Tish grinned. "You were right that today would be fun. This is entertaining. Maybe you should invite her to the wedding."

"Wedding?" Orchid's voice squeaked. "Seriously?"

Didn't take long for them to get back together. Shock hit her in slow motion. Orchid could feel the permanency of the idea travel through her brain, thick with denial.

"Yeah, first week in April. Cipriani's," Tish said.

She stared at him in disbelief. "Cipriani's? Where we attended the Effies?"

"You mean you think—" He stopped and stared at her, eyes narrowing. "Is it really so shocking? Not everyone has the same hang-ups as you, you know."

Hang ups? Was being jealous of his engagement a hang-up?

A security guard dressed in a well-cut black suit and slender, matching-hued tie came to face Phoenix and Tish. "You two can come in now. I can't take a third though," he said, eyeing Orchid.

"She's not with us," Tish said.

And they were gone.

CHAPTER 40

IT'S TRUE THAT WE LOVE ONE ANOTHER

Orchid

SATURDAY MARCH 3

Casting eyes up from the luggage belt at Los Angeles' LAX Airport, Orchid registered a face she thought she'd never see again.

"Orchid," pronounced the man sporting her father's likeness in the hue of a perpetual Southern California tan.

"You look just like Dad," she said, suddenly shy, and put out her hand. Uncle Zach looked nothing like the scrawny twenty-four-year-old she'd remembered at her parents' funeral.

"So do you," he said, memorizing her features with a mirror-image of her hazel eyes. He clasped her outstretched hand and used his muscle, will, and the magnetism of shared bloodlines to drag her into an embrace. *He smells like Dad.* Or maybe it was her mind playing tricks. Her eyes suddenly watered.

"Wow, you're all grown up. God, I'm sorry it's been so long."

Her uncle's hair waved the same as hers, only in dark brown, and like her father, it looked good on him. His gaze slalomed down her face, maybe marveling, like she did, how sixteen years could pass with no sense of time, how family is rare and finite yet can slip away, how features and mannerisms marked them as the same tribe.

He took her bag and strode through the airport. "I hope you're hungry. Esty will have lunch ready and expect you to eat."

"Eating's a specialty of mine, though right now, my stomach's a bundle of nerves," she admitted.

"Don't be nervous. I'm really glad you came."

She followed Uncle Zach to a rounded Jaguar, its silver cat leaping forwards, oblivious to the harsh pavement that lay beneath, like Orchid leaping to meeting family members she'd never known.

"Esty wants me to get a hybrid." His hand dismissed the car while his heightened posture caressed it with pride.

"Would you believe, this was the car I always wanted as a kid?" Orchid said.

"Oh yeah? What else did you want as a kid?"

"Normal stuff. A phone, a boyfriend." This fragile moment of meeting thrust into the forefront her memory of wanting parents to love her, unconditional acceptance, to belong to someone. But she wasn't about to say all that.

Along the road, palm trees waved against the bluebell sky, blotting out the ever-present sun. Freeways sprouted double the normal lanes wide. Cars weaved into braided lines as if to prove the need for so much asphalt.

"Beautiful weather," she commented, fiddling with her window, a little down to feel the temperate air, then back up because her uncle had turned on the air conditioning. She glanced at his neatly pressed golf shirt and khakis.

His devilish grin produced folds at the corners of his eyes that looked just like Dad's. After all, he was only six years older than Dad was when he died.

"You'll learn. Only tourists talk about the weather here."

He pulled into a compact parking garage under a series of tightly tucked condos. They walked up carpeted stairs to where Esty awaited, baby in her arms. *Insta-family*. The hugs of strangers, the smells of broccoli steaming, and overly stretched faces was overwhelming.

"Aww, Quentin is adorable," Orchid said, finding that crinkling her nose produced blubbery squeals. She retrieved a gift-wrapped package from her bag and placed it on the staircase ledge. "A little something for him."

"Well, thanks. You must be exhausted. Come sit," Esty insisted, scraping the chair out at the head of the kitchen table filled with a wooden salad bowl, terrines of grains and platters of vegetables.

Orchid washed her hands at the kitchen sink, then, feeling like an alien among her newfound family, she accepted the seat of honor.

"Did Zach tell you we're vegan? Hope that's okay," Esty said, ladling scoops of food onto Orchid's plate as if to make up for the family meals missed over the last dozen-plus years. "The quinoa is organic. I just baked the kale chips this morning. This soy-ginger sauce is for the veggies."

"I'm vegetarian so this is great. Thanks for doing this. Especially when you must be so busy with the baby." She pointed a chin at Quentin, who was nodding into an open-mouthed sleep, cradled in the hollow of Esty's arm.

"We don't mind," Zach answered for his wife, face twisted with regret. "I feel terrible that we lost touch. I was still in school when your dad died. I called your aunt and she always said you were fine. It's not an excuse. Just, you know, I'm sorry."

Zach tilted his head expectantly at her, looking just like Dad, and then picked up his fork to slice the soft broccoli crowns. His words were sincere. He was only twenty-four when she'd been orphaned. And she could see he was trying now.

"Hey, it must've been hard on you, too. Dad dying so suddenly and all."

He nodded over his plate, corners of his mouth pulling down the corners of his eyes. Esty placed a hand over his.

"Yeah, it was such a shock. Your mom, too, they were both so young. The last six years of his life, I was in school here in LA, so I didn't see them much. But when I was growing up, your dad was the best. He'd drive me to school in his sports car, and talk with me about girls."

Zach lifted his eyes to Esty's. She squeezed his hand and then pursed her lips into a little air kiss. "What? You knew girls before me?"

"None," he pronounced, returning her air-kiss. *These two are adorable.*

Zach spooned greens into the small space she'd managed to empty on her plate. "What do you remember of your parents?" he asked.

Orchid swallowed. This was the reason she kept everyone out, so she never had to answer these awkward questions. Maybe this case was different. Maybe family calls for a new level of honesty. So, she aimed for disclosure.

"It's going to sound terrible, but not a whole lot. I remember vacationing at an amusement park, family holidays, and stuff like Dad helping me with math but having a hard time understanding how the basics weren't totally obvious to me."

"Yup, your dad was a math whiz. He couldn't get how post-grad students didn't understand multi-variable calculus, so you were in good company," he said with the teasing tone of an admiring little brother. This tidbit of insight lightened the load of idolizing her dead parents, bringing her dad a little closer to human.

She dipped a shiny sugar snap pea into the sweet-tart sauce.

"But mostly," she admitted, "when I think of them I remember their accident. Sometimes, I start with a happy memory, but then I always end with them dying. It makes me not want to think about them."

Esty looked down at sleeping Quentin. "That's really hard on a little kid to see something like that. On anyone, really."

"Maybe I was always sensitive, but seeing the car crash . . . it seems like I can't watch the news or see anything gruesome."

Zach nodded. "You know what I always tell myself? That was a single instant in lives that were mostly filled with intellect and love and fun. And if your parents thought back on their lives, I doubt the accident is what they'd dwell on."

His pronouncement rewound the scenes of her childhood until the early happy ones spun before her with the same tempo as the bloody accident and sterile years with her mother's sister.

"How is your aunt?" her uncle asked about her other side of the family, no blood relation to him, as if paused at the same spot on the reel of her memory.

"She's retired. She travels between Florida and a place she owns on one of the islands, I always forget which one." Orchid sliced a bulgur stuffed pepper, sliding pale seeds to one side of her plate.

"And how about you? Zach says you're not married?" Esty asked.

Orchid noted her un-ringed left hand gripping the tablecloth, not wanting to think about Phoenix in this place where she had a new chance to be accepted. "Nope, I'm single."

"You're still young. You know, we started dating when I was thirty-three and Zach was thirty-seven, so you never know when you'll meet your guy."

Air whistled between Orchid's teeth.

Zach raised his fork. "You still down about that guy?"

"Yup, he's engaged to his ex."

Esty broke in. "You're a beaut. That guy must be crazy."

"Yup, or I am for holdin' onto a pipedream."

"There're a lot of nice-looking men in California."

"Three thousand miles is a bit far for dating," she tossed out, experimenting with baring her teeth to the newly wakened little boy, extracting squeals from him with each face she made.

Esty looked at Zach. "Are we ready for Orchid's surprise?"

Was *surprise* a euphemism for something bad?

Zach stood with his Dad-like grin. He waved over the table. "Leave it," he said to his wife. "Let's go."

They packed into Esty's Prius, Orchid squeezed next to a backwards-facing Quentin. They continued their non-verbal flirtation. Pink tongue. Squeal. Bottom teeth. Squeal.

"I refuse to ride in that gas-guzzling monster," Esty explained, peeling past the Jaguar and taking local roads through Santa Monica.

They parked on a downtown street with brick sidewalks in front of a sage green awning. Zach popped out with swagger, swinging Orchid's door wide while Esty scooped up Quentin. He nodded towards the café tables, surrounded by people inside and out.

"Let's go in," he said.

A bakery? Sure gets these guys excited. Her sweet tooth didn't mind.

As they crossed the threshold, the smell of yeasted bliss mixed with roasted coffee beans and babble of conversation relaxed Orchid. *Home.* Then, the trio burst into celebrity.

"Zach!"

"Esty!"

"Quentin got so big!"

The name etched in the plate glass window suddenly penetrated her mind. *Sweet Paige at a Time: Organic Bakery* was their shop. *Of course.*

They navigated customers and staff to guide Orchid to the back kitchen.

"Sit," Esty said, pulling out a chair for each of them at the wooden table as Zach arrived with a plate of oatmeal cookies, whole wheat scones and mini apple tarts.

"What a great place," Orchid complimented, taking in the gleaming ovens and crumb-free floor. She bent a cookie in half and slid it into her mouth. Crisp oats on the surface blended with the moist interior, both still warm. *Yum.*

"Everything here's sweetened with agave or stevia," Zach said proudly, swiping the remaining half of Orchid's cookie.

"Is this the only organic bakery in the area?"

"Unfortunately, no. There's another place, all upscale and fancy." Esty wielded a rounded knife to crumble the scone into bite-size chunks.

"What does *page at a time* mean?"

"I had some vague idea that literary types would hang out at cafés like this and write, so I thought we could organize readings and stuff. But I never did anything with the idea," Zach admitted.

"Do you have a business plan?" Orchid asked, straightening with excitement over the potential of the place. They chatted into the afternoon, her business schooling kicking into gear.

By the time Orchid packed to leave the next day, she'd typed them a PowerPoint presentation.

"Check out all these great ideas you guys have." She angled her laptop screen for them.

"I love the name change," said Esty of the title page for *Sweet Paige: Organic Café.*

"It keeps your essence while broadening the appeal across day-parts," Orchid agreed. "Your financials are solid and you have a good start on your point of difference. There are a couple of avenues you could take: either build your physical presence in neighborhoods where this kind of place will appeal, or invest in a delivered business that leverages your profitable sweet lines. And you definitely need to play up that literary angle," Orchid summarized, paging through to the end of the document.

Zach put an arm around his niece. "You are a marketing genius," he said.

Esty hugged Orchid, *sans* baby for a change, as Quentin napped in his pack-and-play. "Sorry I can't come to the airport. Never wake a sleeping baby!"

"Thanks for everything. You two are great together."

"Well, we can't wait for you to come again."

Zach directed them to the Jaguar. The silver cat now seemed to leap with confidence, not recklessness.

On the freeway, Zach tapped the steering wheel in syncopation with a guitar ballad. Their age difference just twelve years, he was more like a cool older brother.

"I wish you weren't going," he said.

Orchid slumped to let the sun warm her turned face and absorb the goodbyes in the undulating palm fronds. "Yeah, me too."

"Esty and I talked. You know, we missed all those years together. We can't get that back but, hell, why don't you move out here?"

"What?" Orchid sat up to stare skepticism at him. Maybe irrational ran through their genes.

"Hear me out. LA is great, you'd love it here. In the beginning, maybe it wouldn't pay as much as Estée Lauder, but we'd love for you to start up the new line, run the marketing and strategy of the whole place. Who knows, it could be more lucrative in the long run."

"Seriously?"

"Come work for Sweet Paige. Like you said, we could take it national. It'd be a real family business then."

The idea of family was foreign enough, never mind family business. And now, an invitation to live in a new place, to be near family she didn't realize she'd missed like an essential part of her.

She glanced at her bare left ring finger through teary vision. "That's really generous of you. Guess there's nothing I couldn't leave behind in New York. Let me think about it." She bent an arm to bring her phone closer, not seeing the time. "We'd better get to the airport."

CHAPTER 41

GIRL, YOU HAVE NO FAITH IN MEDICINE

Orchid

THURSDAY MARCH 14

"I already network," Orchid said to her boss, Joan, whose Botoxed forehead indicated the pressure of working in the beauty industry after the age of retirement.

"Yes, you're networking internally. I'd like to see you build your contacts outside of Estée Lauder." She placed one short leg over the other, and rested against her desk chair, lips stretching while nothing else moved. "Because, you need to keep this hush-hush for now, but Lauder China is planning to offer you an international assignment in Beijing."

"No way."

"Congratulations. Three to five years, full expat package. I don't have to tell you how rare an offer it is to work in the fastest growing market. Human Resources will call you with the details."

"Thank you so much." Orchid's imagination unfurled with excitement. A pang reminded her there was nothing keeping her here in New York.

"Great," her boss said, clapping her heavily ringed hands together. "You have no meetings this afternoon, right?"

"No meetings," Orchid said, staring at her boss's tailored pants suit, chains of gold and diamond earrings so heavy they strained her earlobes. She should've noticed before. That was a day-to-evening outfit. *Crap.*

"So, we're leaving here at four for an agency anniversary party," Joan said.

Orchid sighed, looking down at her hip-chic leggings and boots under a layered skirt and white summer mini. Mixing and matching pieces from her closet this morning, she pulled together an ensemble that pleased her with its uniqueness. Perhaps feeling Phoenix's absence more than she wanted to admit, she'd assembled the outfit around the dress she'd worn when they first met at the agency presentation nine months ago.

"Network in New York while you still can. No excuses," Joan said.

Orchid stood to gather her papers. "Okay," she said, tugging down her mini and slipping out of her boss' office. *Lots to think about.*

At four, Orchid closed her laptop and shoved it into an oversize patent leather bag bound with burnished hardware and grommets as if the contents would have to ninja fight their way out to escape the Fort Knox of purses.

They picked their way through melting piles of snow to walk south along familiar streets. Orchid continued their earlier conversation.

"So, tell me about this assignment."

"I don't want to spoil all of HR's news, but it's a marketing director role, reporting to Lauder China's marketing head. You know him, right?"

She nodded, flabbergasted at her good fortune.

"You'd have regional responsibility with a cross-functional team from Singapore, Japan and China."

"I'm pinching myself."

"Now don't make me break my promise of silence. We can talk more after HR calls."

"Okay," Orchid said, respecting her boss' wishes by changing the subject. She brushed lint off her dark coat. "Whose anniversary party are we going to?"

"counterAgency. You met them at a pitch presentation last summer."

A thump sounded so loudly in her ears that she thought a baby grand had fallen on the sidewalk beside them. Looking up from the snow-covered ground—no piano—Orchid stared at her boss, disbelieving.

"You know, the agency I'd worked with before?" her boss continued.

Orchid snapped her jaw shut and nodded. Was she ready to see Phoenix during a work function? He'd never returned her messages and once she realized he was engaged—*engaged*—she respectfully left him alone. Knowing Joan had worked with counterAgency, Orchid kept her crush a secret. Now didn't seem like the right time to bring up some schoolgirl fantasy. No doubt, he'd be professional. She'd do the same and get out of there as soon as she could.

They stepped into the warm building. Joan signed them in and led the way to the elevator. "Five years is a pretty good milestone for a boutique agency," she said.

Arriving at counterAgency's floor, a pumping bass line reached them through the enclosed elevator. The doors slid aside to a refreshingly open space, at once warm with the buzz of people chattering, and cool with modern architecture. Sheets of glass contrasted with exposed piping and white-painted brick.

The receptionist greeted them. She tottered on five-inch heels, vibrantly red from underneath, to check a preordained list. "Estée Lauder? Okay, gotcha!" She took their coats.

Orchid peered around the clean white surroundings splashed with pockets of neon blues and greens. Memories swirled with reminders of his personal décor. She didn't spot the person she both wanted to and was apprehensive seeing. *I have it bad.*

"Would you like caw-fee? A drink?" the receptionist offered.

"White wine," the women replied, Orchid automatically choosing the less enamel staining variety. Perhaps her boss employed the same logic.

Dex ambled over, touching cheeks with her boss. "Joan, how are you? Lovely to see you as always. You look smashing," he said, his eyes nearly closing as his cheeks spread to express pleasure. A tall woman hurried over from another group and hugged Joan with excitement.

As Joan conversed with her acquaintance, Dex leaned over to Orchid. He touched one chubby cheek to hers, his beard bristly against her skin.

"Hello, Orchid, need another?" he asked, pointing to her empty glass. She was pleased to see a friendly soul in a place that held the potential to flatten her.

"I must've been parched," she said, following him past a buffet laden with food to the temporary bar set up on the other side of the expansive area at the center of the agency. Corridors of offices fronted with clear glass walls lined three sides of the space. Soaring rock ballads crooned over the hubbub of wine-fueled conversation. The music swirled with the minimalist design, creating a cool atmosphere that seemed to be able to materialize creativity from anything, ordinary or extraordinary. The imprint of Phoenix.

"So, how've you been?" Dex asked, his bulk taking a spot in the snaking line of thirsty guests.

"Pretty busy with work. How are you? And Fiona?" She looked up at him, intuitively trusting the burly fellow whom Phoenix had always spoken of with the highest respect. He donned a decidedly unfashionable red sweater vest over a checkered blue and white shirt in the pattern of one of her dishtowels, paired with baggy jeans. Topped off with a bow tie in casual twill, he pulled off the look with the panache of an executive creative director.

"We're good. Too bad we haven't seen you much."

"Much? As in nine months since the Effies?"

"Yeah, we thought we'd see you more often after that," he said, inching up towards the guy taking orders at the bar.

"Me, too."

He looked at her funny, but they didn't have time to explore the reason. It was their turn. "Another white wine?"

"Vodka, double, rocks, splash of something, anything," she said, needing liquid help to forget her unrequited obsession, who was engaged to be married in weeks.

Dex handed her a tumbler, and led them to a spot by an aggressively green ficus to talk above the din.

"Cheers," he said, touching his glass to hers.

"Cheers. To Phoenix's wedding." She downed half the drink, waiting for the near-instant numbing she was sure to experience on an empty stomach.

"Wedding? What wedding?" he asked, his bushy brows pulling his normally drooping eyes up with them.

"To Tish?" she pronounced, glancing at him askance. "In April? At Cipriani's?"

Dex's face twisted, like a schoolboy trying to untangle a complex math equation. "April? Cipriani's? He's not getting married."

"He's not?" She saw them. Arms wrapped around each other. Phoenix's eyes filled with tenderness and desire.

Before they could delve into this surprising revelation, Joan bounded over, striding as easily on four-inch heels as if she'd been barefoot on new-mown grass.

"I've come to say goodbye to my favorite creative genius. But you're not going to let me go without saying hello to your hotshot founder, are you?" she teased.

"Ha, of course not. Let's see if he's done with his call," Dex said, leading them down a corridor opening up to a series of offices featuring floor to ceiling plate-glass windows. The walls along the corridor were also clear glass, leaving unobstructed views of Midtown under late afternoon sun.

Orchid tipped the glass up to her mouth for the last few icy drops of courage and, leaving the tumbler on a tray, followed them.

The end of the corridor opened to a large, glass-walled conference room. Inside, Phoenix leaned back in a cream-colored leather chair, face tilted up, talking at a conference phone on the elongated table. He commanded the space, the room, the whole agency. Liv perched at the edge of her seat nearer the door, bent over an iPad, partially blocking Orchid's view of Phoenix.

Noticing the trio, Phoenix put up two fingers. Catching her boss' action, Liv turned towards the glass wall. Her glance traveled from Dex to Joan, and then settled onto Orchid. Behind half-moon spectacles, her eyes narrowed.

The call ended. He stood straight and strong and strode to meet them just as Dex ushered the women into the conference room. They nodded their hellos. Phoenix's shirt sleeves were pushed up to his elbows. Orchid stared at him, not comprehending.

Oh no! His eyes affixed on hers. Then he met the group just inside the door and greeted Joan. Orchid could make no sense of their conversation, as every word was muffled under the weight of another revelation, one that annihilated news of the non-wedding or move to China.

Her stomach twisted as she squeezed her eyes. She swallowed to mitigate the shock. Feelings swayed. *Poor Phoenix.*

"Bye, Joan," he said.

Oh God, he was standing so close. His voice reverberated through her. She forced herself to look at him. She met his eyes and she read her own transparency in his expression. His mouth turned down in dismay, his nostrils flared and quivered for a whisper of a second, his gaze cast upon hers and hardened as he took in her demeanor.

Stop. Phoenix is alive. He pulsed with life, energy in every wink of the eye and animated gesture. He was more than okay. His presence filled the room, dwarfing them all.

Phoenix whom she'd fallen for. Phoenix who'd abandoned her. In between, he'd been broken.

Joan turned to go. "Are you coming?" she asked.

Orchid faced her boss. "Not yet, you go ahead," she said.

Dex escorted Joan out.

Slipping her Fort Knox bag off her shoulder and onto the ground by her feet, Orchid stepped towards Phoenix. Liv took a position in front of him, blocking her access. *Move, wench.* Liv's lips pressed into a tight line as if she could read Orchid's thoughts.

"How'd you enjoy the show?" Phoenix asked, his speaking to her like honey to her ears.

She tumbled head first into his deep blue gaze. "Show?" she asked, still addled.

"Dolce?" he reminded her, his voice cool.

"I wasn't feeling well. I had to leave early," she said, truthfully, remembering her roiling stomach over the thought that Phoenix would soon be married. "How's Tish?"

"I haven't talked to her since then. She's probably running around with last minute stuff for her wedding." *Her wedding.*

Orchid nodded and took a step to the left, trying to skirt Liv. The persistent assistant parried well, mirroring her movements so she could get no closer to Phoenix.

"Are you okay? What happened?" she asked. Suddenly, she wanted to touch him, comfort him, because she could feel his pain. Perhaps her overreaction to trauma wasn't just her own demon. She was experiencing empathy. She stepped closer, drawn to smooth away the hurt she could see in his eyes. She wanted to do so for him, and for herself.

He glanced down at himself, as if he'd forgotten what might cause her to ask.

Liv looked from Phoenix's ducked head and tight lines around his eyes to Orchid slipping closer. A flush of pink rose from her neck over her cheeks until it reached her hairline. She stretched her petite stature taller, growing rigid, hands balled, and then exploded.

"You have some nerve!" she shouted, stomping the two steps to reach Orchid, fists jabbing with every word.

Instinctively, Orchid stumbled back, avoiding the child-sized knuckles. "Hey, I didn't do—"

She'd forgotten her computer lay in the bulky bag on the ground. The heel of her shoe caught on the metal grommets and her ankle twisted on the Fort Knox of purses, toppling. She slammed to the right, one shoulder crashing against the delicate case along the transparent wall. With a sharp sound like crystal chandeliers in a windstorm, she broke through the fragile surface.

Shards exploded and stabbed her hair and skin.

Phoenix and Liv stared at her, frozen with surprise, then horror.

She swayed, fighting to right herself against the frame of the case.

"Oh, my God." Phoenix sprinted to Orchid's side, glass crunching below his feet. He yelled at Liv. "Call an ambulance!"

Liv fled.

"No, no hospitals," Orchid said, clawing against a strange heaviness to stagger to her feet. "I'm okay," she reassured him. She didn't understand why her vision blurred and her legs buckled.

Muscular arms supported her torso and slowed her slump to the ground. She held him too. She inhaled his scent that had only echoed in her imagination these past six months.

"What happened to you? Are you okay?"

Phoenix looked her all over, then whipped the shirt out from under his waistband and pressed it against her forehead.

"Don't worry about me," he said, "let's focus on you right now."

Cradled against his crouched stance, she followed the path his eyes took to see her white outfit spattered with red streaks, new rivulets crossing old ones to form a kaleidoscope of ever-changing streams. Feeling faint, her eyes closed.

"Orchid," he said, voice tight, "you stick with me, you hear me?"

She looked up at him. "No doctors."

He pressed harder at the source of the red river. "It's going to be okay," he said. His tone was compassionate in contrast to his prior aloofness.

"Hey, hey," he said, comforting her physical pain when it was the emotional pain crushing her. He cradled her with half an arm as he tried to stanch the flow of blood.

Dex and a few guys with a white stretcher crowded into the conference room. One of the EMTs ripped open a packet of sterile gauze and took over applying pressure. Phoenix moved back as they hoisted her onto the stretcher.

"No," she insisted, twisting wildly away from the man holding the bandage.

Phoenix stepped by her side, taking her hand. "Shh," he said, "You need me to come with you?"

She nodded weakly and lay back onto the firm white surface. She held onto his hand. "Don't leave me," she said, and the meaning of the words struck her. *Don't leave me—now, ever.*

"I'm right here," he said.

They wheeled through the corridor, then crowd, rendered mute, to the elevator bank. Joan stood with another woman, mouth agape.

The motion of the swinging stretcher made her dizzy, and she shut out the world. In the dark behind her eyelids, Orchid could feel the swaying to the elevator, the rush of movement downwards, and through it all, the warmth of Phoenix's hand. The medics hoisted her into the back of the emergency vehicle, breaking her connection to Phoenix.

She tried to sit up to protest. He clambered in beside her and she relaxed into the pressure of his palm against hers.

In the ambulance, despite the stinging pain, Orchid couldn't stop looking at Phoenix. Even if she died, seeing him study her bandaged forehead with care was worth it.

"I want to be cremated," she said from the back of the ambulance.

"I don't want to waste space in the ground."

"You're not dying," he said, squeezing her hand.

"Then I don't want to go to the hospital," she said, feeling an impish humor cross over her face.

"Too late," he said.

"I'm sorry if I ruined your party."

"You kidding? With that crowd, I promise you they're still boozing it up without us."

Her chest squeezing a little less hard, she was able to study him closer. Fine lines had deepened between his brows. A flash of gray shone in his dark mane. Smooth flesh stretched taut over bone where his hand had been. He glared, catching her staring at the asymmetry of his left arm.

"Are you okay? Does that hurt?" Her reach wavered, then stretched for the arm on his far side.

He edged back, keeping out of her radius. "That's not really your thing, remember?"

She processed the tight set of his lips, trying to make her fuzzy brain fathom something nearly within grasp of her consciousness. *Not really my thing? What does he mean?*

They arrived at Roosevelt's ER where Orchid was whisked inside for registration and care. The scent of antiseptic, flickering of cold overhead bulbs, and sound of tinny voices paging doctors yanked Orchid back to a place sixteen years ago. Even though she wanted to shut out the place, her eyes widened.

Phoenix read her face and leaned down as they wheeled her to a room. "You are a strong woman. You run multi-million-dollar brands, travel the world, sway unit presidents to invest in your business and cook like a champ. You are going to be fine."

"Thanks, but maybe this isn't such an easy place for you to be, either," she said. "When did that happen?" She indicated his arm peeking out from under the rolled white shirt cuff.

"Would you believe, the day you left for China."

Her inhale hitched. *Gray day. Plane in the sky. Phoenix on the ground.* Unimaginable. His wry tone hinted at pain.

"While I was away? What happened? Why didn't you tell me?"

"Why are you surprised? I figured I didn't need to tell you after we saw each other in December," he said, confusing her more.

"December?"

"At the holiday party."

The nurse interrupted to settle her into a bed, clean her wounds, and measure her temperature, blood pressure, and pulse.

"Need me to call anyone for you, honey?" the nurse asked.

"Oh, my boss!" She sat up, remembering. The movement started the gash bleeding, drops hitting the white sheet. "Ouch." She closed her eyes, unable to look at the red stain.

The nurse eased her back against pillows.

"I'll text Joan not to worry, that you're in good hands," Phoenix said, pulling out his cell phone and typing a message with his right thumb. His left arm hung limply like a forgotten appendage.

Orchid swallowed, her fogged brain unable to process Phoenix's altered state. His eyes met hers. "You look like a horror movie extra," Orchid said, hoping he would think she'd been staring at his bloodstained outfit.

"We must've been cast in the same film," he said lightly, coming over to take her hand. "Too bad about that dress. I have fond memories of that outfit."

His closeness made her already addled brain float higher. "You remember! I didn't even know I was seeing you today. Joan sprung it on me at work."

"Serendipity again."

Before she could respond, a pretty blond woman knocked and marched in. Phoenix stepped back from the bed to make space for her white-smocked, efficient presence. Orchid missed Phoenix's proximity.

"Hello, Ms. Paige? I'm a plastic surgery resident here," she said, shaking Orchid's hand.

"Plastic surgery?" Orchid asked, alarmed. "Will I need surgery?"

"Probably not, but let me take a look." She removed the bandage and examined the wound site. "It's a deep laceration. Looks like seven to nine stitches should do the trick," she declared.

"Stitches?" Orchid asked, her voice careening.

The doctor eyed her. "Probably three internal, six external. We'll give you a local anesthetic."

"Can I see a mirror?" Orchid asked, feeling faint.

The nurse looked around, then pulled a round mirror out of the supplies cabinet and handed it to her, handle first.

Orchid's breath caught in her throat at her reflection. Cuts gashed along her left cheek, speckling her skin dark red with drying blood. Those were minor compared to an inch-long raw slice, diagonal above her left brow. The flesh lay split open like the first cut into a hunk of raw meat, red drops pooling into the cavity. Phoenix stood at her side, observing her observe herself. She dropped the mirror face down onto the bed, ashamed for Phoenix to see her like this.

"There is nothing wrong with the way you look," he said, his words frozen over.

She couldn't examine why he was acting cold right now. The pressing questions shot out, directed at the doctor. "Oh my God, I'm hideous. My face is disfigured. Will I have a scar? Please tell me there won't be a scar."

The doctor explained. "You have a pretty clean cut. The scarring will be minimal. You'll have to adhere to wound care basics. Staying out of the sun will help. We'll go over all the details with you."

Orchid didn't hear what the doctor had to say. Her mouth hung open watching the door swing shut behind Phoenix. Her lagging brain finally surfaced what her subconscious had pieced together. He'd been injured when she left for China, after which, he'd refused to see the woman who couldn't look at a cut on her foot or pictures of physically imperfect soldiers.

There should be hope. If only she could tell him whatever feelings over his injury he projected onto her weren't true. Then, fear of losing that chance bathed her in cold sweat, as she realized she'd just called her inch-long gash "a hideous disfigurement."

CHAPTER 42

HYPOCRITICAL KISS

Phoenix

"Why?" Rina asked again, as if studying for a test. She crossed one leg over the other, her movement giving away her emotion as much as the rising tone of her voice.

"Because we're not right together. Because you can do better." Phoenix placed the glass she'd given him onto her coffee table. He probably didn't deserve the drink, seeing that he was breaking her heart.

"We get along great. Why do you think I can do better?"

Phoenix studied her ramrod posture and silky brown-blond hair. Rina really was very pretty. And smart. They'd enjoyed many pleasurable evenings in this compact one-bedroom apartment. He could see how they could be a good match. He tried to explain to the stoic woman before him.

"Because, Rina, I don't love you as much as I could. You should have someone who is wild about you."

Tears escaped the corner of her eyes, plopping onto her pressed gray suit.

"Don't cry." He reached out to her. She yanked her arm away, looking more furious than he'd ever seen her.

"You're heading back to Canada soon, anyway," he continued, thinking of the April end to her six-month assignment.

She straightened further. As he figured, latching onto logic ameliorated this actuary's dejection. "I was going to ask you about that. I'd extend my stay if you wanted. If that's the reason for this . . ."

She'd reached the bargaining stage of acceptance.

Seeing her pain, he wondered if he was wrong to start something that pleased but never sparked passion in him.

"When we made love, did you love me?"

He recalled that first night. He'd been so worried she'd reject him. Instead, she'd patiently allowed him to find his way. *Love, though? No.* He aimed for diplomatic truth.

"You made a huge difference during the hardest time in my life. You saw me as a man no matter what I had or was missing. You encouraged me to work harder, to give up my cane. You didn't care about my injuries. I love you for all those things and more. But you deserve fireworks and dreams of the future, and we don't have that."

As Phoenix spoke, Rina's tears dried in salty lanes along her cheeks and clothes. She looked him in the eye. "Fireworks and dreams of the future? Maybe *you* didn't have that. But *I* did."

He gazed at her pretty features, puckered and drooping in a mixture of sad and angry. "Sorry."

They sat in silence. Rina stared out the window and absently blotted a tissue under her eyes.

The memory of Orchid popped up, unbidden. Seeing her yesterday put his relationship with Rina into stark contrast. What he had with Rina wasn't enough. What he could've had with Orchid couldn't be resurrected.

Finally, Rina turned to him with renewed self-control. "Should we stay friends?"

"Sure. We could still have your birthday dinner with your co-workers."

"Okay, see you then," she said.

Her checklist complete, she stood and grabbed his glass. She headed to the kitchen, where he could hear her clattering ceramic and glassware in the sink. He cringed as a particularly loud crash sounded like something had broken.

Then he stood, taking one last look around. He left, feeling oddly unburdened.

CHAPTER 43

SEVEN NATION ARMY

Caleb

E ven with the snow melting, the afternoon traffic was slow enough to catch Caleb's attention with each jingle of the doorway bell.

Well, hell's bells. He did a double take at a dark-haired woman shaking snow off her boots as she entered the shop. Not that her pleather leggings, biker boots and army surplus jacket seemed out of place here. More surprising was that the last time he'd seen Orchid's familiar face was while screaming into it.

She looked around, swiped her smooth locks out of her eyes, and spotted him. He pushed himself out of the consultation chair at the back of the shop and made his way to her. No sense pretending he hadn't seen her.

"Orchid," he acknowledged.

"Caleb, how are you?"

"Fucked up, as usual," he answered calmly.

"Me, too," she answered. He eyed the bandage on her forehead, wondering if it was the reason for her self-deprecating sigh. She looked different, her expression serious, as if she only recently had matured from a girl into a woman. He didn't think it was only a matter of the wound. There was some determined emphasis in her stride. He sensed she was on a mission.

"If Mom were here, she'd say I owed you an apology."

"Because you yelled at me for wronging your brother, even though it was the other way around? Because you thought I'd be shallow enough to avoid him after his accident, when I didn't know anything about it?"

"Somethin' like that," he replied.

"Okay, I'll take that acknowledgment as an apology. Thanks."

"What are you doing here?" he asked, changing tacks, loyalty sitting squarely with family.

"I need to apologize to Phoenix."

"You're fishing for an apology from me when you owe one to him?" He shook his head. "Tell him yourself."

"I would, except he doesn't return my texts."

"So you came to ask me? Maybe there's a reason he's ghosted you, darlin'." He wandered back towards his table of paperwork.

Orchid ignored his last remark and stayed planted like she owned the place, from the black-and-white checkered floor, crisp linens on tables, and walls covered with photos of body art.

"Wow, so . . . pretty," she said turning towards the pictures. "No, more than that. Evocative, powerful."

He glared at her with suspicion as she studied the wall of tattoos of people's faces. "Jack Nicholson, Marilyn Monroe, Johnny Depp . . . "

Walking slowly toward him, gazing at the myriad pictures, she appeared to be a young gallery visitor. A laugh of pleasure burst out of her, pure and innocent. "Children and animals!" She turned from the pictures of pugs, cats, and chubby-cheeked toddlers executed in the blue-green of tattoo ink and faced him.

"Children and animals are a surefire way to pull at heartstrings in advertising."

"Phoenix teaching you tricks of the trade, huh?"

"Yeah," she said with earnestness. "He taught me a lot." She flopped onto one of the hulking black vinyl tattoo chairs.

"He taught me about kindness, what it means to be a gentleman, how to use humor no matter how bad the situation looks."

She grew quiet. He continued sorting papers, one pile for unpaid bills, another for invoices to be mailed, junk tossed right into the recycling bin.

"Is your shrink away?" he asked, using sarcasm to try to harden the vulnerability on her face. He didn't want to get sucked in. It was hard to avoid because whatever she was thinking, she was being real.

She laughed, a pretty sound, unlike the raucous ribaldry that often ran through his place.

"You're the shrink I need, because you know him better than anyone else." Brown eyes looked at him full of hope. His hands paused over the piles of paper, stilled by feeling like he was the hero in an un-filmed action adventure.

Knows him better than anyone else? Christ, am I really that person for another human being?

She leaned forward, one elbow on his workspace. When she rested her chin onto the palm of her hand, she pulled back, surprised. "Ow! I keep forgetting," she said, putting one hand up to her bandaged forehead.

Caleb drew himself straighter. Phoenix would want him to protect her, just as he himself had tried to protect her.

"What happened?" he asked, drawn in despite himself.

"Have you ever been to his agency?" she said, answering his question with a question.

"Yeah."

"I crashed through a glass case there."

"What?" He stood, chuckling darkly. "You want a tattoo of that?" he asked.

"Very funny," she said.

"Why'd you do that?" he asked, sitting.

"I didn't mean to, I tripped. After his admin threatened me." Her face fell and then she jutted her chin up, like a little girl acting tough to get herself through a difficult spot.

"Tiny little Liv?"

"I think he let her think that I'd been a bitch to him, too."

"And you're sure you haven't?"

"I only found out about his accident four days ago. So how could I have been a bitch about it?" Her voice hardened and she looked out the window, fingering the frayed piping of her army jacket.

"But?" he encouraged.

"I guess I said something insensitive when I last saw him." Her chin dropped.

"After you knew about his—"

"Yeah. After I cut myself, he went with me to the hospital. And I guess I was worried about how my face looked. I think I called it hideous and disfigured."

"How'd he take that?"

"He left."

Good. Smart man.

"If that's the case, seems damned straightforward to me. What's the point of chasing someone who doesn't want you?"

"But that's the thing," she insisted, straightening. "I don't think it's so straightforward. My stupid comment didn't mean anything. I've got to let him know that we should try again."

Damn, she's tenacious.

"Don't you freak out over every little scratch?"

She ran a hand through her hair. Her eyes grew large. "He probably thinks I do, but I swear, after the initial shock of seeing his arm, he was just Phoenix to me. All I could think was how I'd missed him. I mean, I feel terrible for him, but it's not going to freak me out." Her fist pounded the armrest for emphasis. "You've seen us together. What'd you think?" she pressed.

"Yeah, I guess you had something. At that triathlon, and down the shore. But that was all before, you know." He was surprised he couldn't name the time that dominated his life last fall. He looked out the window at piles of shoveled snow. He worried about Phoenix taking a tumble.

"I don't know. Tell me what happened," she said, her eyes growing even more expressive.

He stood to stretch, looking up, thinking. Only with Sascha had he shared the images and regrets that still dogged him. A pressure built. He wanted to unload the memories. Not for her. Rather, for himself. He talked while he paced.

"Freakin' call came to my shop in Jersey," he said, remembering the day. "I couldn't believe it, I couldn't picture it. I couldn't even drive, I was so messed up, so Sascha drove me. Mom said I needed to come say goodbye, just in case."

Orchid appeared to have forgotten to breathe, eyes frozen wide.

He stopped, gazing at the pattern of the black-and-white checkered tiles on the floor, his mind elsewhere. The whine of a siren whizzed by and faded, reminding them of the city past the clear glass door.

"Then I saw him, and it was him, but he looked bad, not moving, tubes and shit. Scary, you know?"

She nodded, even though she hadn't been there and couldn't have known.

"I didn't know you could be hit by a train and survive."

She yelped.

He strode, pacing around the shop in the darkening shadows of late afternoon, agitated. "What? You didn't know?" He stopped walking, hands on his hips.

"So he really was hit by a . . . train?"

"Yeah, saving a homeless guy. He woke when *I* was with him, and *I* had to tell him. He was so broken up, I didn't know what to say. Then Mom came in and she told him it was okay. But I didn't do anything. I couldn't make him feel better. I still can't." His voice cracked, having stated the worst part, the part where he'd let his brother down.

"Saving a homeless guy?"

Emotional when he didn't want to be, and suddenly aware of responsibilities he didn't know he'd held towards his brother, he headed to the shop door. He turned around the sign so that, from the outside, it read CLOSED.

"It's after five, I'm closing up." He moved around, locking up the safe and cash register.

"Here's the thing," she said, getting in his face to make him look at her. "I think we have something special. I think he thinks I can't deal. I think he thinks he's protecting me."

"Yup. Sounds like him."

Caleb wrapped a scarf around his neck against the cold wind and shrugged on his warm, lined leather coat, relishing the smell that reminded him of rides in open air.

Stomping one booted foot, she put a hand to her forehead. "So, are you going to let your brother sacrifice himself for no good reason? When he has a chance to be happy?"

"You sure you can make him happy?" He infused her romantic dreams with some reality. "That's some tough shit," Caleb warned. "He's not the easiest guy to live with, and he's probably even more ornery now."

"Because of his arm?"

He grabbed his keys. "Vamoose," he told her, indicating the door.

"Just do this, Caleb. For me . . . for him. Find me a chance to see him so we can talk." She followed him out, buttoning her coat. He swung onto his bike parked at the curbside, revving the engine.

"I'm outta here but I'll think about it. And to answer your question, yeah, probably missing a hand makes him ornery, but how come you aren't giving any credit to his missing leg?" He accelerated away from the curb in a wide arc, pulling a U-turn before the oncoming traffic reached them. "Ciao, babe," he called to the gape-mouthed beauty staring after him.

CHAPTER 44

LOVE, INTERRUPTION

Orchid

SATURDAY MARCH 16

Orchid walked Uptown, head bent against the cold. There was no way she was going into the subway system and board a train after what she'd just learned.

Missing leg? She realized that it didn't change her feelings for him. Of course, it shouldn't matter. How little credit did he give their relationship to hide that from her?

Her resolve withered when she imagined the full extent of his injuries. Then, she was angry for even pausing. *He's still Phoenix, right?*

How had he kept all this from her while she was in China? Not for the first time, she reexamined the time they were apart. She'd been climbing the Great Wall while he was immobile in a hospital bed, trying to protect her with silence. She'd cherished his protectiveness, but now it seemed like his Achilles heel.

She found herself at Mandy's building. The doorman called her friend's apartment, then sent Orchid up.

Mandy opened the door dressed in stretchy leggings and an oversized T-shirt.

Mandy glanced at Orchid's bandaged forehead. "Did you get in a bar brawl or have you taken up wrestling?"

Orchid hugged her friend. "Long story. How are things with you?"

Mandy guided her through the warm apartment. "Oh, we're all good. Same old. Hubby's worried about his job, as usual. Part-time daycare's going fine, when it's not closed for snow days, that is."

"Yeah, heck of a winter, huh?"

Mandy patted the barstool nearest the kitchen and then grabbed a wine bottle from the fridge.

Orchid felt a little better in the familiar chaos. "Where's Matty?" she asked, and reached for two crystal stems.

"Down for his nap. Hopefully, he'll sleep for a while. So, what's up with you?" Mandy filled the glasses high, commensurate with how rattled Orchid looked.

"My company wants me to move to China."

"No way! Congratulations, right? But you know you can't leave me."

"Don't worry. There's at least two trips home a year."

"Cool, so why are you not sounding excited?"

"Phoenix," Orchid said with a sigh.

"Weren't my orders for you to move on?"

"Yeah, except it's not what I thought," Orchid said. "He didn't call me because he was in a train accident and didn't want me to worry, or he thought I'd reject him or something stupid like that."

"Train accident? Sounds serious. Is he okay?"

"Hard to say. He looks okay. He looks good, actually. I've only seen him a few times since I came back. Remember at that holiday party? I guess I was so focused on the girl he was all wrapped around that I didn't notice much else."

"Yeah, what happened with that girl?"

"Turns out I misunderstood. That was his admin, and they weren't dating." Orchid took a sip then replaced her glass onto the counter. "So, my boss took me to a party at his agency."

"You go, girl."

"Only when I see him, I look down and realize he's missing his hand."

"Oh, no!"

"Yeah, poor guy, right?"

"Yeah, and poor you. How are you feeling about all this?"

"Stupid sensitive me. I had a minor freakout. But then, I was so worried for him, like did it hurt, was he okay. Then I thought that maybe that was why he stopped talking to me and he just needed to see that we're still good together, and we can make it all right again."

"Sounds good. And if that were the case, I'm guessing you wouldn't look so glum, right?"

"You know me too well. So, it gets complicated. Phoenix's not returning my calls, so I went to see his brother to ask for his help."

"You've got me on the edge of my seat here. Hot brother willing to help out?"

"I dunno," Orchid said, "except he tells me that the accident took his leg, too."

"What? Oh my god! That's messed up."

"I know. I feel terrible that this happened to him. And I wasn't even around when he was going through all this. And then, he doesn't even want to tell me. He kept it secret for six months. Just from me, 'cause he thinks I'm a total dolt."

"Aw, Orchid. You're not a dolt. He knows about what happened to your parents?"

"Yeah, I think that's why he didn't want to tell me. Plus, I freaked over a cut on my foot with him once. He knows I don't watch the news. And I couldn't look at pictures of injured soldiers, and . . ." Her voice trailed off realizing how damning the evidence must have appeared to him.

"Hey, just curious here, how could you not tell before? About his leg?"

"Well, he walks perfectly fine. He was wearing pants, and you really can't tell anything's different. After I found out about his arm, I looked it up online. With adaptations, he can probably do what he wants."

"Holy crap, this is unbelievable. Are you okay, honey?"

"I'm okay. He's the strong one. I can't believe everything he must've been through. And here's the kicker. Last time I saw him, I called my cut hideous and disfiguring." Orchid pointed towards the bandage on her forehead. "He walked out."

"Uh-oh."

Her own part in this began to dawn on her. "You know what sucks? I can be pissed at him for thinking he gets to decide what happens to us. But, honestly? I'm pissed at myself too. I thought I had it down pat. Avoid anything unpleasant. Don't read the paper; don't watch the news. Live my sheltered life working in beauty."

"Who could blame you?"

"I do. I thought I was smart keeping myself safe. Now it's cost me any chance with Phoenix. Life is messy, and I need to grow up and face that. Otherwise, he was right all along."

"You want messy? Come by next time Matty has a blowout diaper."

Orchid swilled her wine, and stood. "That one's all yours, hon, I have my own mess to deal with."

At home, Orchid pried open her laptop and typed in her password. The information from Caleb didn't reconcile with her perception of Phoenix. He moved with fluidity and grace. He'd sprinted to her side and held her when she was hurt.

Orchid typed *multiple amputee* into the blinking search bar. Pages of links filled her screen. She tried not to look away. *They're just pictures. Nothing bad is going to happen.* There were stories about military veterans and their prostheses, about amputees surfing, training for 5K's, skateboarding, and rock climbing. The guys looked tough and tenacious.

One article described a soldier who was blown up by an IED and lost both legs and a hand. She paged through quickly, learning that he spent a year at Walter Reed, adapting to driving and living on his own. It was a hard recovery. Yet, he felt the experience made him stronger. Even if he could, he wouldn't change a thing. His only wish was that people wouldn't judge him based on how he looked. Orchid winced recalling her insensitive comments last she'd seen Phoenix. He wasn't likely to interpret her judgment kindly.

Her perspective shifted. Avoiding these images hadn't brought her parents back. Looking at them didn't make bad things happen. And she wasn't some overly sensitive person who was repulsed by other people's imperfections. She felt their pain with empathy.

Did she want to curate an artificially rosy existence? *No. I just need to find Phoenix to tell him how much I care.*

He wasn't letting her get in touch with him, so she shot hope into the atmosphere for the goodwill of one tattooed giant.

CHAPTER 45

HIP (EPONYMOUS)
POOR BOY

Caleb

Phoenix peered down the corridor even though his office was too far to be able to see the receptionist's desk. "Caleb's here?" he asked, confused.

"You want me to tell him you're busy?" Liv asked, one hand over the mouthpiece of her phone.

"Remind me again. I've got a two o'clock, right?"

Glancing at her computer screen, Liv nodded. "Right."

"Send him in."

Caleb arrived at the heels of the office receptionist, toting a paper bag.

The receptionist warily eyed his scowl, black jacket, jeans and untied combat boots. She shifted nervously.

"Oh my gawd," she said, "will this snow ever end?" She stopped snapping her gum long enough to flash her wide, perfectly bleached-white teeth.

Caleb grunted and strode towards Phoenix. The receptionist turned and slouched back towards her spot in the waiting area.

Phoenix stepped out of his doorway to greet Caleb with a brief one-armed hug. "Hey. This is a rare and pleasant surprise."

He turned to Liv. "Caleb, you remember my executive assistant, Liv? Liv, you've met my brother Caleb."

They shook hands. Caleb deigned a quick "Hey," then pointed at Phoenix's office, situated behind Liv's desk. "Should we sit in there?"

"By all means," Phoenix said, leading the way. He indicated two swivel chairs adjacent to the floor-to-ceiling windows overlooking Midtown.

Caleb waited for the door to shut behind them and joined his brother, plopping the bag onto the low table between the chairs. He shrugged off his jacket and tossed it over the back of the chair, where it promptly slid off the slick plastic surface. Caleb left it, sinking into the chair and leaning forward to open the paper sack. Rich, meaty odors emitted from the oil-spotted bag.

"Hungry?" Caleb asked.

The smells triggered the feeling that it was lunch time. Phoenix nodded. "Two Boots, nice. It reminds me of you sneaking food into my hospital room."

"Rules mean shit," Caleb said, dumping the contents of the delicious-smelling bag onto the table.

"C'mon, we're in an ad agency. No clichés allowed."

Caleb rolled his eyes. "Breaded chicken, catfish po'boy, or meatball parm? Or are those too cliché for lunch?"

"Touché. I'll take the chicken, if you don't mind."

Caleb pushed one wrapped sandwich towards his brother and opened another for himself.

"Thanks," Phoenix said, peeling back the paper and taking a bite of the dense white roll compressed around lettuce and still-hot chicken breast.

Caleb looked through the glass wall toward the row of offices stretching down the corridor back to the reception area. He swallowed a bite of meatball sub and wiped his mouth with a brown paper napkin. "I still can't believe you made this place. Look at that," he said, pointing towards Liv with his sandwich-clutched hand. "You have a secretary."

"Executive assistant," Phoenix corrected. "You did the same. Built a business. Different product, same principles."

"It's not the same. I don't have a secretary," Caleb said, chewing while studying Liv typing rapidly.

"I'll send her to your place for a day. She'll scare away your clients with her efficiency," he said, laughing. He finished one corner of his meal and rolled up the other portion inside its waxed paper wrap.

"Is half enough?" Caleb asked, eying the leftover food.

"Half a guy, half a sandwich," Phoenix said. The image hit him in the gut. He shook his head to clear it. "So, what are you doing here?"

Caleb ignored the question and glanced down. "How's all that going? How're you feelin'?"

Protective shield up high for the workday, Phoenix didn't feel like heading straight for vulnerability. He hated these questions and the implied pity that went with them.

"I'm okay. You?"

"Yeah, I'm decent," he said, balling up his empty wrapper and arcing it into a wastebasket. "I saw Orchid again."

"You did? She okay?" Phoenix pictured the gash above her hazel eyes. He'd thought to send flowers and a note after her accident. Peonies were her favorite. But there was no point.

"Yeah, she came into the shop."

"With her fear of needles, I doubt it was to get a tattoo." On the heels of pleasant memories came one of her staring at his residual limb on the day she claimed she'd learned about his injury.

"She came in to ask about you. She was clueless about your accident."

"So what?"

"Sounds like you wronged her big time."

"I was going through some shit, if you remember."

"Come to think of it, guess I was pretty shitty to her too."

"I don't want to talk about Orchid," Phoenix said, glancing at his watch. "I've got to prep for a meeting."

Caleb shrugged. "No skin off my back. But I thought you guys would've been good together."

Phoenix plopped back onto the chair and ran a hand through his hair. "Yup, I thought we would've, too. That whole thing blows."

"Maybe she's changed? Maybe she just needed a minute to get used to the idea?"

"Since when did you become a Orchid supporter?"

"She's got feelings for you. She wants to talk."

"Last time I saw her, she called a little cut on her forehead *hideous*. She said she was *disfigured*. I can't imagine how disgusted she'd be over my scars."

"Seriously, man. Who you trying to protect? Her? Or you?"

Some truth in that question struck him. He wanted to believe in his altruistic intentions in keeping her at bay. It didn't have to do with his own fear of rejection. She wouldn't be able to deal.

Phoenix rose from his chair, anger over injuries he thought he'd accepted. His face flushed. "I told you, I don't want to talk about this." He strode to his desk and slammed a drawer open, pulling bound papers from it.

"You're throwing away a good thing," Caleb said, standing.

"Then you go out with her," Phoenix said, glaring at his brother.

"I think I will," he said, and pushed his way out the door. "Bye, Liv," he called over his shoulder.

How can Caleb have such a different interpretation of what's possible? Phoenix thought.

CHAPTER 46

YELLOW SUN

Phoenix

THURSDAY MARCH 21

"Mom?"

"Yes, Phoenix, it's me. It's a wonder you recognize my voice, given how long it's been since you called."

"Absence makes the heart grow fonder," he joshed, stretching on his sofa.

"Someday, I'm going to be gone and you're going to miss me," came her familiar refrain.

"Aw, I miss you already," he said. He popped in his air pods so that he could flip through news headlines on his phone while talking.

"Good. Because we're seeing each other next week."

"Next week? You coming for a visit?" He sat up, running through his mental calendar.

"Easter with your aunt and uncle and cousins. Have you forgotten?"

"Is it Easter already?" he asked. *Isn't Easter in April?*

"March 31st, the earliest it's been in five years."

"Oh, okay, thanks for the reminder. I'll be there. They want us down on Saturday, right?"

"That's right. I'll be flying in that day. George is going to pick me up. Are you bringing anyone?" Mom asked.

Unbidden, Orchid came to mind.

"Nope, there's no one to bring."

"Not Rina?"

He'd rarely thought of Rina since they parted ways. "Rina? We broke up."

"Uh-oh. What happened?"

He recalled their easy companionship. Weekends now felt empty. "It wasn't any one thing. You know how you always said you and Dad fell madly in love the moment you met? We didn't have that."

"Well, it's not love at first sight for everyone. Dad and I were lucky. Honestly, how many times have you had that happen?"

"Once." A dark-haired beauty pricked at his memory. He pushed the images away. "Never," he corrected himself.

She puffed some air. "Well, which is it? Must be a complicated love life."

"I couldn't even begin to tell you," he admitted.

"Who was it? Tish? I liked her."

"No, not Tish. Someone else you've never met."

"As long as it's not that horrible woman who abandoned you because of your accident. What's her name? Orchid?"

"She didn't abandon me. I've told you."

"Leave, abandoned, never showed up, all the same wretched selfish thing," his mom spat, surprising him with her vehemence.

"She's not selfish," he protested, wondering why he was defending her.

"You've always been overly generous in your estimation of others. You need to protect yourself first."

Phoenix was too tired to correct her. He didn't want to talk about it. "Okay, Mom."

He nearly chimed in with his good-bye when she started up again.

"How's the phantom pain?"

"It's usually not too bad."

"Is the mirror box therapy helping?"

"Yeah, amazing how the brain can be tricked into thinking a missing limb is still there. That guy who invented the technique is pure genius."

Phoenix had been skeptical of the idea that seeing his right leg in a mirror would fool his brain into thinking his left leg was still there. Minds are mysterious. Somehow, it did diminish his pain.

"Maybe I should come out early, or stay with you for a bit after Easter."

"You're always welcome here, but really, there's no need. How's your business? It's been busy, right?"

"Yeah, people in this town take on redecoration like spring cleaning. I've got two clients who need whole rooms redone before the holidays."

"Then I'll just see you at Easter."

"Remember, if you change your mind, feel free to bring someone next week."

"I'll keep that in mind." *When hell freezes over.*

CHAPTER 47

HELLO OPERATOR

Caleb

THURSDAY MARCH 21, NEW BRUNSWICK

"Hey, Mom. How are you?" Caleb answered, twirling the cord attached to the old-fashioned handset Sascha had purchased for their shop.

"I'm well. Thank you. I've just spoken with your brother and I'm sharing the same reminder with you."

"What's that?" he asked.

"Have you forgotten? Easter with your aunt and uncle and cousins, at their shore house. Make sure you've booked both days."

He suppressed a groan, sinking into the black vinyl armchair, its fluffed surface sighing under his weight.

He stared at the pinup calendar on the wall. "Okay, I'll be there, Mom."

"Good." She paused a moment. "I'm a little worried about Phoenix."

"Oh yeah? What's the matter?"

"He doesn't tell me how he's really doing. Have you seen him recently?"

"Yup. We had lunch at his office."

"Well, that's nice. How is he?"

"He's the same stubborn person he's always been."

"He sounds a little down to me."

"Of anyone I know, he's got a right to be down." Caleb shook his head, imagining how he'd feel in Phoenix's situation.

"But it's more than his injuries. He told me he broke up with his girlfriend."

"When I saw him, we had an argument over a girl," Caleb said, thinking of Orchid even though Mom's comment referred to Rina.

"Uh oh, you're not—"

"Oh, c'mon Mom, of course not. You guys are never going to let me live down a couple of stolen girlfriends," he complained. "It's just he's got some crazy notion, like he needs to be perfect, and he's not good enough for any woman. That accident messed with his head."

"He's always held himself to such high standards. I don't know where he gets it from."

"Really?"

She ignored the sarcasm. "Are you bringing anyone, dear? You know Harry's invited Lucy."

He thought for a moment, an idea striking him. "Yeah, maybe I'll bring a girl, too."

"Is it Sascha? She was good for you."

"Yeah, she's good for me. But she's not coming."

"Why not?"

"It's a long story, but you know we broke up a while ago."

"So, should I ask your Aunt Betsy to put you and your friend in the same room or separate rooms?"

"Separate rooms. Definitely."

"Oh, is she not pretty enough for you?"

"She's a pretty one alright."

"If she's not your type, maybe your brother would be interested."

"You're closer to the truth than you know, Mom."

"Now I'm intrigued. Who is this mystery woman?"

"Wait and see, Mom. You've always said patience is a virtue."

"Good news," Caleb growled.

Orchid stared at her phone's screen, surprised to see Caleb's name. "Yeah, what is it?"

"You wanna see Phoenix?"

"You know I do."

"For a whole weekend?"

"Wow, really?"

"Yeah. There's an annual Easter weekend with my aunt and uncle. You want to go as my guest?"

She paused. This wasn't exactly the intimate one-on-one she'd imagined. "So who's going to be there? Besides your aunt and uncle."

"My cousins."

"Yeah."

"My mom."

"Oh, no! I've never met her. From what I hear she's tough."

"You want this chance or not?"

"Um, yes."

"Pack light. We're going on the bike."

"On your motorcycle?" she shrieked.

"What do you think? That I'm picking you up on my high school ten-speed? Yes, of course, on my Harley."

Orchid hung up the phone and started planning. What was she going to wear? Never mind that, what was she going to *say*? The thought of apologizing for hurting Phoenix with her callous remarks made her feel a little sick. Could he forgive her for being so thoughtless? She'd have to be brave because this might be her only chance.

An hour and fifteen minutes under a helmet was plenty of time for her carefully smoothed hair to grow damp and lifeless.

Orchid spent the time on the back of the bike hanging onto Caleb, and thinking about Phoenix. She imagined him with her. *What adaptations would he use to operate a motorcycle? Is he driving himself today?* When she'd asked Caleb about his brother, the taciturn twin's answers were less than illuminating.

"He's fine."

She pictured how she'd greet Phoenix. Hurtling sixty miles an hour towards him, an epiphany gripped her; *he needs reassurance that being with him is no compromise. That, despite my unthinking remarks at the hospital, I see nothing ugly in him.*

Familiar streets passed by. They drove past the kitchenette where she and Phoenix had eaten and romped in the water last summer.

As Caleb slowed the Harley in front of the Victorian house facing the water, the plump woman Orchid had seen in pictures emerged from the house. The cousins whom she'd met on the Fourth of July, Harry and Stew, followed.

The woman tiptoed up to kiss Caleb on the cheek. "You beat your brother here," she said.

"Well, there's a first."

Then she turned to Orchid. "Betsy," she trilled. "Caleb's aunt." They shook hands.

Harry and Stew, finished greeting their cousin Caleb, came over to Orchid.

"Hey, stranger," Stew said. "What, did you switch sides?"

"No switching sides . . . and don't go starting that rumor. My big brother seems to have lost his mind, so we're just trying to help him remember what he's given up," Caleb answered for her.

Orchid looked at him with gratitude, then turned to kiss both men on the cheek. "How's your girlfriend?" she asked Harry, remembering his stories from their July Fourth outing.

"Lucy's upstairs," he responded. "She's a talker, I'm warning you."

While they chatted, Stew picked up Orchid's bag. "I've got this," he said.

"Thanks," she said.

The house opened to a series of bedrooms and a laundry room on the ground level. Betsy pointed out the room she'd set aside for Phoenix, then led them to up two flights of stairs to a bedroom that Orchid remembered from the previous summer. While Stew deposited her bag and Betsy led Caleb down the hall to his room, Orchid looked out the framed window at the view she and Phoenix had admired together. Nine months ago, he'd cared for her here when she'd cut her foot. Now it was her turn.

CHAPTER 48

ICKY THUMP

Phoenix

SATURDAY MARCH 30

The street was visible from the main windows of the living room. Betsy and crew came outside soon after Phoenix pulled into their driveway.

He stepped out of the car, stiff from sitting for the last hour and a half. He was missing Dad, unsettled by an emptiness he couldn't quite articulate.

His cousins Harry and Stew greeted Phoenix with half-hugs, back slaps and high fives. Aunt Betsy pointed at the open door to the ground floor. "I put you down here, as your mom requested."

Just like Mom to make a big deal over me. Something about being back at the spot he'd last visited with Orchid, or maybe the increasing keen of physical discomfort, was making him irritable.

"Great, give me the gimp floor."

"Well, you look wonderful."

Phoenix grabbed his bag, then looked up to see Caleb bounding down the porch steps. At his elbow was a dark-haired beauty he wasn't expecting to see. Her kohl-rimmed gaze darted to him then back to Caleb.

No freaking way! Caleb and Orchid?

Caleb paused on the stairs to place a hand behind Orchid's back and whisper something in her ear. She listened intently then leaned her head against his shoulder. Even in her betrayal, she was gorgeous.

Thunderous denial boxed his ears. *No, no, no.* The whole son. The uninjured brother. The Walker who could walk. Of course. Caleb had what he didn't. The inequity narrowed his throat until air molecules had to fight to enter single file.

Caleb split off to talk with Stew. Orchid approached. Phoenix eyed the bandage on her forehead, remembering his worry for her in the ambulance. He wondered how the wound was healing. *Nope, don't care.* She searched his face, guilt in her expression. She looked sexy in a pair of shorts under a hooded jacket showing slender legs. His fingers curled around his suitcase handle, remembering the feel of her smooth skin beneath his hand. *She has some nerve, showing up here with Caleb. They should at least have the decency to date behind my back.*

"Phoenix," she said, voice as soft as if it were only the two of them together. "I'm so sorry. Last time we saw each other—"

Of course she's freaking sorry.

"Save it," he huffed, cutting her off. He wasn't sticking around to hear more. Dragging his bag behind him, he stormed to the open door, calling over his shoulder to his brother. "That didn't take you long, bud."

Aunt Betsy hurried to follow him. She pointed down the hall to the first bedroom.

"Thanks," he said, placing his overnight bag on the luggage rack in the closet.

"Do you need anything?"

"No, thank you." he said, loneliness compressing in his chest. After all the women in his life, why was the treachery of this ebony-haired woman so painful?

"We're heading to the beach for a stroll, then serving cocktails before dinner. Would you like to join us?"

"I'll join you for drinks but pass on the beach." He looked at his feet, fond memories of the shore battling the uncertainty of balancing in the sand on a stilt.

CHAPTER 49

ANOTHER WAY TO DIE

Orchid

"**N**ot going well, huh?" Caleb asked Orchid, dropping next to the spot where she moped on the living room sofa. Her side of the cushion bounced up as if he'd sat on the opposite side of a seesaw.

Her voice quavered. "He doesn't want to listen. I can't even get three sentences out. I haven't been able to apologize for what I said at the hospital, and I feel terrible about that. How could I keep making him mad?"

"It's a tough situation."

"He looks so good. He's doing well, right?"

"Tough to say. He doesn't really talk about it. But I don't blame him for that. I've been there with him through all this, and I still don't know how I'd react if it were me."

"Me either. But I do know I'd want him with me every second I was in the hospital. I couldn't imagine pushing him away. I'd be the most selfish person."

"Maybe. But you know he's strong. He probably thought it'd be too much for you."

"Did you see how he looked at us when he arrived?"

"Like I'd tattooed him in his sleep?"

"More like he'd seen a ghost."

"Embodied in you," he said, chuckling darkly.

"I'm so tired," she said, leaning against him and closing her eyes. "Probably from the bike ride, the sun . . . "

"The guy who hates you," Caleb said, adding to her list.

Orchid must've drifted off to sleep. The hubbub of people returning from the beach woke her. She picked up her head from Caleb's chest and opened her eyes to look into . . . Phoenix's glare as he stood facing the two of them.

"How cozy," he said, hand balling into a fist.

She jumped up to her feet to follow him as he headed towards the stairs. "Phoenix, can we talk? Please?"

She was so close behind him when he whirled that she stepped back in surprise. His eyes burned her with disdain.

"How. Dare. You?" he asked. "How dare you show your face here, with my family? Do you feel no shame? I thought you were lots of things. You fooled me into thinking you were kind and innocent. But now, the way you're flaunting yourself, I don't even recognize you."

Shame flamed her cheeks. "I'm sorry. I just wanted to talk with you. To tell you I didn't mean to hurt your feelings. In the hospital, I wasn't thinking—"

Holding the railing to traverse the steps, he moved more quickly than she'd expect. He was already halfway down the stairs. "That homeless guy at least had the decency to leave me alone."

His accusation, flung at her up the reverberating stairwell, took a moment to sink in, then snatched her breath. *I'm worse than the guy who took his limbs. I should have just left him alone.* She looked down at the empty landing.

He was gone.

She turned, almost falling into the solid mass of Caleb behind her. Betsy stood between her boys, mouth agape.

The front door flew open. A gentleman's booming voice filled the room. "Hell of a flight delay. But now I've brought the lovely Veronica, and it's cocktail hour!"

He stopped, looking around at the frozen faces.

Veronica didn't heed the chill. She barreled over to hug her sister Betsy, bestow a peck on Harry and Stew's cheeks and then stepped over to Caleb. She flung her arms around him. "Caleb, give your mother a hug!"

He leaned down to return her embrace. "Hi, Mom."

She turned with open curiosity and an outstretched hand to Orchid. On automatic pilot, Orchid shook her hand. "Orchid Paige, nice to meet you."

"Veronica Walker, Phoenix and Caleb's mother," she said, looking as if she'd remembered something distasteful.

Hearing their mother pronounce Phoenix's name, picturing how much she must love her boys, made Orchid feel faint.

"I remember you," she said, tone sharp.

Orchid looked up and startled as Veronica stepped towards her.

"He said you didn't want to see him when he was—"

Orchid could hear from her ascending pitch where this was going. "He didn't want to see *me*," she interrupted, at the same time that Caleb spoke.

"I thought the same thing, Mom, but Phoenix didn't tell her," he said. The memories slammed her. She winced.

"So, what are you doing here now?" Veronica asked.

Caleb put a meaty arm over his mother's shoulders. "I invited her here to give her a chance to talk with Phoenix."

Harry chuckled. Then he covered his mouth and turned away. He and Stew took the stairs two at a time to join a singing Lucy whom the group could hear playing a video game upstairs.

"Not going well?" Veronica asked archly.

Orchid shook her head, looking down.

The older woman leaned in with a voice so low it doubled in

power. Her words punched Orchid in the stomach. "He has been hurt enough. If you hurt him, I will find you wherever you are and I . . . will . . . kill . . . you . . . with . . . my . . . own . . . hands."

Mouth agape, Orchid tried to recover enough to say she would never hurt Phoenix. On purpose, anyway.

Caleb, the only other person with a chance to hear the threat, spoke first. He nodded darkly. "So now I know where I get it from," he said, and steered his mom towards the minibar set up in the corner of the living room.

George finished rimming glasses with lemon. He held up two tumblers as if offering sacrifices to gods. "Chivas," he said, handing one drink to Veronica and the other to Caleb.

Orchid, stumbling, took the stairs up to her room where she shut the door to the shame of being in a place where she was wanted by almost no one and misunderstood by nearly all.

A shower, smoothing wet tresses and a fresh outfit soothed a fraction of Orchid's chafed nerves. A knock sounded. *Phoenix?* She hurried to open the door. He'd been limping a little, and though she wanted to see him, to explain, she also hoped he hadn't trekked up two flights to see her.

A fair-skinned redhead stood, her teeth gently working her lower lip. "Hey, I'm Lucy, Harry's girlfriend," she said, with an easy swing of her ponytail.

"Oh hi, I'm Orchid," she said, moving aside so Lucy could enter.

"Yeah, I know." She entered the room and flopped onto the bed. "I am so glad you're here."

"Really? No one else seems to be."

"Yeah, it takes the pressure off me, you know?"

"How's that?" Orchid asked, turning back to the mirror to apply eyeliner. She felt comfortable with this easygoing outsider, who, like her, was not related by blood or marriage.

"I don't want to be the only nonfamily member here," she said, echoing the same dynamics Orchid observed. "That's why I didn't come at Thanksgiving. Harry's parents are intimidating, you know?"

"Oh?" Orchid asked, peering into the mirror to curl her lashes from the base to the tip.

"Well, George is completely famous on Wall Street, and they're like bajillionaires."

Orchid chuckled. "You're messing up my makeup by making me laugh," she said.

"Although it turns out I could've come at Thanksgiving. I didn't know Rina would be there."

"Who's Rina?" Orchid asked.

"Phoenix's ex-girlfriend. He brought her to Thanksgiving for their first date after meeting at a Starbucks or something."

Orchid turned, forgetting about the mascara.

The details slapped her. *Ex-girlfriend? Thanksgiving?* He'd dated after his accident, when she couldn't get excited about any of the guys she'd met. Though he was acting like the one wronged, she wasn't sure which of them deserved the title more.

She faced the mirror to brush base powder all over and feather on lipstick in a shade of purple that matched her eggplant-hued dress.

Harry popped his head in the door, no knock. "Hey, dolls," he said. "Din-din."

"Are we feeding me to the wolves for dinner?" Orchid asked, dabbing a final touch of blush on each cheek.

"That's right. It's like a shark's cage three days late for mealtime down there. What's wrong with everyone? Thinking you're with Caleb?"

"What?" Orchid whirled, forgetting the brush in hand, incredulous. "Who thinks that?"

He counted off on his fingers cheerfully. "Let's see. Phoenix. My mom. Who told my dad, who is totally confused about why you're even here."

"Oh, no," Orchid said, "I can't go down there."

Lucy looped one arm through Orchid's. "Oh, you have to. No one's going to notice anything stupid I'll say with you there!"

Strengthened by the buoyant couple on either side, Orchid inserted her feet into silver heels and descended the steps.

Most were already seated at the oval dining table, replete with fine porcelain, crystal and layered linens. The remaining guests straggled in to find empty seats.

Orchid slipped in next to Caleb, who was engrossed in conversation with Stew and George. Veronica, seated between Betsy and Phoenix, ignored Orchid's arrival.

Lucy sat on her other side, and Harry took the last empty chair, next to his girlfriend.

The conversation quieted as Betsy suggested prayers. She reached out on either side to hold hands with Veronica and George. Everyone else followed suit. As Orchid took Caleb and Lucy's hands, she gauged Veronica holding Phoenix's shortened forearm with absolutely no trace of self-consciousness. *Could I be so nonchalant?*

Orchid bowed her head for George's words.

Then, a server arrived with a steaming bowl of soup for each person.

"Watercress," trilled Betsy.

"Bon appetit," boomed George, the French phrase reminding Orchid of her trip to Cannes with Phoenix. She looked up at him to catch him gazing at her. As she caught his eye, he looked away and returned to converse with his mother.

She had no appetite, so she turned to Caleb.

"Working on any cool new tattoos?"

"We're working on a kick-ass one for a hunter. It's like the designs you'd find on high-end gun handles."

"Really?" Orchid asked.

"You getting one?"

"Haha, very funny," she said. The server took her untouched bowl and placed a plate in front of her.

"Veggie lasagna with béchamel sauce, and white asparagus," Betsy said. "Even though there's no rule about it, we avoid meat on Holy Saturday."

"I've never seen a gun handle," Orchid said to Caleb. "What does the design look like?"

Caleb pulled out his smart phone. "Just Google 'Geoffroy Gournet'," he said. He showed her pictures of heron in flight, foxes chasing birds through a forest, all densely packed into a few square inches.

"Wow," she said.

She looked up to see Veronica break open a roll, butter it and place it on Phoenix's plate. Phoenix turned to murmur his thanks.

"Yeah, he's a master engraver. Works out of a shed in his backyard. Sometimes one piece will take him months," Caleb continued.

Orchid nodded. She wasn't listening. She was floored by what else Phoenix might need that she wouldn't even know to offer.

That night, Orchid scoured the Internet like she was about to defend her post-doctoral thesis. She looked up medical knowledge, therapies and daily living adaptations that she'd previously only skimmed, through metaphorical fingers, half-hiding from the information. She saw the hard work of amputees in rehab. She read about military research on prostheses to help wounded vets returning home. Some of the images were hard to look at. Finally, filled with a realistic set of knowledge, Orchid felt both saddened and hopeful for Phoenix.

Then, on a whim, she typed *Phoenix mythology* into the search engine. She skimmed the top results *mythical, sacred, dies and is reborn.* "A phoenix obtains new life by arising from ashes." Orchid blinked. How prescient. Phoenix truly was reborn by arising from symbolic ashes.

It was nearly midnight. Orchid tiptoed downstairs in the quiet house for a cold drink. She passed the echoing stairway down to the basement level. She heard a sound like a groan.

Padding on bare feet to the basement, she listened. To the left, soft snores emitted from one room. Then, the sound came again, from the room directly in front of her, the room Betsy had pointed out as Phoenix's.

The door ajar, Orchid tapped the solid surface. "Phoenix, you okay?"

No answer in the darkness.

CHAPTER 50

BROKEN BOY SOLDIER

Phoenix

*A*ww, shit. This was going to be a bad one. *It's all in your head. Just get up and get the meds.*

As he forced himself to a seated position, groaning, he caught sight of a figure peering through the faintly lighted doorway.

"Who's there?" he asked, doubling over in pain.

The figure flew to his side. "Phoenix, are you hurt? What do you need?" asked a familiar voice, strangely soothing even while its honey-sweetness brought the bitter taste of betrayal to the back of his mouth.

He squeezed hard, trying to replace the feeling of a bulldozer grinding his missing toes into concrete with the more manageable pain of his hand kneading the hell out of his leg.

"Phantom pain?" Orchid asked.

Her knowing and saying the phrase with composure surprised him long enough that he was able to pause. "Meds. In my bag. In the closet," he said, spitting the words out between the throbbing.

She ran over and then back to his side within the space of two spasms. "How many?" she asked mid-stride, the bottle already open.

"Two," he said, though part of his brain screamed for the whole container.

She wrapped his hand around two oblong pills then sprinted to the bathroom. He'd already swallowed them by the time she'd returned with a glass half full of tap water. He drank it anyway.

"What else can I do? Can I massage you?"

Rina would never baby me. She'd tell me to take my meds and suck it up.

His pain steepened, exploding through his mind. He couldn't speak. He fell back onto the mattress, banging his leg, praying for relief.

Orchid's hand, smooth and cool, found his leg and rubbed, tentatively at first, then firmly, rhythmically. He resisted, pulling away a little. *I don't need anyone.* Then, though he hadn't asked for it, touch by touch, her caress comforted.

With time, his pain eased until he returned from pure feral animal instincts to human sized agony.

Orchid was grateful that Phoenix could communicate what he needed. Fetching the pills was something she could do in the face of his pain. His expression twisted her gut as if pain were winding its way through her own body. She'd read about massage therapy, and so she pressed her fingers to his skin, trying different angles and pressure to ease the agony. The strong muscle reminded her of his performance at the triathlon, running out of the water, leaping onto his bike, sprinting along the final stretches of the race. The sweetness of those memories overshadowed the flashes from her parents' car crash.

Beneath her hand, his writhing slowly calmed. After long rhythmic minutes massaging his leg, she felt him relax under her touch. She didn't know if the improvement was due to her efforts, or the medicine she'd run to get for him. So she traced her movement again. She smoothed her thumb and palm from below his knee, down the side of his calf and under the rounded bottom. When she ran a finger along the crooked path of his scars, she could feel the fine, thin skin where his wound had grown together.

Phoenix lay heavy and asleep, eyes closed, breathing calm.

He'd ignored her for six hellish months. Now he was before her, at least, without him yelling in her face or with another woman wrapped around him. Perhaps if he'd been awake, she'd give him a piece of her mind instead of sitting so close. Her hip rested against one leg while she caressed the other. Were these precious minutes stolen?

She daren't shift her weight, lest she wake him. Drawing warm air in through her nose, Orchid savored the faint scent uniquely Phoenix. A clean male and spice scent.

Outside, the world stilled in the night air. Only the insistent thump of the ocean pounding against sand accompanied their middle of the night quietude.

Ghostly rays from the moon whitewashed Phoenix's face. She studied his strong brow, straight nose and full lips. Sitting so close, she saw new lines had formed in the past six months. The hollows beneath his eyes shadowed darker, with a hint of tightness. The fine crease between his brows had deepened. Asleep, he looked vulnerable.

Her hand had stilled, so deep was her concentration on his features. He lay limp, one arm across his chest, the other above his head. She'd often wondered how he slept. Orchid reached forward, drawn to the silky waves of hair. She let his smooth locks slip through her fingers.

It was late.

Her eyes wanted to shut with fatigue. Her chin nodded towards her chest. She was worn out, not only physically, but also with highs and lows of the day's emotions. Yet, she didn't want to go.

She pictured the Phoenix she'd first met, confident and capable. He was still those things, yet he had changed, and not just physically. He seemed more mature, less boyish, with a tinge of resignation. Of course he'd changed. She had no idea the adaptations he made on a daily basis. She'd changed, too. The knowledge of what he'd been through made her stronger. She could do that for him, be that for him.

Orchid eased up from the bed. Her gaze swung around the room. It landed on a leather club chair by the window. Orchid padded over and sank onto the cold, smooth surface. Phoenix, now half a room away, seemed too far. She sprang up. Determined, Orchid gripped one slippery arm, and pushed the furniture until she'd shoved it right next to his bed. She covered him with the sheet and thin blanket. Morning would give them an opportunity to talk, for her to correct misperceptions. Then, comforted by the sound of Phoenix's deep, even breathing, Orchid dropped into the chair and into slumber.

Phoenix had no sense for how long she stayed like that, ministering to him. Sometime later, with only pale moonlight to sepia-tone the room, Phoenix woke with the relief of feeling no pain. He must've dozed off. The meds numbed everything.

Glancing over to see the time, he saw Orchid asleep in an armchair pushed beside his bed. Though his first inclination was to dredge up anger, he found her presence strangely comforting. A truth struck him. There was no way that she and Caleb would date and then flaunt it in front of him. Neither of them was cruel.

Seeing her delicate features, luminescent skin and smooth hair, peaceful in repose, filled him with a different kind of pang from the one that had filled his consciousness earlier. A faint scent of her rose soap wafted from her skin. He found himself examining his feelings, turning them over like discovering a long-lost beloved object. The truth was, he'd missed her. Her face angled towards her chest, relaxed, sweet. An impulse bubbled up to take her in his arms. He knew her expressions, the way her brows knit when she was cross, the way her cheek dimpled just before she was about to be mischievous.

Tonight, she cared for him in his vulnerable state. In every stroke, she imparted affection. What if? The thought hung in the air above his semi-conscious state. *What if we can build more memories together, new moments? What if we can reclaim a little of the tenderness?*

He became aware of the starfish clock at his bedside. The silver arm ticked forward like a sentinel that was never off duty. Its cold glint reminded him of the solid, concrete world beyond the walls that enveloped them. Only in the darkness of night could all outcomes seem possible. He looked down at himself and a clearer thought came to him, ethereal, floating before him like pure truth.

Broken.

He'd spared Orchid disappointments, limitations and nights of pain. Come morning, in the unflinching daylight, his constraints would lock back in place. He was an idiot to think otherwise. He'd made the right call. The clarity of his logic narrowed to that one conviction.

CHAPTER 51

PRICKLY THORN BUT SWEETLY WORN

Orchid

With little sense of time passing, bright sunshine filled the room, lightening the whitewashed walls, indicating that it was no longer early morning. Orchid stretched, trying to straighten the kinks in her back. The starfish-shaped clock ticked past eight.

Peeved at her stiff joints, Orchid turned to check on Phoenix. He must've heard her stir because he pushed up to a sitting position. He looked at her and scooted back, levering with one hand to situate his rear against a pillow.

Despite knowing that a prosthesis supported his six-foot stature the day before, and massaging his leg in the darkness, the sight of him sent a shock through her. Sheets kicked off during the night, he sat in shorts and a T-shirt, gorgeously carved like a Greek statue, every muscle etched and strong, pale ends of limbs against burnished copper linens. One well-shaped foot gone, his form ended bluntly beneath his knee, lines of scars visible. A flash of a speeding train's metal rims crushing his flesh whipped through her mind, like a slap in the face. The way he maneuvered on the bed hinted at the everyday challenges he must face.

The fraction of an instant flash-froze, as if captured on film. Her mouth open, back bent on her way to standing upright, her eyes affixed on Phoenix. She was unable to move, like a department store mannequin left contorted in an awkward position.

Then the pain in his eyes as he watched her reached down her throat to rattle her from the inside.

He yanked the sheet over to cover his legs.

She was not going to let him think that she judged the way he looked and found him lacking. She snapped her jaw shut and straightened. Her trembling legs were the only deficit in her composure.

"Hey there, how are you feeling?" she asked, perching on the edge of his bed. He was so close. Just lean forward and she could press a cheek to his. Then, just a turn and she could caress his full lips. The indentation her weight made caused him to roll towards her, his leg coming to rest against hers. She looked down, smoothing the sheet over the muscular thigh nearest to her, wanting to comfort away the distrust in the furrow of his brow. "All better?"

He pulled his legs a few inches away, so they were no longer touching hers. "Yeah, better. Thanks."

"I'm glad. Is it always so bad?"

"Not always. That was a bad one. Like an eight."

"Eight?"

"Out of ten," he explained. "On the pain scale, eight means excruciating or something like that."

"Excruciating?" It was worse than she'd guessed. "Oh, I'm sorry. I wish you didn't have to go through that."

"I don't want pity, and you didn't have to stay," he said, ice creeping into his voice.

"It's not pity. I wanted to take care of you like you took care of me last time we were here," she said.

His glare narrowed, forecasting an end to their civility.

"I don't need anyone to take care of me." He threw off the sheets, then pivoted away from her and shimmied to the other side of the bed.

"Of course not. I can see you don't need anyone, just . . . I just wanted to be here for you." She stood to come around to his side of the bed. He grabbed a silicone liner from the side table. She kept talking, not wanting to lose this opportunity to right his misperceptions.

"I have a lot to tell you. I never dated Caleb, I'd never do such a thing."

The tightness around his eyes eased a little. "I know. I believe you." He spoke as he rolled a gel cover over the smooth end of his left leg.

"Good. And I'm sorry for what I said at the hospital. It was stupid and insensitive. I was only thinking about me, and I feel terrible for that."

He blinked, the lines around his mouth taking up whatever tension his eyes had surrendered. The hum of a nearby washing machine heightened, speeding into a final spin.

"I need to apologize for what I said about you being worse than the guy who caused my accident."

"Right." She breathed out with one short exhale.

He shoved his leg into the socket of the upright prosthesis. "I was so angry that I wasn't thinking straight."

The wash slowed, clicks announcing the change in cycle.

"Kind of like me, at the hospital."

He paused to gaze at her forehead. "You all better?"

"Yeah. The stitches came out a week ago. "

"That's good, I was wondering how you were doing." His face smoothed into a grin. "How are we always causing so much trouble?"

"Was it a huge deal to clean up your place?"

"Haven't you seen? We had to raze the building to the ground."

"I hope you made Liv do her share, since she was the one who tripped me." They joined in laughter. Her eyes met his.

"I've missed you," he said.

His admission emboldened her. She deserved to know. "If you missed me, why didn't you tell me that you were hurt? Why didn't you tell me you were in the hospital when I came back from China?"

"You know why."

"Because you didn't trust me."

"Because I couldn't give you what you wanted."

"How did you know? You didn't even ask me."

"Have you seen me? I couldn't give any woman what she wanted."

"But then you dated Rina."

"I don't want to hurt your feelings, and I wasn't even looking, but Rina was just who I needed after my accident."

Rina was just who he needed? The specter of another woman lanced her. Orchid pictured some wraithlike angel, a perfect model of patience and care. The inherent criticism in his words cut deep.

"What do you mean, Rina was just who you needed?"

"She had no reaction to my injuries. She just saw me as a man. She made me laugh at myself."

Orchid shot to her feet. "You ever think maybe *I* could've been that person? You don't think I could've seen you for the amazing man you are? You know what's crazy? You didn't even tell me what happened! You didn't trust me! You could've given me a little more credit, you know. For being more than just squeamish Orchid. Maybe remembered my good side, too?"

His blue irises darkened. "The difference is she'd never known me any other way. You would've had a lot to get used to. I did what I thought was best. After we saw each other at the holiday party, it seemed like the right call."

"At the holiday party? What do you mean? What was best? To lie to me? To hurt me?"

"To protect you. You don't know what it was like after I got hurt. Things got pretty bad. It's still not the easiest. It didn't seem like you—" He shook his head.

"So this is it," her voice dropped, interrupting him, somber over having her theories verified. "You thought I couldn't deal."

"That's right."

"Well, aren't I here now? Dealing just fine?"

"Caleb said you came to apologize. There's nothing to apologize for. I'm the one who's sorry. You've come for nothing."

"It's not nothing. I've missed you too. Let's try again. Pick up from before China."

He pushed off the bed and stood, peering down at her. "Orchid, stop this crazy talk. Don't do this."

"We had something special," she argued.

"I'm not the same."

"I'm not either."

He shook his head and hobbled towards the toilet.

This was her last chance. "The stupid thing is, I fell in love with you and I can't stop." She flushed with surprise. Did she say that aloud?

He paused to look at her. His eyes blazed cobalt. "There's nothing between us. I'm sorry."

Phoenix limped into the bathroom and shut the door.

The washer chimed its song to indicate the end. *The end.*

CHAPTER 52

CAUSE AND EFFECT

Orchid

O rchid stumbled up to her room, replaying their exchange. *Abandoned. Again.*

She was an idiot for divulging every last vulnerability. But this time felt different. She didn't need him to make her happy, just as he didn't need her to make him whole.

Sure, she could wallow and seal herself off for another half year. Or, she could choose not to. Phoenix's rejection *was* sad, especially since a part of her intuited that it wasn't a reflection on her. Beyond the sadness, though, was strength, and the knowledge that she'd survive—even thrive. Her well was deep. She could love again.

For now, she had to go face him and his family.

Orchid tore off her yoga outfit and pulled a dress over her head. She could do this, take part in one last meal. She'd take the high road.

The streams of silver and vanilla-hued fabric fit her perfectly. For Easter, the season of rebirth, she'd chosen an outfit that wasn't black, a feat considering her wardrobe. She slipped her feet into silver heels and strode over to the mirror to re-apply makeup over puffy eyes.

A knock at the door. She calmed herself with a lungful of air, then tore it open to find Lucy and Harry.

"Wow, I love your dress," Lucy said.

"Yours, too," Orchid said, glancing at the spring green floating chiffon. It wasn't one she'd ever wear, but the color and style suited Lucy.

"Ready?" Harry asked, offering each of them an arm.

"Sure. I'll be your shield for any stupid comments, right?" Orchid said dryly to Lucy.

"That's right!"

Downstairs, the table was set more ornately than a Martha Stewart *Living* shoot. Pale lavender linens complemented cream china and robin's egg blue walls to create the feeling of being inside a Fabergé egg.

"Betsy, you've outdone yourself," Orchid said, touching cheeks with the hostess.

"Oh, thank you," she said, beaming. "Did you sleep well?"

"Not bad," she said, stretching a back made sore by the awkward angle of the armchair.

Caleb strode over. "I bought you guys time this morning," he said with gruff pride. "You were asleep in Phoenix's room and I figured you'd want to talk, so I had the rest of the crew leave for Easter Mass without you."

"Thanks." Orchid stretched upwards to throw her arms around his neck when he stepped back, one hand up.

"I also straightened everyone out that we never dated, so you don't want to start rumors, do you?"

"You're the best, thanks," she said, backing up to allow proper distance between them.

Orchid hesitated and then walked over to Veronica. "Good morning, Mrs. Walker. How are you?"

"I'm well. I understand you spent the night in Phoenix's room?"

Orchid blushed. "Um, not like that . . . I was—"

"I know. I didn't mean anything. Just, actually, thank you for helping him."

She exhaled. "You're welcome."

"Was he better by the morning?"

She nodded, throat tight remembering his calm sleep and then the finality of his rejection. "Once he fell asleep, he seemed okay. I wanted to stay just in case he needed anything."

Veronica relaxed. Orchid could see the caring mother behind her tough exterior.

Betsy came to take her sister by the arm. "Brunch is served!"

Orchid ended up between the Walker brothers, Caleb on her left, Phoenix on her right. The tempo of her heart as he settled beside her told her that his dismissal had done little to cool her ardor.

Prayers weren't awkward. Orchid didn't experience the nonchalance Veronica exhibited during the previous day's benedictions.

Instead, holding Phoenix's arm was as intimate as holding his hand.

George made his rounds balancing the fat bottom of the green bottle. "No empty glasses," he admonished.

"Happy Easter," he said as he refilled Orchid's flute, waiting for the bubbles to subside.

"You too."

Betsy observed them. "What do you normally do on Easter?" she asked Orchid as George moved to Caleb's glass, perpetually empty.

"Um, sometimes I go to my friend Mandy's house."

"Where do your parents live, dear?"

"My parents died when I was younger." Based on experience, she tried to keep her tone matter of fact.

"Oh dear! I'm so sorry."

"Thanks."

"Surely you have other family. Grandparents? Siblings?"

"I've got an uncle in California and an aunt and grandparents in Florida," she said, gesturing expansively to make it sound like more than it was.

"Well, that's good."

"I actually just became reacquainted with my uncle. He was

pretty young when my folks died," she said. "He's invited me to move to LA to work on a family business."

"Are you moving?" Caleb asked.

"Maybe," Orchid said, realizing all options were viable now. "Except, my company's offered me an assignment in China."

She could sense Phoenix staring at her profile. *What does it matter, since there's no 'us' anyway?*

"Well, that's exciting," Betsy said. "Which will you pick?"

"I'm pretty excited about both," she admitted, hit afresh with the memory that nothing held her in New York.

"Definitely, go to China," George boomed. "LA for family, or working in the fastest growing economy? No contest." He launched into stories of deals he'd made in Asia, and the talk turned away from Orchid.

Following the meal, Caleb stood to thank his aunt and uncle. He and Orchid would be the first to leave. "We're going to ride in daylight," he said.

Each person offered a hand or a hug in farewell. Except Phoenix, who'd disappeared into the underbelly of the house. *Goodbye.*

Riding behind Caleb back to the city, Orchid compared her expectations for the weekend with reality. She'd hoped to see Phoenix, *check*. She wanted to speak with him, *check*. She needed to apologize for misunderstandings, *check*. Most of all, she'd mined deep, sifted through the wreckage of her past to find the best person she could offer, and opened every last vulnerability to hold back nothing, to give all. *Every . . . last . . . dream.*

Hopping off the bike in front of her building, Orchid expressed her gratitude tinged in melancholy. "Thanks. You did your part, but I guess it wasn't enough."

Caleb looked at her from under bushy brows. "No?"

She shook her head, looking down. "I told him how I felt, and he had nothing for me in return."

"Sorry, babe. You were expecting more?"

"Yeah. I thought there was more."

"Me, too, actually."

She looked up, knowing it changed nothing. Still, she wanted to hear someone else say that she'd had reason to hope. "Really?"

"Why else would I go to so much trouble?"

"Yeah, why did you help me?"

"Well, it's not all for you," he said. "I get the feeling that my brother's holdin' himself to some impossible standard. I'm trying to give him a chance, too."

"What do you mean?" she asked, intuiting an echo of truth she couldn't articulate.

"Ever since the hospital, seems like he's been trying to be someone for us. He was always holding it together, even when we barely could."

"That kind of breaks my heart," she said.

"Yeah, me too."

"You're a really great brother, you know that?" she asked, briefly flinging her arms around his neck. "I guess this is goodbye for us, too. Take care of yourself, and Phoenix."

He gave her a quick squeeze, and hopped onto his bike.

Caleb and Orchid leaving hollowed Phoenix's insides. He looked down, numbly predicting he'd see a gaping cavity devoid of life-giving organs. After they'd left, Veronica claimed the empty spot on the sofa next to him and twined her arm with his. "I've missed you," she said. "Everything okay?"

"Nothing time won't fix," he said, oddly heavy considering his innards had been suctioned out.

"Is it over that woman?"

"She's not a bad person, Mom."

"I was about to tell you the same thing. So how come she came to see you, then left with your brother?"

He sighed, exhaustion weighting every word. "She has a history that makes the two of us impossible, but I'm the only one honest enough to see it."

"Caleb told me about it."

He leaned back, closing his eyes. She pushed a lock of hair off his forehead.

"So, I have a story to tell you," she said, her voice quiet and soothing. "Imagine, twin brothers, schoolboys in the same class, with the same teacher, with the same math test. One gets a 97 percent and petitions the teacher to allow a retake, convinced he can do better." She paused. "The other gets a B- and gives up, since he hates school anyway.

"Which way is right?" she asked.

He recalled his and Caleb's divergent paths. Had their differences in motivation been evident even in elementary school?

"Of course, both the perfectionist and the dropout are going to have issues," he said, eyes still closed.

"Well said. So maybe it's time you were okay with something less than 100 percent."

He opened his eyes to stare at her.

"Or rather, maybe it's time you believe someone else could be okay with less than perfection."

He swallowed over the hard lump in his throat, blinking.

"She's got standards," he said. "I don't know if B- is going to be enough for her."

"I may be biased but I don't see anything less than an A here."

She sat up to look at him directly. "From the look on her face, I don't think Orchid sees anything less than 100 percent."

Tears surprised him, heating his eyes as they sprang to existence. He blinked through the prickling sensation in his scalp as he worked to keep them hidden.

The sun shifted, the distinct colors of the room muting to speckled grays in the afternoon dusk.

"She said she wants to try again. She said she loves me." His throat tightened as he remembered her expression that morning. *Aren't I here now? Dealing just fine?*

"And what'd you say?"

"I told her there was nothing between us."

His mom studied him, pressing down the spot of hair that always lay against the grain of the others. "Some imperfection is a bit endearing," she said, looking at the errant wave.

"Christ, Mom," he exploded, stabbed by the impossibility of what he couldn't have. The source of his emotions hurtled sixty miles an hour away from him, her feelings growing cold faster than Caleb's motorcycle could take them back to the city. "I'm a double amputee. I've got one hand and one leg. Do you think sensitive Orchid is going to find that freakin' endearing?"

His mom remained calm despite his outburst. Betsy and George slunk out to the kitchen. He was glad that his cousins and Lucy were nowhere to be seen.

"I don't know Orchid as well as you do, but do you think her experiences could make her more empathetic about all that?"

"Remember I had nightmares during those early days in the hospital?"

"I remember. You didn't talk much about them."

"I dreamt I was crawling through a fire and no one would help me," he said, obscuring the details about his family's imagined callousness. "Except Orchid."

"You see?" she asked. "You knew even then that Orchid cared for you."

"In my dreams, Mom, she saved me from the fire, yes. But she did so at her own expense. She threw up looking at me. She carried me . . . *out of pity*," he spat.

"I didn't know," Mom said. "I'm sorry."

Her stare reminded him of the desperation in her eyes as he'd fought to regain the small slips of independence in the early days—transferring to his chair, eating independently, and dressing.

"You know that's just a dream, right?" she asked.

"The dream feels more real than reality. Like that's what's going on for her behind all that fake bravado."

She lifted his hand, warming it against her cheek. "No, honey, that's what's going on for *you* behind all your bravado."

The room empty, alone with his mom, real tears came. "I'm scared, Mom. Scared to try, and then she's going to figure out that this sucks."

Veronica nodded. "You know what I'm scared of?" she asked softly. "I'm scared you're letting that train take more than it already has."

CHAPTER 53

WHO'S LEAVING WHO

Phoenix

MONDAY APRIL 1

"Hell of an Easter weekend," Phoenix said from behind his desk.

"Oh yeah? Bunny forget to bring your basket?" Dex flicked a wrist to pop balled paper into the air, then caught it.

"Orchid showed up with Caleb."

"What do you mean, 'showed up with Caleb'?"

"I thought the same thing at first, that they were together. Turns out he was doing her some favor, because she wanted to talk to me."

"I knew it!" Dex pounded his fist onto the desk between them.

"Knew what?"

"That she had a thing for you. At the anniversary party, she was all doe-eyed. But I don't get it. Wasn't she a bitch to you? And why was she thinking you were engaged to Tish?"

Phoenix shook his head. "My life is a mess."

"If we ever pitch a soap opera, we're coming to you for material."

"I cut her out of my life. After the accident. Don't judge me."

"No judging here. That was a hell of an accident. It'd screw anyone up, for a bit anyway. So, you know Fiona's going to want all the details. Why'd you cut her out of your life, and what happened when she showed up for Easter?"

"Isn't it obvious? That is one sensitive woman. Remember she was the one who couldn't look at military ads? Who was bleeding all over the office and still tried to avoid the hospital?"

"So what?" Dex huffed. "She's also the one you said was special and sweet. The one you brought to Cannes and came back like you were smitten."

"Yeah, that was all before I ended up half metal, half man."

"All right. So what happened at Easter? Is she all freaked out, or cool, love my metal-man?"

Phoenix got up to walk to the plate glass overlooking Midtown. "Crazy woman says she loves me." The words hit him hard. "She doesn't want to admit it, but she's still traumatized on the inside."

"Yeah? What makes you think that? Did she faint? Freak?"

"Naw, she was cool. She even stayed with me one night."

"You sly dog."

"Cut it out." He paced, agitated. "You know her parents died, right? Some terrible car accident. She witnessed it, and seeing people hurt reminds her. So what am I going to do, torture her every time she's with me?"

Dex stroked his unruly beard. "Honestly, all decked out in Armani, you don't look that busted up to me."

Phoenix looked down, from tailored suit to buffed shoes.

"It's more like you're bionic. Cool in that Ironman, Six-Million-Dollar-Man way," Dex said.

Phoenix considered this. He'd achieved all those goals he'd set with Nadine.

"Hey, if she's telling you she loves you, you might want to hold onto her. Fiona only tells me that after she's had a glass of wine. Or four."

And then he saw it.

The pieces of the puzzle he'd been focused on, Orchid's horror over her cut, while true, was just one side of the image. Flipped to the front side, he recognized new connections. Orchid massaging away his pain, seeing his missing pieces and, after these many months, still offering her care. Caleb, Mom, and now Dex each advised the same thing. The loving textures and hues of Orchid's care had been there all along, just obscured by his own prejudice. She saw nothing less than 100 percent. Maybe he could do the same.

CHAPTER 54

MISSING PIECES

Orchid

Two days frozen and then Orchid's thaw came in wet salted waves.

She first pictured Phoenix whole and angry. Gorgeous and stunning too, even while pelting her with sarcastic and biting accusations.

Next, she saw his pain, and the inequity of what he had to deal with. Her own source of pain was that, despite the finality of his abandonment, she still cared for him.

It wasn't how he looked that shocked her. Rather, seeing him ambulate without prostheses produced pained images of his difficulties. His scooting, hand past bum, gave a glimpse of daily challenges.

At home after work, bag slung over a chair, mail tossed on the table, her everyday tasks laughably easy, the dam broke. Misery tightened in the space beneath her eyes, watering her view. The sympathy he wouldn't want clenched high in her throat. It erupted in baby pockets of sobs. "It's not fair." And then despair squeezed sobs at a faster tempo. "No, no. It can't be. Don't take that away. Undo it. Make him whole, the way he was. For his sake." The sobs turned ugly, blurring her view of the room.

The denial stage of grieving.

The tears unleashed vulnerability. The frozen of the last two days washed away with the warm water. In its place, a quiet and growing acceptance. He'd survived and now thrived.

Yet, what concern was it of hers? He was no longer in her life.

Then, that evening, a pale hue still touching the sky, the phone sounded. She stared at the lit screen, her surprise dotted with both anticipation and concern.

"Phoenix?"

"Hey, Orchid, how are you?" His voice, light and unencumbered.

Ugly pained air expelled. Fresh clean air inhaled. "I'm okay. How are you doing? How are you feeling?"

"I'm feeling fine. Why do you ask?"

"I was a little worried about your phantom pain."

"Don't worry about that. Those have become pretty rare nowadays."

"That's good to hear. Everything else okay?"

"Things are great. I'm calling to see if you're free Saturday."

"Free Saturday?"

"To attend Tish's wedding with me."

She regained her footing with sarcasm. "What? Are Liv and Rina busy?"

He laughed. "I prefer you, in case I need to find the men's room."

"I am good at finding the men's room. So tell me the truth, are you just taking pity on me?"

"What? Friends can't invite friends to events?"

She paused, her heart at risk.

"Hey, I was kind of an ass last time we saw each other. Can I make it up to you?"

No. But at least I can say goodbye before China.

"Okay, thanks for the invitation. What's the dress code?"

His chuckle brought a smile to her face. "Since when did you care about someone else's dress code? I'm going black-tie and I'm sure you'll come up with something uniquely Orchid."

She hung up, vowing to keep their final evening together light. More important than her outfit or a nail appointment, she began to erect a scaffold around her bandaged heart.

What's appropriate to wear to the wedding of your crush's ex-girlfriend when you're still in love, despite a tumultuous relationship?

A full-length Free People dress in a modern interpretation of Scottish tartan, the pattern turned forty-five degrees, low in the front and low in the back, seemed to hit just the right vibe. Orchid sipped an iced vodka cranberry cocktail as she dressed.

Her doorman called at five. *Right on time.*

Heading down the elevator, she mentally checked if she had everything she needed: *lipstick, phone, keys.*

Her legs moved on automatic pilot off the elevator. Holy hell, he'd gotten hotter in the week since she'd last seen him. Attired in a well-cut dark tux, offset with a crisp white shirt and trim, dark tie, he looked like an ad for men's cologne. It wasn't just his physical beauty. The corners of his eyes crinkled with happiness. He met her halfway through the foyer and captured her around the waist. Dipping her, he kissed her cheek. She stood and looked up at azure eyes smoldering a familiar hole into her racing heart.

"Well, how are you, hungry bird?"

"I am great. You?"

"Super happy to see you," Phoenix said, guiding her through the lobby doors.

A driver with a burst of billowing white hair exited the car and opened the door for them.

Caleb, waiting in the back seat, scooted over for Orchid. Phoenix slipped in behind her. As the car started moving, Caleb handed her a flask. She eyed him. "It's a wedding. We need fortitude," he said.

The three of them passed the Scotch. There were few other places Orchid would prefer to be than wedged between the Walker brothers in the back of a stretch limo.

The car pulled in front of Cipriani's. *How surreal,* she thought.

She turned to Phoenix. "What are the chances, from the Effies to Tish's wedding?"

"Yes, it did take some work to convince the bride to choose her locale based on us," Phoenix said dryly. The idea of *"us"* gave Orchid an undeserved thrill.

"What'd we send her?" Caleb asked, sporting a rarely seen tuxedo that covered most of his arm tattoos. He pushed open the massive door before Phoenix or Orchid could reach it.

"The week before a wedding, registries have slim pickings. We were able to snag some linens and a honeymoon crack-of-dawn bike expedition from the top of a volcano."

"Nice," he smirked. "Sheets for her bed from her ex."

"Tom's got nothing to worry about. Tish has seen the damaged goods."

Orchid slipped a hand around the shortened left arm of his suit jacket to twine with his elbow. "Hey, you look pretty great to me."

The hall was festooned with garlands of white roses, and an usher at the entrance greeted them. "Bride's side or groom's?" asked the awkward teen, sparse facial hair sprouting between pimpled skin, feet oversized like a puppy's.

Seated two-thirds of the way back, they could still see the *huppah,* or Jewish wedding tent, clearly.

They were just in time. The bridal march began and flower girls lobbed petals onto the carpet more randomly than a Jackson Pollock painting. Bridesmaids on the arms of suited men came in widely varied body types. Clothed identically, they looked like mismatched furniture upholstered in the same bad chintz.

All the players in their expected places, Tish and her parents entered the room to a collective sigh at the beauty of the bride. The guests heaved to their feet. Caleb rolled his eyes at no one in particular.

Tish played the part well. With a simple silk gown that draped from her bosom in one flowing line several feet behind her, she looked the picture of a contemporary bride. Tish paused mid-strut, sensed her moment, then raised her bouquet high in the air, emitting a face-splitting "Hoo-yeah!"

Appreciative applause and sprinkled "Hell-yeah's" echoed through the hall.

The breaking of glass was followed by a kiss and catcalls as if the attendees had just been freed from a decade in a nunnery. Throughout all of it, Orchid wondered if it'd ever be her. To find the love of her life, and have him be willing to commit. Wasn't looking good.

After the ceremony, the trio shuffled along with the crowd towards the banquet hall. Phoenix scored a champagne flute, handed it to Orchid, and grabbed another for his brother, then himself. His blue gaze held hers as they clinked glasses. *God help me, I'm still in love*, she thought. Phoenix swallowed his bubbly and returned the empty glass to the silver tray.

In the receiving line, Phoenix greeted the mother of the bride.

"*Mazel tov*. Tish and Tom look very happy," he said, leaning down for a hug. Orchid's imagination wandered, thinking that Tish and Phoenix had looked happy. Orchid and Phoenix, too.

"Thank you. They are perfect together." Tish's mom smoothed her sequined gown. "I'm sorry about your accident," she said to Phoenix while studying Orchid.

"I appreciate that. I'm doing much better now. Do you remember Caleb, my brother?"

"Congratulations," Caleb said, and bent to touch cheeks with her.

"And this is Orchid, my friend."

"Nice to meet you. This is a beautiful wedding," Orchid said.

"Thanks. You know this one's a troublemaker?" she said, nodding a chin towards Phoenix while shaking Orchid's hand. Her tone said *teasing*, but the words hit Orchid like the truth.

"Um, yeah," Orchid agreed. "I've experienced that firsthand."

"I like a place where *I'm* not the troublemaker for a change," Caleb said.

"Thanks for all the votes of confidence," Phoenix interjected. "We better let you go," he said to Tish's mom. "Congrats again."

She smiled, and turned to a young couple next in line.

"Troublemaker, huh?" Orchid said to Phoenix as they picked up their tented name cards outside the reception hall.

"Have I got stories," Caleb added.

"That was the old me," Phoenix said.

As they made their way to a table, several women waved at them. "Tish's sorority sisters and their spouses," Phoenix whispered.

"Phoenix!" shouted a freckled redhead, as if he wasn't already headed directly for her.

"Gail," he said, leaning in to kiss both cheeks. "I'd like to introduce you to Orchid Paige."

"Nice to meet you, Orchid." She turned to Phoenix, curious. "Is this your girlfriend?"

"Definitely not," Orchid muttered just as Phoenix shook his head. His denial, expected as it was, cut her.

"This is my brother, Caleb."

Gail studied him from thick hair, to the tips of serpent tattoos showing above his collar, down to his muscular physique. "You have good taste in brothers," she said, and then extended her hand.

Caleb bowed his head.

They sat, Gail inserting herself in between the Walkers. "Just broke up with my beau," she offered. The waiter came by to fill glasses next to their salads. "White, please," Gail and Orchid called. "Red," Phoenix said. "Both," declared Caleb.

While Caleb consumed the appetizer, greens and several rolls, Gail questioned him about his barely visible snake tattoos, exclaiming over every new piece of information.

"Oh, you own your own tattoo shops?" she asked, amazed.

"You have how many tattoos?"

"Your motorcycle has the same design on it?"

Phoenix cut the salmon filet with his fork.

Caleb raised one hand for more wine. Gail ate a few bites of crisped spinach and turned to Phoenix. "Tish told me about your accident. How terrible."

"Yup," he mumbled, his fork chasing a slippery sphere of oiled potato around his plate. Orchid buttered bread and placed it next to him. He put down his silverware and acknowledged the gesture with a quick hug around her shoulders. If that was the payment for a roll, she'd butter an unending bevy of them so he'd never let her go.

Tish and Tom came by with a flurry of photographers and videographers. In hyper-amped hostess mode, she rapidly exchanged personal dialogue with each guest.

"I'm so happy you came!" she said to Phoenix and then Caleb, as the men stood to kiss her cheek.

"Congratulations," Caleb said.

Tish hugged Gail. "Best seat in the house," she winked.

"You remember Orchid, right?" Phoenix said, stepping back from an embrace with the bride.

Up close, Tish's makeup was running underneath each eye, giving her the appearance of a Raggedy Ann doll dressed in white. They shook hands, assessing each other with unspoken competition.

"Congratulations to you both." Orchid nodded politely towards Tish and Tom.

"Maybe you'll catch the bouquet," Tish mused.

"Unlikely," Orchid responded, with a tinge more acid than intended. *Tonight is for goodbyes,* she reminded herself. *Goodbye, Phoenix.*

The photographer, misinterpreting their exchange as an indication of friendship, gestured for Orchid and Phoenix to join the wedding couple for a photo.

Orchid caught a glimpse of emotion shadow Phoenix's face. He deftly stepped around her and slipped his left arm behind her. Automatically, she mirrored his action and snaked her arm around his waist. Tish and Tom, conditioned from a nighttime of posing, tucked in close to her to face the camera.

As the flash captured the toothy foursome, her understanding clicked.

Phoenix didn't want his loss to be visible in the picture. He'd positioned himself to hide his arm from the photo lens. Orchid suddenly remembered the way Tish and Phoenix were intertwined at Fashion Week. The way he'd draped his coat over his arm at the holiday party to camouflage his injury. A weight of sorrow threatened to pull her through the parquet floorboards. *You don't have to hide yourself.*

She was still stunned by this insight when the newlyweds moved to the guests sitting on the other side of Caleb.

Phoenix pulled out Orchid's chair for her. She looked up into his eyes. *Are you okay?* she wanted to ask. He studied her expression and his mouth compressed. *I don't want pity*, he seemed to say. He sat.

"How long was your recovery?" Gail asked Phoenix, reaching for another roll.

Orchid slid into her seat, and shook her napkin on her lap. Phoenix looked cold, closed off. Orchid's intuition elbowed her. *Gail's headed straight for a touchy subject.*

He gulped the last of his wine. "Three and a half months, including outpatient rehab." He put up a hand to flag a waiter.

"You are so amazing, to go through all that. I can't even imagine. I would've just died."

Orchid's mouth gaped open. Gail made it sound as if his life situation was impossibly dire. Phoenix's eyes narrowed.

A gentleman in a dark tux came over and refilled Phoenix's glass.

"I guess some people are just stronger than others," Orchid said to Gail, wine inspiring a tinge of haughtiness.

Phoenix raised his head. His expression cleared and he looped an arm around Orchid.

Gail looked stunned. "Uh-huh." Then she turned back to Caleb.

Phoenix leaned to kiss her cheek, his lips brushing the tender side of her neck as he pulled back, leaving her more flushed than he'd likely intended. "Thank you," he said.

"How come people make it sound like your accident is the end of the world?" Orchid blurted in a whispered hush.

"Happens all the time," he said.

"Well, that doesn't seem fair. You can do everything you want."

He looked at her appreciatively. "Not quite everything," he said, pointing towards his arm with his fork.

"Well, enough of everything that it's far from the end of the world," she whispered in his ear.

He put down his fork and pulled her closer. "Well, I kind of love you for seeing that."

She leaned her shoulder against his. He smelled great. "You know me, I'm team Phoenix," she said, trying to joke away the emotions gripping her. *He means the innocuous kind of love, right? Like 'love you like a sister, love your point of view, love your apple pie, can I have the recipe' kind of love? Right?* Thankfully, tonight was for goodbyes, because the muscle pumping oxygen through her body couldn't survive just being friends with Phoenix.

His cheek pressed to her hair, he issued words above her head. "In a way, I don't blame Gail for having those sentiments. There was a time when I thought this was the worst thing that ever happened to me."

She swallowed. It was the first time he'd volunteered his point of view on the topic. "Past tense?" she asked, careful not to spook him.

"Now I'm focused on stuff I can still change."

She released a breath and looked up at the face she loved. "Me, too. I've accepted the assignment. I'm moving to Beijing next month."

"Next month?" He let go of her to watch as the DJ called the bride and groom to the dance floor, his expression unreadable.

"Yeah, they're getting my work visa now. I'm glad you invited me tonight, so we can say goodbye," she added, unable to interpret his faraway look.

"You happy?" he asked.

"Yeah, I'm excited. It'll be an adventure. Maybe a clean slate's a good idea for me." She looked down, struck that Phoenix was one impetus behind her escape. *Will leaving the country be enough to heal the ache of what nearly was?*

Servers took their plates and replaced them with chocolate Chambord cake that been cut earlier, during a kitschy interlude that included the requisite smearing of icing onto the groom's face.

When the DJ invited guests to join in the dance, Phoenix looked down at Orchid, mouthful of chocolate cake nearly at her lips. "May I have the first dance?"

She took the bite, wiped her mouth, and nodded. "Absolutely."

They weaved through the round tables to the dance floor, this wedding their last opportunity to be together.

Once they joined the crowd, the music picked up the pace from a slow song to percussion. Orchid couldn't keep her feet from moving to the beat. She bopped to the rhythm until they found a spot in the increasingly full ballroom. Phoenix, always a bae, still had sexy moves. His style exuded much of his pre-accident sass and attitude. Orchid sensed other women checking out his physique. She threw her head back, staring openly with pride. He was a man not afraid to move his hips. Only because she'd seen him move before, she could detect the slightly more limited range.

"You're a great dancer!" she shouted over the music.

"You too!" He smiled, a beautiful wide happy smile, and for a moment, they were meeting as if for the first time, all tension and drama dispersed.

"You need the men's room?" he asked. She laughed.

The music switched tempo to a slow number and Phoenix paused, looking at her, hand outstretched. She joined him, pressed up close, wanting to be nowhere else. *Screw how much this is going to hurt tomorrow.* He kissed her hair.

"I'm all sweaty," she said.

"It's okay," he said. "You'll have to dry clean that crazy dress."

She buried her face into the side of his neck. "You smell great," she said. "Would you bottle that for me, so I can have it with me always?"

He laughed. "Would you like a drink?"

"Yeah, a drink sounds really good."

She took his hand and followed his lead as they weaved through the crowd of couples swaying to the music. "No wine," she said.

"Okay, I know just the thing."

He leaned in to speak to the bartender. "Patrón doubles. Bud chasers. Two."

When the drinks arrived, he handed her one. "*Pour vous.*"

"*Merci,*" she said, taking the shot glass and putting a cool finger under each eye at the memory of their trip to France. It'd be a miracle if tears didn't spill at some point this evening.

They clinked glasses and tossed back the shots. The liquid flowed hot and smooth down her throat. Better say goodbye drunk. That was a good idea.

"Paris was a beautiful trip," she said, sinking into a bar stool to tip her beer bottle to his and take a long draw.

He sat next to her. "Yes, it was. You remember how much you loved that underground market?"

"We went two nights in a row."

"No one believes us when we describe how unusual that place was."

"Well, we know," she said. Sadness gripped her chest at having just this one last night for reminiscing.

He put his bottle down and touched her under the chin. "You okay, hungry bird?"

He was killing her with his endearments, looking so handsome, and being so thoughtful. She wanted to remember everything with him before she left, even though seeing him was pummeling her gut from the inside.

"Yeah, I'm okay. It's just we have so many memories," she said, sniffling.

"Yup, some kind of crazy roller coaster all right," he said, handing her a cocktail napkin for her nose, then putting up his hand for another round of booze.

He toasted her again and they threw back the second set of Patrón shots.

"Remember coming here for the Effies?" she asked.

"Yeah, I had a great time that night, even though we didn't win anything. At least, the agency didn't win any awards. I won having a beautiful woman agree to come to a triathlon with me."

Okay, now he's trying to make me cry. "The triathlon was where Caleb told me about how you left Tish."

"You know, she came to see me in rehab and was so horrified, I thought if tough, mouthy Tish can't deal, there was no way you were ever going to be okay with this. Or if you were, you'd be fooling yourself."

"I'm not fooling myself."

"Look how happy she is now," he said, glancing over at the general direction of the dinner tables. "Told you it wasn't me; it's finding the right person," he said, referring to their early conversation denying Caleb's aspersions on his relationship with Tish.

"You think she found the right person?"

"Tom seems like a nice guy. But I thought we were talking about us."

"Us?"

"Yeah, like our happy memories. The club, down the shore, Paris."

"That was great, and that was what, nine, ten months ago?"

"Yup, and we've made happy memories recently, too. Like tonight."

"And then there was that whole mess in the middle of those happy memories," she said.

"Mess, like you thinking I was dating my assistant?"

"Mess, like us not talking, and you not calling me back. And don't forget about falling through your glass case and you thinking I'd date Caleb and all that. That mess." Now she was laughing, kind of crying too. *Ciao. Au revoir. Zai jian. Goodbye.*

He looked up, and then stood to take her in his arms. Holding her tight, cheek pressed against her hair, he laughed. "No more messes, okay?"

"Okay," she said. "Six thousand miles between New York and Beijing should do the trick."

His gaze drifted to an empty spot above them, like he was lost somewhere inside. "You tried so damned hard to get us together. You're amazing, you know that?"

"Is amazing a euphemism for stupid?"

He trailed a finger down her arm, bare below the plaid sleeves, tracing a line of longing. "Hardly. You had faith in me. Even when I'd lost sight of that and not because of you, but because I didn't think I could be enough."

She searched her mind for possible interpretations of what he was saying, trying to slow her hopefulness in case it was going to be obliterated. Again.

"And then you told me the most amazing thing. That you'd fallen in love with me and hadn't stopped."

"Well, that was last week," she joked.

He looked at her, measuring the meaning in her eyes. "I hope it's not too late to tell you something. Because I'm learning from you. I'm learning to be courageous. Courageous enough to tell you how I've felt all along even though I've been scared shitless of being rejected for not being . . . enough."

"No chance of that," she said, memorizing the planes and contours of his face.

"You know, I thought you being sensitive, squeamish Orchid meant you'd never be able to deal." He ignored her intake of breath as she prepared to defend this tired argument. "But actually, you being sensitive means you have more empathy than all those people who say they'd never be able to make it through what I did."

Orchid wasn't sure she could speak. He brushed his lips against her ear.

"I love you."

The shock of the words required her to replay them in order to absorb his meaning. Her hand over her mouth when she didn't remember raising it, the tears she'd predicted came. Hot, salted droplets cascaded heavy like liquid metal, one for every moment apart, for every stone of his suffering, for each missed opportunity. She threw her arms around him. He returned the embrace, no buttered rolls needed.

He tilted his head back to trace a thumb over her cheek, reading her right. "I'm sorry I hurt you. Forgive me?"

He held his breath waiting for her answer. She nodded, her throat too tight to speak.

"Tell me we can try again. Long distance, or I'll find business in China."

He's willing to go around the world for me. Tears welled, spilling off the precipice. She burrowed into the safety of his shirt.

His voice rumbled through her. "It's only fair to warn you not everything's going to be easy being with me. It's not going to be the same as before the accident, but do you want to try?"

Unable to resist the rush of the improbable tipping towards reality, she tiptoed up to touch lips to his soft, full mouth. Holy scent of soap and spice. "It has to be easier than not being with you."

His lips curved up at the corners over straight, white teeth, brightening his face. He pulled her closer, his chest against hers. "How I've wanted this."

He bent and touched his lips to hers until every subatomic particle bloomed to its fullest glory. He tingled her skin with a kiss like no other, one that evoked thoughts of an expanding universe and the study of numbers beyond infinity.

"Me, too," she said.

He tightened his hold on her. Time ticked forward to unearth each lost intersection, devotion and affection.

He was hers, and she was his. Not a thing missing.

NOTE TO READERS

Dear reader,

I've always loved happy endings. Phoenix and Orchid worked hard for theirs!

And you'd really make mine if you'd consider sharing your thoughts in a book review. Simply write a review on Goodreads, Amazon, Barnes & Noble, and Target.com

Or tag me from your blog or social media post.

Think of it as free goodwill, and a much-appreciated kindness!

Also, I'd love to hear from you. Sign up for my newsletter on my website at www.carolvandenhende.com, or look me up on most social media platforms.

Happy reading,

Carol

Carol

ACKNOWLEDGMENTS

Who knew that books are a team sport? *Goodbye, Orchid,* wouldn't exist without the conviction and support of family, friends, and dedicated professionals, many of whom have become friends. First, thank you to those who serve in our military, and inspired me to write a hero who, despite his injuries, is more than whole. This book will raise funds in your honor. Infinite gratitude to those who helped shape Phoenix's experience, especially my sensitivity readers: Purple Heart-decorated veteran Sgt. Bryan Anderson who role models his motto "live, love, thrive;" disability advocate Heather Abbott who raises money for victims of trauma, and lifelong friend and plastic surgery Chief Dr. Lynn A. Damitz. They deserve credit for the accuracy of Phoenix's recovery; any errors are mine.

Huge appreciation to those who shepherded this manuscript to publication, including the talented team at Koehler Books who recognized the potential for *Goodbye, Orchid* to change minds and lives: publisher John Koehler, executive editor Joe Coccaro, designers Kellie Emery and Skyler Kratofil. There isn't enough chocolate in the world to thank my earliest supporters: literary agent and publishing advisor Larry Kirshbaum who unfailingly believed in my story, and in me; editing partner Ellie Maas Davis whose brilliance helped shape the story from the start, and then concocted the book's title over a Zoom brainstorm; bookstore entrepreneur Shari Stauch, who connected me with Ellie and Koehler Books; and Springboard Global Enterprises' CEO Nadine Vogel, an ardent disability advocate who introduced me to Heather.

An unexpected benefit of writing is joining a community of authors. There are more people who've touched my writing than space permits me to name. To start, thank you to NJRW (Nancy, Miriam, Shirley, Vicky, Stacey and many others who've offered your knowledge and support), Women Who Write (especially my critique partners MaryLee, Genie, Lynn, Mary Kenny, Alice, Kathleen, and also longtime supporters Ginger and Dana), editor Deb Cooperman, the writers' organizations where I've taught and learned, and the many who've shared marketing advice, like Sourabh Sharma, Ann Dayleview, Casey Hagen, Karin Tanabe, Steve Ginsberg, Justin Coble, Derek Murphy, and Laura Rosenberg.

My beta readers helped tremendously to keep the work authentic. Thank you to the keen eye of Christine Tsai (Phoenix's black moment is for you), Tobie Kramer, Rachel Mack, Debra Battista and Rebecca Green; the creativity of art director Chui-Man Lee; the authors' perspectives of Meredith Stack Ross and Leslie Wirtley (RIP); the dedication of Carol DeVito to finish the manuscript in one sole weekend; the advice of Caridad Piniero; and to readers like Dr. Rebecca Li and Emma Boushie who encouraged me by simply falling in love with the story.

This book is dedicated to my family, who permitted me late nights and vacation time to write. You granted me freedom; there is no greater gift. To the authors who transported me to new worlds during my childhood, I salute your imagination, for you nourished mine. Lastly, thank you, dear reader. Phoenix and Orchid expanded my heart. I hope they've found a place in yours.

DISCUSSION QUESTIONS

1. The opening chapter, in which Phoenix suffers an accident after leaving Orchid at the airport, begins the story at a critical juncture. What clues foreshadowed the difficulty Phoenix and Orchid would encounter after that?

2. The title *Goodbye, Orchid* is evocative and enigmatic. How does the theme of hellos and goodbyes echo throughout the story?

3. For most of Caleb's life, he often feels inferior to his twin. How does Phoenix's accident change Caleb's understanding of himself?

4. After the accident, Phoenix's stated rationale for leaving Orchid is to protect her. Later, when Caleb starts to advocate for Orchid, he asks his brother, "Who are you trying to protect? Her, or you?" Do you agree with Caleb that there are other reasons for Phoenix's refusal to see Orchid? Which ones are you most sympathetic to?

5. Orchid has lost a great deal in her early life—her parents' death, abandonment by her uncle. How do you think these experiences shaped her, and contributed to her drive?

6. Discuss the depiction of Phoenix and Caleb's relationship as twins. They've taken divergent career and life paths, yet in what ways are they alike?

7. What does the novel illuminate for you about adapting to a disability? How do you perceive Phoenix's experience after reading the whole book?

8. One key turning point in Phoenix's recovery is Caleb's surprise trip to Walter Reed Medical Center. How much did that visit change your perceptions of Phoenix's injuries?

9. After Phoenix returns to work, he meets and dates Rina. Did you root for them to stay together or break up, and why do you think that is?

10. Several people in Phoenix's life protect and care for him. For example, his mother Veronica, his assistant Liv, his business partner Dex, his brother's ex-girlfriend Sascha. How does each of them contribute to or hamper his recovery?

11. Phoenix ends up hurting the person he's trying to protect. Is that transgression forgivable? If so, is that because of the extent of his suffering? because his intentions are noble? Or other reasons?

12. Who grows the most as a result of dealing with the accident? Is it Phoenix, as he learns to relinquish his perfectionism? Caleb, as he accepts the weight of responsibility for helping his brother? Or Orchid, who overcomes her aversion to trauma, and grows to understand her hyper-sensitivity as empathy?

13. After the initial shock of learning about Phoenix's accident, Orchid takes matters into her own hands. How do you feel about her decision to enlist Caleb's help, and the ways in which she tries to connect with Phoenix over their Easter weekend?

14. In the last scene of the novel at Tish's wedding, Phoenix tries to find the right moment to tell Orchid how he feels, while Orchid, believing this is goodbye, tries not to get swamped with emotion. How does each of their final actions reflect their love for one another? How does this affect your feelings about each of them?